REACH

WHO DEFINES GOOD AND EVIL?

Q.K. PETTY

REACH

First edition. August 16, 2019.

Written by Q.K. Petty.

Table of Contents

A Note to the Reader:

Thank you for reading Reach. I hope that you enjoy reading it.

Chapter 1: To Truly

EVERYONE wants to be the hero of their story but does anyone ever want to be the villain? The thought surges through my mind. It's the year 2026, and we've not changed a damn thing. We're still fighting. People are still looking for something to believe in. Individuals are still trampling each other for power.

The idealists contend the world will change. Someday. Idealists. This world desperately needs them, but they're so few. What there's too much of are those who don't care if this shitty world changes. Those who are oblivious to the struggles of the many.

I have just arrived in Mobile, Alabama. I'm here to find a biblical artifact that has been missing for hundreds of years. I'm also in search of a new Captain that I can train since my previous Captain has been promoted. Yet, as I look around the streets of Mobile, I only see hopelessness. Hopelessness caused by endless violence.

Still, I'm intrigued by Mobile. It's my first time here but it strangely reminds me of home. It rains almost every day; it can be 70 degrees at night and the humidity makes it feel like 110 degrees. Also, the scent of salt coming from the Gulf of Mexico stays in my mind even while I sleep. Reminds me of the Louisiana bayous—that same dark, witchy, Cajun vibe.

What a seductive scent. Like a swamp woman haunting my dreams.

But there's no sleep for me on this restless night.

I walk down Dauphin Street and pause in front of two towering commercial buildings. The Opener, which looks like a local wine bar, is tucked between them and catches my eye. It's a hole in the wall. Brick walls and two cracked windows on either side of the door.

I swing the door open and, to my surprise, it's nothing like I'd imagined. There is light jazz playing in the background that brings a vibrant energy to the room, but it isn't too loud to overpower the conversations inside. People are still able to talk in their room voice. There are only a few couples inside, the room is too small to fit more than about thirty. Some are wearing dress clothes and others are wearing skater casual attire. They're laughing, smiling, sitting, and conversing as if the world outside doesn't exist. Picasso paintings and wine shelves cover the walls. I might consider making this my new hangout.

I take a seat at the bar in one of those tall, copper bar stools with low open backrests. They look strangely out of place as if they'd been lifted from an 1800s saloon. The sleek countertop relaxes me as I run my fingers along its copper surface.

The bartender wipes down an empty glass and places it in front of me. "Black's your thing, huh?"

I lift an eyebrow. "Say what?"

"Well, you're decked out in all black. Look like a priest." She twists her strawberry blonde hair into a bun and taps a slim, pale finger on the empty glass.

She reminds me of my unemployed college friend who graduated a few years back.

"Symbol of death. Maybe I'm the god of death?" I give her a little smirk.

She smiles back. Flirting? "I don't know. You're not gloomy and you don't look like a skeleton . . . "

I bust out laughing. "If you only knew, sweetheart. Get me a glass of white wine. Your choice."

"Definitely not the god of death. More like a fruitcake."

"Hurry up, woman."

She brings me a glass of white wine. I swallow it down with one big gulp and a warm sensation floods my body. The weight of the world lifts off me. It's been such a long time since I've relaxed.

"Damn, that's some good wine!"

I turn my head toward the entrance. A tall dude of medium build walks through the door like he owns the place then sits at the end of the bar.

"Hey, Mary," he says as if they have been friends since kindergarten.

"Yo, Orion. How you been? Haven't seen you in a while. How's the fam?"

This guy is giving off a weird vibe. It isn't a sad, or evil feeling; it's more of a calmness. I feel at peace and alive around him. Way different from the people I normally deal with, but he reminds me of my colleague, Sarah.

"Wow, you finished that wine fast. Here's another," Mary says to me enthusiastically, handing me my second glass of wine.

"Oh, thanks."

I grab the glass and again swallow the wine in one gulp. Mary looks at me with both eyebrows raised. With a confused look on her face, she says to me, "Uhh . . . would you like another?" I feel so relaxed that I barely hear what she said to me.

"Are you okay? Why do you keep looking at Orion? Kinda felt you were a little off. What type of guy orders white wine, anyway?" Mary says with a creepy smile. I glare at her, trying to read her. She turns away. "Never mind."

My vision is starting to swim but I continue to study this guy. He has blond hair with faded sides, medium length at the top and combed to the left. He's very clean, with skin that looks like it has never been exposed to the sun. He looks too young to be in a bar.

He must have felt me staring at him because he turns to me. "Hello?"

He doesn't come off as wary of me or rude. He actually sounds curious. I slide to the seat next to him, and he asks my name. Without making eye contact, I tell him, "Eden . . . Eden Dowler."

Mary walks right up and starts chuckling. "Oh, so you're hitting on him now, are you? You got the courage to talk now?"

I look at her seriously. "Not now."

She sees I'm serious and walks away. Meanwhile, Orion is looking at me with a mix of confusion and wonder.

"I'm Orion Bachman. It's very nice to meet you. You look like a guy that has a story. Would you like to tell me?"

"You remind me of my colleague Sarah. Do you have any relatives named Sarah?" I give him the kind of look that would kill a bird. He looks at me blankly, like he really doesn't know what I'm talking about.

"No, I don't know anyone named Sarah. Sorry," he says with a smile.

Something is off with this guy. I just don't know what it is or maybe I shouldn't have drank the wine so fast. It might be the wine.

"Where are you from?" Orion asks.

This guy is always smiling. Either he's a serial killer or just a nice guy.

"I was born in Cairo, Egypt, which is also known as the City of the Dead, sad to say."

"What a gloomy place to be born. The City of the Dead,"

Orion remarks.

His tone is sincere. He's sympathizing with me, but I have a feeling there's something behind his calm and happy demeanor. I grab the bottle of wine from behind the bar, pop it open, and take three big gulps. I look at Orion with eyes so wide open it feels as though they're about to pop out of my head.

"Wooooooo. Well, I'm the Grim Reaper. Death. You should run, boy," I tell Orion.

He looks at me like I'm drunk, which I am, and says, "Are you hitting on me?"

What's this guy's deal?

But Mary's loud voice interrupts my thoughts again. "I knew it!" she blurts out. "You have a crush on Orion, you woman." She starts to laugh at me, but I don't think it's funny at all.

"What the hell are you talking about?" I say to both of them.

Mary's face suddenly becomes serious, then she looks at me and says, "Nothing's wrong with being a woman, jeez. What are you, a sexist?"

Still gripping the bottle of wine, I say, "I just can't win with you, can I?"

She smirks. "Nope. You can't win this battle, Death."

Orion chuckles then sips his wine. I get up and walk towards a table at the back of the bar. I can still see Mary and Orion but can't hear them.

Why is this Orion guy so optimistic? I look down at the bottle I'm holding and say, "So that's what it feels like to be around someone who is never alone and has the good life. Huh?" I've always been alone, everyone close to me has died. But this guy makes me sick. "Man, I'm drunk!" I yell from my table. Mary looks my way and happily yells, "Shut up over there, Emo!"

I rest my head in my palm for a moment, then my attention

turns to Mary. *Man, this girl is ridiculously strange.* I leave four hundred dollars on the table, then I get up and walk towards the door.

"See ya later, Emo," says Mary from the bar.

"Hope to see you around," Orion says.

I keep focusing on the door so I don't miss it and, without a word, raise my hand up and wave. Walking on the streets of Mobile makes me feel relaxed, despite the distinct smell of the gulf.

Crack! I feel a sharp pain at the back of my head, and then I'm kissing the ground.

A raspy voice says, "You're trying to find it, aren't you?"

I grab the back of my head and touch something wet. "Who the hell wants to know?"

I get kicked in the chest. "We don't take too kindly to those who try to get in the way of Seditio."

I cough up blood. I crack my eyes open to see the face behind the voice. He's a white man with black eyes, a shark tooth tattoo on his neck, rough skin, and long brown hair which he had in a ponytail. He is dressed in a blue suit with a white, long-sleeved dress shirt. What I can't stop focusing on is the massive scar over his left eye. Next to him is an older man with a black suit and oval-shaped glasses and he is holding what looks like a 13-inch piece of steel pipe.

I look up with a sadistic smile and chuckle.

"What's fucking funny?" he says to me with a grating, hillbilly tone.

"Nothing. Just your pretty smile."

He looks down at me and his comrade hands him a bat. He smiles at me, baring his yellow teeth, and says, "Let me give you a prettier smile than me, boy."

Bam! Smash! Crackle! He hit me in the head four good times. Then, he grabs my head and smashes it on the curb. Blood is dripping all over the sidewalk. People are walking by but all I can hear is someone saying, "Move along, unless you want the same fucking beating."

He continues to beat me. Then I hear another voice. "What the hell are y'all doing to him? Get off of him!" I can hardly open my eyes, but I know that voice. Orion.

"What the hell is y'all's deal? Leave him alone," Mary yells at them.

"Get away," I say to Orion.

"What? You need my help," he shouts with concern.

Mary looks at me as though she's seeing a rotting deer on the side of the road.

"I got this, idiot," I bark. I look at Mary and Orion, then barely crack a smile. Then the man with the tattoo pulls out a silver nine-millimeter gun and points it directly at me. I slowly stand up.

"Sleep!" He pulls the trigger and the bullet hits the right side of my chest. I feel the hot lead in my body.

"Noooooo!" Mary cries out.

I fall to the ground and feel my warm blood leaving my body. "Hope you're smiling in Hell," I hear

I laugh out loud. The man looks at me with surprise on his face. "What the hell? I shot you in the chest. How is this funny?" Then he shoots me again, the bullets landing an inch or two around the first shot, one after the other. Five times.

"Can you smell it?" I ask the man. "The flowers. They smell so nice. I think they're Cypress plants."

"There are no fucking plants here, you psycho. Just fucking die." He snatches the steel pipe from his comrade and swings it violently, aiming for my head. I grab it two inches from my skull and give him a piercing look.

"You cannot kill he who already rides the pale horse," I say with an eerie tone.

He backs away with a terrified look. I stand up slowly as

blood trickles down from my mouth.

"That felt good. Thanks for making me feel alive," I say.

I advance towards him. He backs away for a moment, then suddenly charges forward with the pipe in hand.

"I'll kill you. You . . . you . . . you—" he stops midsentence.

"You see it, don't you? Nothingness. There's no care, no pain, no feeling in these eyes of mine," I say calmly. I grab his throat, take the knife out my pocket, then place it—tip first—right above his heart.

"I can tell that you don't want to die," I whisper in his ear. I push the knife slowly into his chest. "If the God of Death is what you want then I'll be the horseman," I say. Then I shove the knife deeper into his chest and release my hold on his throat.

He falls to the concrete. His comrade stands there, frozen.

"If you move an inch. I will kill you," I say with a stern look. Orion looks at me, but there's no shock in his face, not even a little bit of despair. Nothing. I can't read him.

"Is he dead?" Orion asks.

I look down at the body and reply, "I pierced his lung so his lung is filling up with blood. He will die but it will be slow and painful."

Orion kneels near the man and says, "No. He cannot die. Good or bad, he's still a person. His life is just as precious as mine."

Orion sickens me with his sappy nature. He doesn't understand how the world works. I straighten up and look down at him. "You want to save a man who tried to kill me?"

Orion picks himself up, looking me in the eye. "Yes. Be the better man."

I kneel down next to the man. "You're right. I should be the better man," I say to him. I grab my knife and stab the man right in the heart, then I wipe the blade on my leg.

"What was that?" Orion yells at me as he grabs both of my shoulders. "Why couldn't you . . . ?"

I slap his hands off my shoulder, which keeps him from finishing what he's saying. "The sad thing is that I'm the better man. I'm giving him death," I utter with no remorse.

Mary rushes to Orion's side and says to me, "You need to go to the hospital." I pay her no mind because Orion and I are glaring at each other.

Orion looks me up and down with a broken expression as though he lost a family member. "Death comes so easily for you, doesn't it?" he says in a broken tone.

What is with this guy? He just saw me get shot and beaten into a bloody pulp. To top it all off, I just killed a guy.

Orion puts his hands in his pockets and asks me, "So, what now?"

Mary glares at Orion and slaps him on the back of the head. "Are you serious? He just killed a man.! Why in the world are you so calm?" she snarls.

Orion grabs the back of his head. "Mary!"

I look at him just as confused as ever. Then I remember there's a corpse in the middle of the street.

"I'm going to have to get rid of this body," I say. "Yo," I yell at the man's comrade. He looks at me with dismay. "Come get this piece of shit and take it to your boss. Bury it or whatever."

Without speaking, the comrade picks up the body and places it over his shoulders.

"Run. Like, now," I prompt him.

The man jogs to a yellow 2017 Ford Mustang with black rims parked around the corner. He opens the trunk, throws the body in there, and speeds off.

Knock, knock, knock. Mary's hitting me in the chest. "How did you survive six shots to the chest?" she asks. "We saw them hit you."

13

"I'm wearing something that can't be pierced with just any bullet or weapon. That's really all I can tell you." I say to her.

"Who the hell are you? Who do you work for?" she asks me with eyebrows raised and her hand on her chin. "Wait! Are you the Devil? No, the Antichrist! No! No! You're a freaking alien. I knew it . . . right when you walked in. You were such a weirdo that I felt something was off about you." She speaks so confidently as though she just got an A on a test.

"Your idiocrasy is highly fascinating, but no, dummy, I'm a normal man," I say to her sarcastically.

My phone rings, so I answer it and someone says to me, "Eden. I have gotten confirmation that the Chains of Peter are in Mobile."

This is shocking news. "Are you serious? Why would that be here? I thought this was a cold lead." Mary and Orion give each other quizzical looks.

"In early 1519, Panfilo de Narvaez traveled to Mobile and explored the area. There was a man who stowed away on the boat. This man was a former Judge of the House of David. With him he brought the Chains of Peter to America," the voice explains.

"That can't be right. There haven't been any strange events in this region. I'm the first Judge to come to this area. Where would he hide an artifact like that in Mobile?" I say, completely mystified, then add, "I'm on my way back to the Gate."

"No. We need you to find this artifact. I will be sending you potential leads that can help you."

The call ends and I find Orion looking at me. "What's a Judge?" he asks.

"Doesn't concern you."

I walk right past both of them, glaring at Orion. I can hear them calling out to me but my head is somewhere else.

I continue down Dauphin Street past the old Catholic cathedral. I see my 1965 black Ford Mustang; I unlock it, get in,

14

and crank it up.

"Excuse me," I hear from my left. I look up and it's Orion. I frown and say, "What do you want, Kid?"

He's looking at me with confusion, but there's also curiosity in his eyes. "First, who the hell are you? Second, how can you just kill someone and not care? Finally, sick car, bro. What do you do for a living?"

I can't, for the life of me, understand what the fuck this kid wants from me. "First of all, it's none of your damn business. Second, I've killed a lot of people, Kid. That shit back there doesn't bother me in the least. Third, I kill people for a living. Nothing more, just straight up murder. And what the hell is wrong with you? I literally just killed a guy right in front of you and you have the balls to come up to my car and question me? Kid, you might have some serious issues."

He looks at me, shaken, then says, "Sorry. My curiosity has taken over me."

He backs away from the car and I hear Mary scream, "Orion, you idiot, why are you by that guy's car? He just killed someone. I just called the cops. Stop acting white and get your ass away from him!"

As he is walking away, I receive a call from the Gate. The voice says, "Eden! Have you ever heard of the Bachman family?"

I stop at a traffic light and turn the radio down. "No. I have never heard of this family. Why would I?" I reply.

"When you get back to the hotel room, check your email. I'm going to send over a file to you. Seems like the Bachman family has been in the region from the days when Mobile was established. I will also send you info on four other families that have been around since those times," the voice says

"Roger."

I pull into the hotel. It's a regular old hotel—nothing fancy, but comfortable enough to make me feel like the place is safe. The room is relatively big. In fact, it has everything that a normal hotel room would have: a queen bed in the middle, a double window with dual curtains, a mounted 50-inch television, a desk with note cards on it, a bedside dresser with a lamp, and a bathroom with a single sink and a roll-in shower. I also smell a lemon-like scent, possibly from the cleaning supplies that I imagine were used to clean the room.

All I have with me are a medium-sized bag and my laptop. Right away, I put the laptop on the desk, pull out the rolling chair, sit down, and open the laptop. I put the hotspot on from my phone and log in to the hotspot from the laptop. I sign into a secure server and access the email that was sent to me.

"Hmm. Four families that are linked to the man who stowed away on Panfilo de Narvaez's ship," I mumble. I rest my head on my hand and sigh. My head starts to feel heavier as I realize what's ahead of me.

I stare at my computer screen through my fingers. "So, Bachman, Leon, Helton, and Scott. So, these are the families I need to look out for," I mutter, acknowledging the challenge.

Then I have a revelation.

"Bachman...Wasn't that kid's last name Bachman? Wait! Holy shit. Fate is a cruel little bitch. Isn't it ironic that I would run into you so soon, you little bastard." I say as if Orion was standing in front of me.

Chuckling, I begin to type "Bachman" into the computer and, sure enough, there is a bakery nearby called Bachman Bakery.

"This is too easy. They might not be who I'm looking for, but it is a shot. I can knock out two birds with one stone. He was too curious about what I do for a living."

I lean back into the chair and wonder if he has known this whole time that I'm a Judge. It would make sense if he does because if his patriarch knows that the House of David would come looking for the artifact that he possessed, he would make sure that his family is prepared for anyone that may try to find them and hurt them.

"Stupid kid," I mumble. I grab and firmly pull my hair. "I will find out the secret that I'm looking for and then just kill. Yeah. I'm definitely going to need to check and make sure these other families are involved or have knowledge of the House of David."

I release my hair and begin checking on the other families. The other three families are related to Panfilo de Narvaez by blood. There is only one member of the Scott family left and she is a ninety-year-old woman with no grandkids. The Leon family seems to be a good candidate but it seems that the main descendant was adopted and doesn't have any ties to his bloodline. Finally, the Helton family is a middle-class family with descendants scattered throughout the United States. They seem to be relatively harmless; no members of their family have any criminal records. I don't feel like they would be a threat, but just to be sure, I will check them out in the morning.

Seditio is here, too. Am I going to have a big problem? How would they know that I'm here, unless they were alerted to my arrival?

The fanatic organization Seditio is here as well. Seditio is Latin for "rebellion." They are an extremist organization with the intent to cause disruptions in society. They believe that only dysfunction and chaos can help people understand and evolve. The leader of this organization is unknown. However, rumor has it that they are a relative to the Judge who stowed away on de Narvaez's ship. He didn't agree with what the House of David was doing, and so he branched off. This Judge took with him the stolen artifact— the Chains of Peter—and gave it to de Narvaez. Legend has it that the Chains of Peter have the ability to kill anyone whom the wielder considers a sinner.

Anyway, we don't have confirmation on when Seditio was founded, but we know that they have been active since the 1940s.

The first major Seditio incident recorded was in 1943. They were helping Hitler search for the Spear of Destiny, which was later found by Judge Javier Weekes during D-Day in a hidden German bunker thirty miles from Normandy. Thanks to Javier's assistance in that battle, Hitler never got ahold of that artifact. However, once the artifact was studied and researched, we found out that it had no special value. The spear had no power at all, but, in saying that, the mind is very strong and if you can convince yourself enough then you give the spear more power than it actually has. Members of Seditio are usually very devoted individuals who believe that religion has strayed away from what it was intended to do. They also have members who have suffered greatly and been dealt a big blow in life and just want to watch the world burn. If Seditio is here, then an artifact must be present.

I close my computer and decide to go to bed. I start taking off my clothes, which smell like old meat that has been left out in the sun for three weeks. The smell has become so familiar to me that I do not smell it anymore. I strip naked, toss my clothes on the cover of the bed, slip underneath the blankets, and let my body relax. Reaching for the lamp to my right, I turn it off and close my eyes.

I wake up to my phone ringing incessantly. I grab it and see that Joseph has called me ten times. *What does he want?*

I reject the call and proceeded to the bathroom. I turn the faucet on, cup my hands under the water, and begin splashing the lukewarm water onto my face. It feels amazing on my skin and it wakes me up. I put on my clothes and prepare for the day.

The plan is to investigate the Helton family. I get their address from a quick Google search. It is absolutely amazing to me that I work for this top-secret organization and that all types of information or tools that can help me track someone are easily accessible to me. But I can just search someone's name on the internet and find them in no time.

The Heltons are a middle-class family. There are only three members who live in Mobile, Alabama. Blake Helton is a forty-year-old white male, around six feet, 209 pounds. A firmly-built man with a little belly. From pictures, I see he has liver spots located on the left side of his face, long brown hair, hazel eyes, bushy eyebrows with a cut over the top of his right one, a thick beard that looks like he hasn't trimmed it in months, and strands of grey hair in his beard.

Annie Helton is forty-seven years old, a white female with long lavishly blonde hair, a youthful appearance, about 5'6" in stature, 125 pounds, has ocean blue eyes, deep dimples, and her eyebrows are so blonde that you can barely see them.

Kyle Helton is seventeen years old, 6'1", 215 pounds with an athletic build, dark brown hair with a faded haircut, extremely hairy arms, clean-shaven face, bushy eyebrows, hazel eyes, big pierced ears with long ear lobes, and a crooked pointy nose.

I drive into the Heltons' neighborhood at 2:00 pm. Their house is located in a middle-class suburb where all the houses look the same. They're all one story with black roofs, red bricks, and black mailboxes out front close to the curb. No garages.

I park on the street in front of the Heltons' house. There are two cars in the driveway, a 1970 cream Oldsmobile in mint condition, which looks like it hasn't been driven since it left the lot in 1970. The other car is a 2010 black Tahoe with pollen all over the car. It looks like it hasn't been washed in months. The yard is bare and there isn't anything distinguishing the house from the others.

I walk up to the door and ring the doorbell. It is a beautiful day, the sky looks very clear, and the air smells fresh. A few moments later, I hear a female voice through the door.

"Who is it?" the voice asks.

"My name is Micah Smith with the Department of Public Works. I'm here to ask if you have seen any changes in your water.

There have been reports that there has been sewage leaking into the public water."

The door opens and I find myself staring at Mr. and Mrs. Helton. "That's very concerning," Mr. Helton says. He looks exactly like his picture. He doesn't seem like he has something to hide.

"Yasir! I'm going door-to-door to ask questions and check your water," I say in my most concerned-sounding voice.

"Yes, of course. We will answer anything to help you fix this mess. Come in," Mrs. Helton invites with a warm smile.

"There is no need for me to come in, ma'am. But could you answer a few questions for me, please?"

"Of course," Mr. Helton answers.

"How long have you lived here in Mobile? And when did you move to this neighborhood? Do you have any children or relatives in Mobile? Have you seen changes in your water color or water smell? Have you heard anything from your neighbors about their water?" I asked.

They exchanged glances at each other like they were trying to figure out if they heard me right. Then, Mr. Helton looked at me suspiciously before he replied.

"Well, if you must know. I'm from Mobile—born and raised," he explained. "My wife is from Ringgold, Georgia. I have one son and all of our relatives are dead. We haven't had any problems with the water lately in our house and haven't heard anything from our neighbors, either. Why do you want to know about my family?"

I put my hands on my hip. "Oh, I know some Heltons around this area, so I was just curious if you were related to them. I'm sorry, sir. It's none of my business."

They glanced at each other at first, then nodded their heads at me cautiously. *Maybe this was a dumb idea.*

I don't see any deception in their eyes. I'm pretty sure they are telling me the truth about who they are. However, I have to be completely sure.

"Would you both mind if I check your backyard and your water lines inside?"

"Sure. The sooner you get this problem of yours fixed, the better," Mr. Helton says ecstatically.

He walks out the front door and Mrs. Helton shuts it behind us. We walk past the cars and take a left past two trashcans. I see a six-foot-high wooden gate. Mr. Helton grabs the black latch, pulls it down, yanks the gate open, and walks forward.

It's a very plain backyard with a pine tree and a big shed in the corner.

"I'm not a yard guy, but knock yourself out. When you're done just knock on the back door and we will let you in to look at the plumbing," Mr. Helton says.

"Will do," I say, surveying the area.

The grass was well-trimmed and nothing seemed out of place. I walk around searching for any markings or anything that looks dug up. I see nothing out of the ordinary. I come up to the tree and inspect it. No visible markings or damages.

The only thing left to check is the shed. It's so small it looks like it can only hold a lawn mower. I grab the gold doorknob and turn it. I'm surprised it's not locked. I tug the door open.

I notice a white string attached to a small and dusty light bulb. I pull it and the light comes on. On the left are heavy duty extension cords, a leaf blower, two rakes, and hedge clippers hanging on a mounted rack. On the right are Christmas lights hanging up.

"Wow, could this family be any more fucking dull?"

I shut the shed door behind me and, on my way to the backdoor, I catch a glimpse of Mrs. Helton in the kitchen window cooking. Mr. Helton appears on the doorway with a tentative expression.

"Hey, sir, there are two men out front looking for you," he says.

"What do they look like?"

Mr. Helton stares at me with scared eyes and says, "They're wearing weird designer masks and black suits."

I tell him to lock the doors and hide, then I run to the shed, grab the rake, and break it across my knee. I approach the gate and open it. To my surprise, I see the men in front of me. There were two of them, about 6'3" and firmly built. The one to my left is wearing an Okame mask that was covering most of his head. It is a hard mask with red lips smiling at you, slits for eyes, and pulp red cheeks. I can't see the color of the man's eyes but I can tell by how the mask tilts upward that he has a big nose. The man to my right is wearing a brown wolf mask that has its ears cut off and has eye holes for him to see. I can see his dark brown eyes through the eye holes.

"Hola, gents! Would you like an ass-kicking? Or should I just fuck you up? Or, wait—option C—what if I just kill you? I'm going to go with option C."

I grasp the rake tightly and prepare for a fight. The man with the Okame mask raises both hands and says, "Wait! We're only here to talk. I see yesterday that we got off on the wrong foot. My name is Drone and my partner is Fall."

I raise my eyebrows in disdain. "Those are some dumbass names if I can say so myself."

"You're looking for the Chains of Peter, right? We had the artifact and it was taken from us by an individual in our organization," Drone says.

"I don't know why you're telling me this. You should know that I'm a Judge. And I'm the Judge-who-kills-first-and-asks-questions-later type of Judge. And I know you from that dumb fanatic organization that wears stupid masks, right?"

Fall jerks forward and says, "You know not what you speak

22

of, Peasant. You're just a demon in the field of lost souls."

I glare at him. "Yep. And I'm going to be killing you first."

Drone grabs Fall by the left shoulder and says, "Calm yourself, Brother. We did not come here to spill blood." Drone turns to me. "We just need you to find who stole the artifact and eliminate the heathen."

I retract from my fighting stance to a relaxed form.

"Okay. Do you have information on this person?"

Drone glances at Fall, nods, adjusts his Okame mask, and says, "I don't really know who this person is. However, it has been in the area for a while. This person's father was the former leader of Seditio who was brutally killed by someone we don't know. The child was found covered in blood and raised within the organization, but this child was very problematic. The child wasn't mad or anything. In fact, it was very bright and it learned quickly. It enjoyed reading our history books and was very interested in the crises that's happening in the world, but there was evil within it."

This is all confusing me, but I don't care. I just want to know where I can find the fool.

"Random question. Why do you call the child an 'it?'"

Drone looks at me, tilts his head, and says, "Because this child cannot be human with the ideas or thoughts it has. Yes, it lost its family but it didn't believe in anything but chaos."

I huff impatiently. "Okay, enough backstory. I do not care. Where can I find this thing? Or it? Or whatever?"

Fall walks forward, grunts, and says, "We never met it, but it is about 5'8", slim build, usually wears a black bag with holes on its head."

I start to get extremely pissed. "What the fuck do you mean by you never met it? What am I going to do with this information? You didn't give me shit to go by."

Fall flings his arms out wide. "We gave you information. Aren't you guys good at finding stuff? Find it and kill it. You

23

should be lucky that we are giving you this information and letting you leave unharmed."

I smirk at them. "Oh, thank you for your generous offer and, in return, I promise I won't kill you—just make you both half dead."

Fall goes in for a left-hand swing. I duck, grab his arm with my right hand, and pull it straight down. I jolt my left arm up with an open palm, striking underneath the chin. Under the mask. He flies upward. I release his left arm, grab his shirt so he doesn't fly backward, pull him down, and strike him in the liver. He collapses to the ground gasping for air.

Drone pulls out a gun and says, "I guess you don't want to take my offer, do you, Sir?"

I give Fall a kick in the face to make sure he was out cold.

"It won't work, you know. Shooting me. A member of your stupid organization tried that yesterday and I ended up killing one of them."

Drone fires at my chest three times. I can feel the hot metal fly through my body like it's going through thin paper. I can feel the blood flood out of the wounds. *Glad I decided to bring that little piece of wood this weekend.* My wounds start to heal and I advance towards the man. He's panting like a tired dog.

"I thought they were lying when they said you can't be killed," he says in a frightened tone.

I step over Fall's unconscious body.

Drone drops to his knees like a lion about to devour a zebra. He puts his hands together and starts begging, "I'm sorry. Forgive me. Please!"

I'm right in front of him. He is shaking. I take the mask off of his head and see how terrified he is. He's an older man, about forty-five years old with a scar on his chin, a narrow nose with a piercing on the left nostril, brown eyes, bushy eyebrows, clean-shaven face, thin chapped lips, and big Dumbo ears. Tears are

24

flowing down his face like water from a hose.

"Why are you crying? You literally shot me. But to answer your question—nope. No forgiveness, just death. Bye."

I hold his head between my hands and break his neck. The neighborhood was so silent that the crunch of his bones snapping echoes for a good minute. His lifeless body drops on the cold grass. I stare at his corpse. *Is this all worth dying for? What am I going to do with the information they gave me?*

I walk to the front door but pause after a couple of steps forward. *I probably should kill the other guy too.* I turn around and begin to walk back towards Fall, but I have a change of mind. I don't feel like killing anyone else today.

He is most likely going to tell his buddies and they are going to come find me, but I'll handle him when the time comes.

I walk towards the front door to tell the Heltons to call the cops. I knock on the door and I see them peek through the side window. I barely hear them but I swear I hear them say, "We called the cops!"

I give them a thumbs up, and I notice an old 1995 red Jeep Cherokee Country with beige trim parked in front of the house. I assume that's how Drone and Fall got here. I run back to Drone and Fall and check their pockets. I find the keys in Drone's pocket. I race back to the Jeep and drive away.

I hear sirens from a distance. I find a mask on the floor of the passenger seat and I put it on my face. It's a regular *Phantom of the Opera* mask. *Joseph is going to kill me. He doesn't like media coverage and there are too many dead bodies. This is bad. I need to stay low now. No more dead bodies, Eden.* I feel relieved that I didn't kill Drone. The House of David tries to stay out of the media. So far there have been two deaths in two days.

I drive city to city for twenty minutes and reach a breaking garage connected to the Renaissance Hotel on the third deck. I park the Jeep in a spot away from the security camera. I take the stairs down and drop the keys in a trashcan.

I get to street level and I see a sign that says S. Royal. What gets me about this city more than anything is the smell of salt and water. It reminds me of the Gate. The smell of the ocean, the salt, and the humidity brings me back to where I spent the majority of my life. People are walking the streets just minding their own business and all I can think about is this smell. Dark clouds hover above.

"It's about to rain," I mutter.

I take a right and go on the sidewalk. I walk past a coffee shop and a bank. Mobile feels like New Orleans. The buildings have a Creole style of architecture with broad spreading rooflines, multiple French doors, L-shaped buildings, and wraparound mantels. I read that Mobile was a French colony at one point and it was the first capital of the French colony, La Louisiane. It was founded by French-Canadians Pierre Le Moyne d'Iberville and Jean-Baptiste Le Moyne, Sieur de Bienville, to establish control over France's claims to La Louisiane.

I've always been fascinated by the history of places, people, and things. Maybe that is why it was easy for me to understand the teachings of the House of David. It was stuff that I was fascinated about. I continue walking and I spot a café to my right called Café Joe Cain. I walk inside. I see green, yellow, and purple beads nailed to the green walls. Pictures of men in yellow and green joker costumes are also on the walls, and the smell of king cake floods my nostrils. Besides me, the only other people here are the barista and another guy behind the counter.

The barista is wearing blue skinny jeans and a yellow shirt that says "Café Joe Cain" on the front. She is a brunette with ombre highlights, a piercing on her left nostril, and thin eyebrows like she was still stuck in the early 2000s. She looks at me with excitement like she hasn't seen anyone come in all day. "Welcome to Joe Cain Café!" her voice was cheery and her smile is so big.

26

"Would you like to try our cinnamon mocha hot chocolate?"

I sigh and say, "Coffee. Black."

"Okay, that's $1.50."

I reach into my pocket and I feel loose change. I grab a handful and count. I have a dollar, seven quarters, two dimes, and a shitload of pennies. I hand all of it to the barista. "Keep the change."

Then I notice a book sitting on the counter. I pick it up. It's *The Sun Also Rises* by Ernest Hemingway.

"Does this belong to anyone?"

The barista glances at the book in my hand and says tentatively, "Not that I know of. I don't know how long that's been sitting there. You can just take it if you want."

"Thank you."

I take the book and coffee with me and walk to a table near the window by the entrance. I sit facing the door. I sip my coffee as I look out the window. I see small drops of rain roll down the glass. Suddenly, it begins to rain harder. The raindrops sound so loud against the glass windows of the café, that I can tell the rain is heavy. I feel calm for a little bit. It's a feeling I haven't felt in quite some time.

When I was young there was one thing I loved to do that helped me think, and it was reading. Reading transported me to different worlds. I could travel the seven seas, go to outer space, and be someone else. I used to collect books that I would find in the trash cans in the streets of New York. It's amazing how people are so willing to throw away good books and continue to drown themselves in social media.

Right before I start to read, I hear the door open and, for a moment, the sound of the downpour outside gets louder. I see that girl from the wine bar. She's wearing an oversized blue raincoat, blue rain boots, a red dad hat, and stud earrings. She sees me and her eyes light up with excitement. When we first met I felt like there was something off about this girl. I don't know if she is crazy or something. However, she isn't right; I just have a feeling. I ignore her and start reading.

"That's rude! You're not even going to say hello?" wine bar girl says.

"I only say hello to people I give a damn about," I reply.

She sits across from me and pushes the top of the book down so she can see my face. "Are you always this grumpy?" she asks.

It's amazing to me that this girl has no fear. She saw me kill a man and she's so lackadaisical about it. At least that Bachman kid had some trepidations about what I had done. However, she seems unfazed by blood and death.

"Well, I'm a little upset that you interrupted my reading."

She leans back, crosses her arms, raises her eyebrows, and says, "Uh huh."

I close the book and place it on the table. "So, what do you want? Oh, and what is your name again?"

She smiles at me and replies, "You know my name, dumbass. It's Mary. I usually come here to get some coffee."

I run my right hand down my face. "Okay, well you can go now. I just want to sit here, read my book, and drink my coffee."

But she doesn't move. "What do you want with Orion?"

I look at her with confusion and respond, "I don't want anything from him."

She smiles, looks out the window at the rain pouring outside, and says, "Orion has a lot of friends, but he doesn't see them as friends. They're more like acquaintances to him. They look at him like he's the best thing ever because he's smart. He could go anywhere in the world but he stays here to help his family."

I rub my forehead. "What are you getting at?"

She leans forward, placing both forearms on the table.

"Yesterday, when he saw what you did. He had a genuine interest in you. It was like he was curious about death and killing. I've never seen him so intrigued."

I sit back in my chair. "Maybe the Orion you see isn't the Orion he truly is."

She rests her chin on her hand and looks thoughtful. "Yeah, but you think you would know a guy after screwing him a few times."

I have no clue why she would tell me something like this. This girl is extremely strange. With a smug look on my face, I grab my book and sit up.

"Okay, I don't care about you or your affairs with your boyfriend. If you don't go, I'll cut your life short. Okay?"

She frowns, stands up, and says, "Okay, okay! I know when I'm not wanted. Geez!" She walks to the door and opens it. Humid air hits my face. She puts the hood over her head and turns to me. "I will be seeing you again, Eden."

After she leaves I continue to read. Then, I pause and start to ponder if I should have killed that Drone earlier. *If I kill him, Seditio will retaliate and this will cause more problems for me. Although I guess since I already killed Fall they will be looking for me anyway.* I also have to check on Orion and the Bachman family to see if they have the artifact. The Bachmans are the only other family that could have this artifact. If they don't have it, it's possible that it's lost forever. That would make no sense, though, because Seditio had it and said it was stolen from them. This whole situation is getting more thrilling by the moment. I'll worry about it later. Right now, it's time to relax and enjoy this book.

As I'm reading, I notice a line in the book that is underlined. I guess the previous owner thought this line served some importance.

"I can't stand to think my life is going so fast and I'm not really living it."- Ernest Hemingway.

29

Chapter 2: Accept

MY NAME IS Orion Carter Bachman. I'm the son of James and Elise Bachman and I was born in Mobile, Alabama on December 31, 2002, at 3:00 pm at Providence Hospital. I love my family with every ounce of my being, and I always have. They mean more to me than anything. My father James is a skilled and successful baker in Mobile and my mother loves and supports us like it is her full-time job. Growing up with her, I learned that she also has the tendency of crying excessively to comedic amounts when she's worried about my father and me.

I'm the only child and, like many only children, of course, I'm spoiled. My parents sent me to the best school to make sure I had the best education. You could say that I was a privileged child. I was raised on two principles: Treat others as you would like to be treated, and that every life is special. On top of that, I was raised Catholic, and we went to church every week.

Growing up, it was easy for me to make friends. People were easily drawn to me. Come to think of it, maybe "friend" isn't the right word to use. I was able to make many acquaintances growing up. I made a lot of acquaintances because many people thought I was highly intelligent, plus I was good-looking for a child. My parents actually knew that I was gifted so they made me take an IQ test. I got a score of 150, which means that I'm considered either genius or near-genius level intelligence.

My whole life it has felt like everything came easy to me. Because of my high intelligence, I excelled in school. My father was very much into computers. In fact, every time I saw him, he was fiddling with computers. So, at the age of five, I started to fiddle with them as well. My father saw that I had a knack for software and reinforced my education through coding and computers.

Every day after school my father would practice coding with me. I learned JavaScript, Python, C++, Java, PHP, Go, and Swift. So, in the end, I ended up loving computers, but my real passion continued to be knowing the world and protecting the people that I care about. When I was thirteen years old, a situation on the playground helped define this about me.

I was in middle school at the time, which was a private Catholic school and during recess, we would always play kickball. One day at recess, I noticed that there was a group of kids surrounding another group. When I walked up closer, I noticed that they were kicking dirt, throwing rocks, and spitting on this group of kids. The kids would beg them to stop and leave them alone but the surrounding kids kept going. Those kids were crying and scared for their lives. I asked one of the bullies why they were picking on the younger ones and he said, "Because that one kid is fat and those other two jumped in to protect him."

What a dumb reason to bully a kid. I stood in front of the older group. "If you don't leave them alone, I'm telling." The bullies laughed at me. A skinny, pale, white kid wearing the school's standard uniform said, "Move out of the way, Orion."

"Just leave them alone." They howled in laughter again.

"You're really going to protect these losers?"

"These so-called losers are my friends. If you have a problem with them then you have a problem with me."

The skinny kid raised his brown eyebrows in confusion and lowered his tone. "You're really friends with these losers?"

"Yes." The surrounding kids threw their last rocks at the younger ones and walked away. I reached my hand out to the fat kid. He had tears in his eyes.

"Thank you," his voice was soft but grateful. He dusted off his shorts and wiped the tears off his brown cheeks, then continued, "Hey, my name is Jacob."

They must be new students. I have never seen them before. When did they transfer to the school? Was he really bullied because he was fat?

Then the other boys got up and dusted their clothes and came up to me too.

"Hey, thank you!"

"Hey, I'm Orion. Are you guys new here?"

Jacob stepped forward. "No, we have always gone here. The tall, skinny kid to the left of me is Matthew. And this other weird, tall, drooling guy is Joseph."

How come I never noticed these guys before? I swear they must be new.

"Why haven't I ever noticed you all before?"

They all laughed. Finally, barely breathing, they replied, "Dude. We are the weird kids. The Unnoticeables! No one ever notices us unless they want to pick on us."

"I actually have known you since preschool," Joseph chimed in.

I averted my eyes in embarrassment. I was not better than those kids. "I'm so sorry. I should have known that."

"Dude. You don't have to be sorry. You helped us. From now on, we are indebted to you." Then all three of them bowed their heads and yelled, "THANK YOU!" It was like they were trying to make me laugh, and all I could do was smile. I had never really had friends at this point in my life. These kids were weird, but that's what makes them genuine. This was what friends should be like.

"Hey. Would you guys want to be friends?" I asked them.

Jacob looked the most shocked before stuttering, "You really want to be friends with us? You know we were losing back there, right? Matthew is almost fourteen and still picks his nose."

"Hey!" Matthew yelled before I could respond. Joseph and

I just chuckled.

"And who asks someone to be friends, anyway? That's weird," Jacob added.

"I just thought asking would be appropriate," I said.

Now Joseph was laughing at me too. "Dude, no one talks like that. You're a weird dude. But I'm the leader of this group. Yes, you may be friends with us."

Jacob and Matthew looked at each other and then at him. "Who made him the leader?"

It felt official. "So, are we friends?" Before responding, they huddled up and I could hear them whispering. A couple of minutes later, they broke the huddle and Jacob approached me.

"Orion! Welcome to our group."

It was the first time in my life that I felt like people other than my family were real with me and saw me like a regular kid—not like a genius, prodigy, or chosen one. I gained three best friends that day, and they are still my best friends today: Jacob, Joseph, and Matthew.

Middle school turned into high school and I played every sport. I was good at them all, but I didn't care to make a career out of any of them. I picked up wrestling at six years old and I did that till I was eighteen. I was relatively good at wrestling, All-State one year, and a State Champion another year. I liked it a lot, too, and wanted to do it because it is the basis for all fighting. If you are a wrestler and you have one move, then you're unstoppable.

Wrestling helped me understand that once you get someone on the ground, you control the fight. Honestly, wrestling is all about control. It is the very best skill you need when it comes to fighting because when you know how to wrestle, you can dictate where the fight takes place. If you are a good striker, you can stand, but also you can just decide to take it to the ground.

There is no better foundation than wrestling. Wrestling also helps you gain tremendous mental toughness. When I was training for wrestling, I would read online about how to be a better wrestler and watch videos. I wanted to completely understand the sport. At one point, I even began to overtrain. But, because I pushed myself so hard, I was able to gain a mental toughness that my coach always commended me on.

When I wasn't wrestling or playing other sport, I was reading the Bible almost every day. My parents believed that if you learned about other religions, you reinforce your faith in your own religion. This ultimately lets you be able to decide what you believe in. They never pushed me to believe in God. They always wanted me to have the information so that I could make the decision to believe in God on my own.

One thing they were strict about, though, was my learning Hebrew. They wanted me to learn Hebrew because my grandmother was Jewish, and she wanted me to learn Hebrew so I could be in touch with her heritage. After all, this was the language that Jesus Christ knew.

I'm not very religious, though. If you ask me if I believe in God, I would tell you yes. I believe that there is a being above this. You don't have to agree with me, but I see it like this. If the Big Bang happened, then, what caused the Big Bang? Newton's third law states that for every action in nature there is an equal and opposite reaction. If the universe was just a ball of matter, then it couldn't just have activated on its own. Newton's law states that there scientifically must have been a cause for it, and I believe that whatever caused the Big Bang is God.

But I also believe in evolution, Darwinism, and all things science. People use the excuse that science doesn't explain God, however from what I see, it hasn't disproved God, either. We also won't know until we die, anyway, so until then, I will believe and live life to the best of my ability.

What is the risk in believing, anyway? If you believe, die, and there is a heaven, then you will be fine because you've lived an amazing life helping others. However, what if you live a terrible life and then die? Then you have to explain to God why you've lived such a terrible life. That would be a predicament. If you die living a good life and there is no heaven, well, then you will live on in the memories of those you touched. In that way, you never actually really die.

I just hate people who say they know what life is or what life means, or know what happens when life dies. In general, I like to get to know people and try to understand their point of view. But when someone says something like, "I know what happens when I die. It'll be black and gold and the end. Just like there was nothing before, there will be nothing at the end." I don't understand how people can say that. How can you say there is no God? We don't know that. The universe might as well be God. At the end of the day, we are only aware of what we have experienced.

My parents encouraged me to come up with my own thoughts on what I believed in. I grew up living with my mother and father, but in my later years, my grandfather moved in with us. My grandfather's name is Robert Bachman. He is seventy-five years old and has lived in Mobile his entire life, just like my parents. He's the old average height with a bald head and rough skin from working in a bakery for so long. He's a kind man, but still more serious than my father and mother. My whole life he has been very proud of me and wants the best for me.

My father's mother died when he was sixteen so I never got the chance to ever meet her. My father said she was the kindest woman he has ever met, besides my mother, of course. My mother's parents died when I was around two years old. So, I really have no clue what they look like except for pictures that my mother has.

My goal, though, is to become someone like my dad. My dad is my hero. When I was growing up, he was always helping people out. No matter the situation, he always had a smile on his face. He saw the good in the world even though he knew there was a lot of bad. He made sure that our family had the best of everything and taught me to not to look down on people who didn't have much. He would always say, "We should cherish this life and be thankful that we don't have it as bad as others. We should live this life to the fullest."

Tragically my father died of brain cancer when I was eighteen. I remember the day he died like it was yesterday. My mother and I were visiting him at the hospital. Mom was dressed in a t-shirt and jeans and I was dressed in shorts and a black t-shirt. I can even remember my mother's smile. She was wearing a lavender perfume that was so lovely that it just made you want to hug her so you can get the smell of lavender on you. I was afraid to go see my father. I didn't want to see him like this. I didn't want to see my hero in pain. I didn't want to see death.

We got to my father's room and it wasn't sad or gloomy; it was vibrant and lively. It was a nice day—the sun was shining, the wind blowing gently, and the atmosphere peaceful. His hospital room was standard: a bed, a 14-inch television hanging from the wall, a small table filled with white roses, and two chairs. I looked at my father as we walked in, and he was just sitting up, eyes on the television watching the cooking channel.

He looked pale. His blond hair was gone due to the chemo, his lips chapped, and his wrinkles more prominent than before. He was under the covers and wearing his rectangle-shaped reading glasses.

"Hey, Kid," he said as I walked up to his hospital bed. "How are you?"

Sadness kept me from answering. I thought that my father was indestructible and seeing him like that tore me apart. I didn't know how to react. How could he be cursed with this? How can someone so wonderful die like this? It isn't fair.

"Why do you have to die? Who is going to teach me

things? Who is going to smile when things look bad? Why would God take you from me? Why? Why?" Tears rolled down my face and sadness felt like it was consuming my heart.

My father pulled me into his arms. "Everything is all right, O. You don't have to be afraid or sad. I have lived an amazing life. I got to fall in love, have a wonderful child, and do what I'm passionate about." He hugged me tighter and kissed me on the forehead and muttered the Irish Blessing.

My father was so good at making us feel at peace. A couple of seconds later, my mother came up to the bed and hugged us both. If you were in the room, you would have felt the love.

"I don't want you guys to be sad for me," my dad said. "This is what God had planned for me. I can die knowing that I have no regrets, and I die knowing that my family knows that I'm okay with this."

Just like that, I wasn't afraid anymore. I knew that everything was going to be all right, and I felt that I was now ready to let my father go. We weren't as sad because my father told us not to be sad for him. He said that he lived his life to the fullest, so why is there any need to be sad? My father lived the life that he wanted to live. He died in peace because he did everything he needed to do. We needed to make the most of our lives so when our time came, we have no regrets, no pain, and no sadness. People should be able to accept death. And accepting death doesn't mean you're being friends with it. If you can't accept the pain and sadness that death brings, then you cannot fully live life. That's not what living should be. It was on that day that I started to believe that you should cherish this life and live it like there's no tomorrow.

I don't see my family as very wealthy, however, my friends say otherwise because my house is huge and it's in the Old Historical District in Mobile. Usually, houses in this district were very expensive. Also, we come from old money which means an inherited wealth of established upper-class families or a person, family, or lineage possessing inherited wealth.

My family's business, Bach Bakery, is well-known across Alabama. Bach Bakery isn't a big store; however, we do ship our baked goods all across the Southeast. We've been one of the main bakeries in Mobile since 1904. My father loved this and wanted us to stay local because one of his passions is influencing Mobile, and he wanted the store to be a "Mom and Pop" store. He finally gave in to shipping across the Southeast in order to help make more money.

Besides my dad passing away, there has never been anything really devastating in my life. I have a loving family. I graduated from the University of South Alabama after three years with my dual degree in civil and chemical engineering. I went on to get my master's in fire protection engineering from Cal Poly in one year. Right now, I'm also working on my doctorate in engineering at the University of South Alabama. I got into every school I applied for, even Harvard, Yale, and MIT. But going to those schools doesn't prove intelligence. They're just names and achievements to make people feel good. If you are truly brilliant you can make the best out of any situation you're in. You can even make the situation you're in better. That's what I'm doing with my education. I don't need to go to a top school to prove my worth. I can prove what I can prove here at home. Once I make up my mind on something, I stick to it and figure it out myself.

It was a hot and humid fall afternoon when I was fifteen years old when Mary came into my life. I was riding my bike in the neighborhood to get some exercise and I saw her just walking around. She was in a black suit with a white button-down. At first, I thought she was a guy, but when I got closer I noticed she was a girl with short blonde hair. I have never seen her in the neighborhood before and I was curious about who she was. She had an exotic look and gave off a mysterious vibe.

She seemed to be lost in thought. I slowed down my bike next to her and said, "Hey, are you from around here?" It seemed like she didn't really see me. It was a weird feeling. It's hard to explain. All I know is that she gave off the vibe that she was not from around here.

"Hey, are you alright?" I asked her again. She stopped walking this time and smiled.

"Oh, I'm sorry. I was lost in thought." She laughed.

All I could think to myself was that this was an extremely strange girl. "Are you from here?"

"Hm, no. I'm not from around here. My family likes to move around. I just moved here from California."

She was also very pretty. *Why is she walking by herself? What is she thinking about?* I got off my trick bike and hit the kickstand with my heel.

I reached out for a handshake. "Well, it's nice to meet you. I'm Orion Bachman."

She shook my hand. "Nice to meet you, Orion. I'm Mary Scotland." We walked together down the street.

"So, Mary, what school do you go to?"

"Well, I just got here and my parents haven't really looked into schools yet. What about you? Where do you go?"

"I go to a private Catholic school. My parents are kind of religious, actually."

"I understand completely. My family is really religious, too. They wanted me to be someone I'm not. I was wearing a mask for a while. When I was little they didn't like me for who I was. So, I had a really hard childhood until I broke free of the mask. I was finally able to be who I am."

Something about how she said that really touched me. "Who are you, then?"

She tilted her head up to the sky for a moment, then told me in a sweet voice, "I'm just a girl who wants to have fun. Nothing more and nothing less."

What does that even mean? It was strange to hear her say that, but the way she said it made me believe she truly meant those words. We walked all the way down to my house.

"I can walk you home if you want me to."

She hugged me instead. "No worries. I like to walk and get lost in my thoughts."

I hugged her back. "Are you sure?"

"Yes!" she said as she kissed my cheek. "We will be seeing each other around, Orion."

Since I've known Mary, she's always been very insightful. She's always nice and outgoing. She also has strange tendencies. She's oblivious of her surroundings most of the time and also mysteriously shows up out of nowhere at places she shouldn't be.

I have never been to her house before and I have also never been asked to come over. I feel like she has family problems and I don't want to intrude. I also don't know what school she went to or if she even graduated. It's not like I don't care but I just never felt like I needed to ask too much about her life. She has always been there for me and she's a friend I can trust.

Besides computers, coding, and wrestling, I have also always liked baking. It's one of my passions. I work with my mother in the family business as a baker. My grandfather sometimes comes and helps out, but usually, it's my mom, me, and a few other students.

People tell me that I'm dumb for not pursuing something in engineering, but I like to be able to interact with the community. Through talking to customers and learning about their experiences, I feel like I'm able to learn and relate my situation to theirs.

Ultimately, I want to live life like my father; he lived a good life and he lived doing things he loved. I want people to look at me and know that everything is alright and that they are safe. I want to be the person everyone looks up to. What's the point of living this life if you don't do whatever is possible to make it the best? You have to be able to improve this world for generations to come. Yes, I have had an amazing and privileged life but that doesn't change the fact that I still want and need to change how people see life. They should cherish life and live it to the absolute fullest like my dad.

Death is an inconvenience that should be eradicated from this world. Overall, I understand that death is inevitable, but while we have the gift of life, we must cherish it, love it, and live it. You have to learn from mistakes and push yourself to be the best at all costs. That's how I live my life. And I recognize that I still need to learn a lot to achieve this goal. I will do what I can even if it takes me forever. It's all about finding situations that will help me fulfill my dream. Up until now, nothing has excited me and I'm really bored. In fact, I've been bored most of my life.

One day changed everything for me, though. It was 10 o'clock at night on a lonely, Wednesday in September. I had just finished up at the bakery, and I wanted to relax a little bit at the wine bar. I've done this before many days after work, but today was different, the weather even seemed darker than normal. There was a man sitting at the bar. He looked like he was not from around here. Little did I know then that he would change my life forever.

Chapter 3: Death

IN THE BEGINNING YEARS of my life, I always felt like I was destined to be around death. My mother died giving birth to me. My grandparents showed me pictures of her. She was slender with dark brown hair that flowed down her back to her waist. She had lovely green eyes with a gentle smile. She had deep dimples and a beauty mark above her lip. She was absolutely gorgeous. My father was a tall, slender, Egyptian man with short black hair, thick eyebrows, and dark gray eyes. I remember him having sad, lonely, and droopy eyes.

I was born Joshua Hazarmaveth. Hazarmaveth is Hebrew for "dwelling death." Being born four pounds and two ounces, how could a woman die by giving birth to something so small? Beats me, I tell you.

My old man loved my mother so much, I was told. When she died, he was devastated. Sadness was all that I saw when I looked at my father and a lot of times, he even blamed me for her death. He died when I was five years old due to cancer, so I don't remember much about him. What I do remember is that from the day of my birth until the day he died, my father always looked at me with anger. He would always say things to me like, "You killed her, you little shit."

After he died, I was sent to the Big Apple and my grandparents raised me. They lived in a two-bedroom apartment in lower Manhattan. They were a sweet, kind, old Egyptian couple. My grandma was a plump woman with pitch black hair, sandy skin tone and thick eyebrows shaped like an S. I really loved my grandma with all my heart. She was so sweet to me and always helping others in need. She used to go to the shelter to feed the homeless. Even though I didn't know much about my grandma, my impression of her was that she was someone I believed would go to heaven.

I was a troubled kid, and always getting into fights in preschool. Most of them were because a lot of kids hated my long hair and would bully me about it all the time. I never saw the point of going to school. I knew that I was smarter than everyone else so why should I degrade myself being with idiot bullies?

My grandpa was a tall, strong man with a thick, gray beard. He was also a proud man and I always thought he would live forever. Then again, I was a child; I really didn't know anything. Two years after moving in with my grandparents, my grandpa died from unknown causes. My grandma was heartbroken. I remember every time she looked at my grandpa she had the look of love in her eyes. It was a love I wish I received from my father. She always looked at me with those eyes of love, but not the way she looked at him.

A year after my grandpa died, she died as well and I was alone again. I was six years old with no family. I didn't have anyone. I was a child alone in the world and what I found was that most people don't understand how it feels to be alone with no one there to hold you and to tell you that everything will be alright. The court wanted me to go into the foster care system, but I knew they just wanted to get rid of me. I figured that with me being a young, poor, homeless, immigrant boy, they would either put me in the system or send me back to Egypt. I didn't want to be tossed around.

One day, when we were leaving the courts they decided they were going to put me on the bus. I caught a glimpse of a pocket knife in the caretaker's pocket. He was an overweight, bald, white man in his late forties who had thin eyebrows and a long goatee. I snatched the pocket knife from his pocket and stabbed him in the leg. Once I'd crippled him, I was able to escape into an alley where I found an opening to climb into the sewers. I hid there for what seemed like days, drinking the disgusting sewer water and eating food that people would throw in there.

Once I felt the heat was off of me, I decided to resurface. I found a cardboard box and made it my home. No one came looking for me. I was alone. It's amazing how someone could be forgotten and tossed aside so easily. I was only seven years old, living on the streets, companionless and dirty. You have no clue how lonely and boring it was to be on the streets.

For months, I would go through trash cans looking for food. Sometimes I would find old books. I wasn't a great reader; some of the books I couldn't even read. However, my grandfather loved to read and I think that was passed on to me. The first book I found was a torn-up copy of *Jane Eyre*. I read it over and over, until one day I found *The Odyssey* by Homer. And another day I found a water-damaged copy of *The Great Gatsby*. Books like these allowed me to escape from the loneliness I was experiencing. There's one quote that always registered with me and it was from the first book I found. *"If all the world hated you and believed you to be wicked, while your own conscience approved of you and absolved you from guilt, you would not be without friends."* To me, that meant that everyone in the world isn't pure and if you believe you are bad, then you aren't alone because everyone is some type of bad. The quote always assured me that I'm not alone and that I'm not a bad person.

One day while looking for food, I felt something tug on my leg. I looked down and there was a little boy next to me. The boy was around four years old, almost the same age I was when my father died. He was a skinny African boy with short hair and a dirty face. He couldn't talk, but he looked like he hadn't eaten for days. I looked around for the boy's family, but to no avail.

"What's your name?" I asked the young boy. He looked at me and said nothing.

"Well, then, I never had a pet dog before so how about I call you Dusty?" I said with a grin.

The boy looked at me and smiled. I grabbed some leftover pieces of hotdog out of the trashcan and handed it to the kid.

"Don't worry! I'll protect you."

Months went by and Dusty and I did whatever it took to live. We would pickpocket tourists, break into cars to sleep when it was raining, sleep in hotel lobbies, and even beg. I noticed right away that he was able to catch on to what I was doing quickly. It felt good to have Dusty around; I finally felt like I had a family with me. Dusty was attached to me like a newborn puppy is attached to their mother. Even though it was one person, it felt like the world to me to have someone look at you with love and admire you like you're the greatest person in the world. It was a dream for me.

I finally felt love. However, in every story there is some tragedy, right? And in my story, there seemed to be a lot of it. I always wanted to be the hero in my stories, but it seemed to me that I'm nothing but the tragic hero. My grandpa used to read a lot the short time I knew him, and he was a big fan of Shakespeare's *Macbeth*. The tragic hero would suffer through death and non-ethical decisions, yet would still be justified as a savior in the end. *If you were to write a story about my life would I be a tragic hero? Or if you were to write a story of my life would it be a tragedy?* To be honest, I know that tragedies are the most entertaining type of story but I don't want my story to be one. But since I was born, all I have ever known is tragedy.

One day, Dusty and I were in the subway begging for money. This beautiful woman approached us asking where our parents were.

"We don't have parents," I replied.

She said that was no good and said, "How about you two come with me and we can get some food?" We both looked at each other with excitement and followed her to her car.

She was tall with young, fair skin. We figured she was in her early twenties. She had brown hair that reached her shoulders and was wearing a red dress with white stripes going down it vertically. If I had known that she was a snake in women's clothes, we would have never gotten into her car.

Dusty and I got into the backseat of her luxury car. It smelled like lavender in there. Oh, I remember the smell so fondly. It reminded me of the perfume section of the mall.

Dusty was shaking, which told me he was nervous, so I put our seatbelts on for both of us. The woman started the car and began to drive. I was getting anxious because I thought that maybe we found a home. She was listening to some classical music on the radio.

"Do you know who's playing this?" she asked.

"Lady, I ain't got no idea. Some old fart, probably," I said. The woman laughed and looked at us. Even though she was smiling, I sensed that something was off. It was like she was trying to smile like a loving, caring mother, but it came off as sadistic, murderous, and mischievous. There was no love in that smile. There was nothing but evil intent from this woman. I felt this dark and insidious energy coming from her, and I was getting scared for me and Dusty.

Eventually, she took us through the drive-through at McDonald's. She got me a Big Mac and small fries and Dusty got a kids' meal with chicken nuggets. He never had McDonald's before so the look on his face was priceless. It was his first time eating real food that wasn't trash in a while. I was happy for him but I knew this happiness was about to end.

"You can drop us off here," I said with my mouth full. However, the woman kept her head straight and kept driving.

"HELLO?" I yelled. "Just drop us off here." She continued to drive and paid no mind to us.

46

"We're going to my house. You both need clothes," she said calmly.

I looked at Dusty and grabbed the door handle but the door wouldn't open. I started to panic a little but I didn't want Dusty to get scared, so I put on a straight face and tried to relax. Inside, I was experiencing the greatest fear I have ever experienced up to the moment. My heart was beating so fast it sounded like a drummer pounding on a drum.

All of a sudden, the woman grabbed a bottle of water from her passenger seat and said, "You look thirsty! Here drink this."

"Don't do it," I said to Dusty. I could see all over his face that he was really thirsty. So, he grabbed the bottle with no hesitation and chugged it. The woman tried to hand me another bottle but I waved her off.

I got more nervous the more we continued driving. It had only been about ten minutes and I noticed Dusty falling asleep. I shook him a little to wake him up.

"Dusty? Dusty!" I said. He wouldn't wake up and he just fell over like a log.

Suddenly, the car stopped. "All you had to do was drink the water," the woman said, still calm. "I bought you food. This should be easy, but you're making this so fucking difficult."

I looked at the bottle and I began freaking out. I unbuckled the seatbelt and tried to get out of the car. The door wouldn't budge and the woman just looked back at me with an evil grin.

"We are going to have plenty of fun, Dear," she said.

I began to panic and she reached out to me and pulled me into her seat. I fought back, but she was much stronger than she appeared. Then she reached for a syringe from her armrest. I was able to act fast and shove my elbow in her face.

"You little brat! You broke my nose. You broke my damn nose!" she cried out in pain.

I reached for her door handle and pushed it open. As soon

as my feet hit the ground, I began running. I didn't know where I was going; all I needed to do was get away.

Suddenly I stopped. In the midst of my mad dash to get away, I forgot about Dusty, so I ran back to where the car was parked, but it was gone. I had promised him that I would never leave him and that I'd protect him. But I failed and now that woman has him. "Why is my life surrounded by so much pain?" I cried out to myself. Once again, I was alone.

***

Two years later, I saw the face of that woman on the news. The anchor said, *"Jessica Matkin has been caught today. Authorities believe that she is responsible for over ten deaths of children under the age of ten. Her last victim was a young boy whom she had abducted and allegedly tortured for over two years. When the boy's body was found, police were unable to recognize the young boy due to the severity of the injuries to his face."*

Hearing all that tore me up inside and I did something that up until this point I thought was impossible to do: I turned it off. I turned my feelings off. I became so numb that even though I should have been hurting, I wasn't. I couldn't feel anything.

It was me. I killed him. I killed him when I left him in the car. I left him there to be killed because that is who I am. I'm death and despair. Death is always around me, I'm Death, and at that moment, I realized I should embrace that fact.

As I turned thirteen, my years of living on the streets continued. I was selling drugs, stealing, and sleeping on benches. I smelled like spoiled milk, and my clothes were so dirty that I forgot what they looked like originally. I gained a reputation around the streets of New York. I was the boy that couldn't feel. The boy that would do anything to survive. If someone wanted something done, I would get it done even if it meant that I would die.

One time I needed food. Badly. It had been three days since

I last ate anything. I was walking around Little Italy that day and I was approached by a dealer. He was a tall, Italian man wearing a grey Italian fitted suit with brown shoes. He had black, greasy hair, a twelve o'clock shadow, and a dimple on one of his cheeks. He had a creepy, smug voice that you'd expect to hear from criminals on *Law and Order: SVU.*

The dealer asked me to do a simple task; he asked me to pick up his merchandise from a drug house. Not having anything else to do, I made my way over there, knocked on the door, and waited. The house itself wasn't what I was picturing at all. It was in Midtown, New York in a fancy-ass building.

Eventually, a guy opened the door and a deep voice with a New York accent asked, "What do you want, Little Man?"

The guy was tall, wide, and had a thick beard. He was dressed in black sweats, dark shades, and a backward New York Knicks hat. He was not someone I expected to be living in this kind of place.

"Tony wants his goods," I told him directly. "He said you got his angel's dust."

He peeked out of the door and looked left and right to make sure no one was there, then said, "Come in."

I walked into the house and, to my disbelief, it looked like a regular house. It was clean with great furniture—almost like a house from a catalog.

I took a seat on the couch while the New York accent guy went and got the drugs. When he came back, he handed me the goods first, then all of a sudden pulled out a gun at me.

"Nah, kid, you know what? I'm gonna need that back." He punched me in the face and I fell to the ground.

What he didn't know, though, was that I was prepared. I had kept a blade in my shoe just in case the deal went sour. He began to kick me over and over and over. Strangely, it's the kind of feeling I craved.

I began laughing and the guy barked, "What the fuck is wrong with you, Kid? Do you want to die?"

I got off the floor; blood was pouring out of my mouth. "There is nothing you can do to me that this world hasn't done."

He stepped back and I fell to my knees. Little did he know, I was pulling the knife from my shoe. He reached out to pick me up and I swung aggressively at his throat and sliced it open. A few seconds later, he fell to the ground with blood flowing rapidly out of the deep cut.

"Now, sleep." I reached down and picked up the drugs from his dead hand. Then I made my way to the door to leave, but before I made it out, Tony walked in.

"Thanks, Kid! This piece of shit has been killing members of my crew and keeping the product. I'm glad you took care of him. Here is fifty dollars. Go get some food."

Holy shit, I thought to myself.

As I walked out the door, I could hear Tony kicking the dead body and laughing. The whole ordeal wore me out so I went to the park to sleep on a bench.

It was later that night while I was sleeping that I was woken up by another junkie.

"Give me these fucking shoes," he commanded aggressively.

Without wasting a second, he snatched the shoes off my feet and took off. I chased him down by jumping over benches and even stealing a bike. In a matter of minutes, I'd beaten him senseless. Blood oozed out of every cut on his face. Bystanders looked on in terror, then went about their normal lives once they've had enough.

I took my shoes from his half-dead body and went back to the bench I was sleeping on. I sank down and stared at my bruised hands.

This is nothing. Pain is just something life gives to us to let us know we are alive. This was the first time in a while that I've felt alive.

As I glanced up from my bloody hands, I saw a man walking towards me from a distance. He was nicely dressed in a blue tailored suit and clean-shaven with his hair combed over to the side. I figured he was in his late forties by his physical features: grey bushy eyebrows, crow's feet around his eyes, and a scar above his left eyebrow. He had a strong walk like he had a purpose. I sensed no fear in him despite all the blood on my hands.

He kneeled down on his right knee and rested his arms on top of his left.

"Hello there. My name is Joseph Cain." He had a tranquil voice and he sounded British or Irish, I couldn't really tell. "You've had a hard life, I see. I saw you chase down that man over there. You nearly killed him. Did he take something from you? What did he do?" he wanted to know.

I kept my gaze on the ground.

"How old are you? You don't look older than twelve. Do you have a home?" he said with deep concern in his voice.

I glared at him. "You should go unless you want to die."

He smiled at me. I didn't understand what was going through his head. I saw no fear, no anger, no evil in his eyes. Just gentleness and contentment.

"You couldn't kill me if you wanted, Boy. If I wanted to, I could kill you in an instant. No one will miss you. You will just be another carcass that the world wouldn't miss."

There was nothing I could say I that could hurt me. I was nothing and I knew that if I died no one would miss me or remember who I was. I didn't know what this man was telling me, but if he killed me right now, he would actually be saving me from the hell that I was already living.

"Kill me. I don't care. I welcome death," I said.

He lifted my chin up. "I was like you once. I lost everyone

51

close to me, but unlike you, I had lots of money and a home. I sympathize with you. How about I give your life meaning? Since you only know death, how about you bring death?"

I stared at him, puzzled. "What do you mean?"

He let go of my chin, stood up, and looked to the sky. He knew who he was, knew what he was, and knew what he wanted. I wanted that. I wanted to have that same feeling.

"I'm looking for a pupil," he continued. "Someone I can train and teach. I can give you purpose and after I'm done with you, you'll essentially be my instrument of death."

He looked down at me with conviction. "Instead of wasting your life, become my weapon. It is, by far, better than living on the street and waiting to die."

I thought about what he said and my whole life weirdly started to make sense. I wasn't destined to be around death. I was destined to be *Death*.

"The last adult I trusted killed a friend of mine. How can I trust you?" I said to him. I knew my voice sounded intense. He looked at me straight in my eyes.

"My dear boy, didn't I already tell you that if I wanted you dead, you would've already been dead? Here's the thing, what does a dead man have to lose? You don't care about your life anyway, so why not take a risk?"

In all honesty, he was right. I had nothing to lose. I didn't have anything. I was completely alone in this world. "Teach me. If it's the God of Death you want, then the God of Death I shall become," I declared.

He reached out his hand, smiling. "Indeed! Let's get to work, shall we? My God of Death."

I grabbed his hand, stood up, and we began walking.

"What is your name, Boy?" he asked.

"Joshua Hazarmaveth."

He placed his right hand on my shoulder. "No, that will not

do. Joshua Hazarmaveth is a homeless boy who lives on the street. All he knew was stealing, killing, and eating out of the trash. Not a good name for the God of Death." He raised his left hand up to his chin as if he was contemplating something stressful. Suddenly, he cried out, "I got it!" He looked at me with a smile. "Eden Dowler is your name."

He led me to a fancy four-door car. A guy wearing a black suit, white button-down, and black tie opened the back door. Once I entered the car, I was no longer Joshua Hazarmaveth, born April 20, 1996, in Cairo, Egypt. On that day, September 21, 2009, I became the God of Death for an organization called the House of David. That day, I became Eden Dowler.

Many things became clear to me. I was young but I needed to grow up. Everything that was going on in my life was my story. I was the writer and I could dictate how it ends. What scared me a lot was that I didn't know if I was the hero or the villain of my own story. But I didn't care whatever I was at that moment. I would be the best damn hero or the best damn villain in the world.

While sitting in the back of the car with Joseph, he asked me if I trusted him.

"Yes. Do I have a choice?"

He smiled. "No. No, you don't have a choice."

I averted my eyes and couldn't help but think about some of the doubts coming into my head. *What did I get myself into? How stupid can I be?*

"Trust me, Child. I'm not going to actually hurt you. I'm not going to promise that you won't experience any pain, though. The training will be rigorous and at times demanding, but it is the type of pain that will make you great." He patted me on my head.

I glanced up at him with a confused look.

"You're going to sleep now, okay?" His voice was so calming.

I felt nothing, but I sensed that I would be safer with him

than I would be alone on the streets. Then I started dozing off.

The next thing I knew, there was banging. It sounded like it was coming from outside. I slowly opened my eyes and found myself in a room. I was on a twin bed. It was the most comfortable bed I had ever slept on since I was born. Around me, there was a dresser, a TV, a desk, and one window.

I sprang up and dashed to the window to see where I was and, to my surprise, all I could see was dark blue water that spanned for miles.

Then, I went to the desk and there were books on the desk. Math books, history books, art books, books of weapons, biology books, and anatomy books. I checked the dresser next. All three drawers were filled with clothes.

Then there's a knock on the door and Joseph entered without waiting for a reply. He was dressed in an all-black military suit.

"Your training begins now. From the second drawer, grab the clothes and put them on. Meet me outside in five minutes," he instructed, then he left.

I ran to the drawer to put the clothes out. I was surprised that every outfit was the same: light gray crewneck sweatshirt and a cotton gray sweatpants. I left the room right after Joseph. "Don't I need shoes?"

He gave me a stoic look and told me that, apparently, I must earn shoes. We shuffled down the hall and I lost my balance as the floor underneath me swayed side to side.

"Are we on a ship?"

Joseph looks at me and smiles. "We are indeed on a ship. Welcome to the Gate."

I followed him.

"What is the Gate?"

He continued to walk forward. Right as I was thinking the hallway seemed like it was never going to end, he suddenly stopped in front of a door to the right of us. "The Gate is the Headquarters of the House of David. You will learn more later on, but first, we must begin training." He opened the door and the room had mats everywhere.

"Show me how you fight. Attack me!" he commanded.

I didn't know why he would want me to attack him, but in my moment of hesitation, I lost my chance.

"Okay, I guess I'll go first." He came at me with a swift punch to my stomach. It was so powerful I flew two feet backward, hit the mats, and everything I ate came flying out of me.

"You managed to chase that New York man down and beat him to a pulp, but you couldn't read my movements? I know you can fight so show me," he said gently.

He marched up to me and kicked me in the chest. I slid across the floor, choking and spitting.

"Really? You're just going to sit there and take this?"

I rolled onto my hands and knees in pain and replied, "Well, that was a little unfair of you to attack me when I was already down."

He took a few steps towards me. "In this world, you have to fight to get what you want. If you do nothing, then you will be reduced to nothing. You have two choices: either fight or die. And, Eden, don't get me wrong, I will kill you. So, come at me with everything if you can fight."

He stared at me like he was looking through me. I felt his calm intensity, power, and confidence. I never saw someone look at a person like that before.

He walked back to the spot where he started and positioned himself for another attack. I slowly got up and he came at me again. I felt I was going to die. I couldn't move. *I'm okay with dying, at least I'll get to see my family and Dusty again.*

However, my body had other things in mind. I lunged to the left of his attack then went in to punch him in the face. He grabbed my fist and threw me across the room into the wall like a rag doll. I hit the wall and landed on the ground.

"There you go, Lad! That's what I wanted to see."

I rolled to my side in pain. "You wanted to see me get thrown across the room like a piece of shit?"

He walked up to me and reached his hand out to pick me up. I grabbed it.

"Language! I wanted to see what you would do if you faced death. And you didn't disappoint. You moved. Your instincts made you move. Few people are able to do that. Humans normally have two options in a fight—submit or defend. You, my dear boy, are one of the few who has that instinct to fight."

What Joseph was saying to me wasn't making a lot of sense. On one hand, I wanted him to kill me because I craved it but on the other hand, I thought maybe he was right. Or maybe I wasn't worthy to die just yet. Death is for those who have lived a great life and have done things where they can finally accept their fate and move on. Maybe I don't deserve to die yet because death does not want me.

"That will do for today," Joseph said. "I wanted to test your skills and see if you have that instinct. Let's go meet some other Captains."

"Who are Captains?"

"Captains are under Judges. They are the individuals that will replace Judges when the time comes. You, my dear boy, are my Captain and one day you will replace me. I should have explained it earlier. There are twelve Judges, and under the twelve Judges are their Captains. Since the founder was a very religious man, he decided to create twelve Judge spots to symbolize the twelve apostles. You'll find the number twelve has a big presence in the House. Anyway, Captains are chosen by the Judge and, normally, there are two Captains to a Judge. Judges are rare. Normally, those nominated as Captains never become Judges.

Judges must be nominated by the King of Hearts, the leader of the House of David. Captains must show courage, honor, skill, valor, and must also successfully complete missions that seem impossible if they want to become a Judge. Eight of the twelve Judges must nominate the Captain with the King of Hearts giving the final say."

Wow. And Joseph thinks that I can be a Judge. I'm just a homeless boy without an education.

"I became a Captain when I was seven years old. My father was a very wealthy businessman in London. However, he liked to gamble a lot and he lost all our money. To survive, he sold me off to sex traffickers. I was a sex slave from the age of five until seven. Luckily, a Judge at the time was searching for an artifact and saved me from that terrible place. From that day forward, I was free. I dedicated my life to the House of David.

"I was promoted to a Judge at the age of twenty after completing nineteen missions and finding four artifacts. When I saw you that day, I saw a part of myself and I wanted to give you the same chance to make a difference. But you need to understand that you are not only Eden. You are also a weapon who serves the House of David. Do I make myself clear?" he paused and studied me. "If you fail me then I will kill you myself and throw you overboard."

His threats don't scare me; I'm already dead. "What is the House of David?" I asked.

He put his hand on my shoulder. "The House of David is an organization that collects biblical artifacts so that others with evil intent can't use them to manipulate people with faith." He continued to talk as we walked towards the door. "Now, don't make me regret this."

"I understand. I don't make promises."

"Good. Never make a promise you cannot keep. However, you will not fail me."

We walked down the hallway and entered a massive room.

It looked like a library. I have never seen so many books before in my life. There were books everywhere, up and down the walls.

There were about twenty long, wooden tables straight ahead of me with chairs all around them. At the first table, there are two people: an older woman and a young girl. The younger one was slender and attractive. She looked around fifteen years old and had bob-length brown hair with long bangs that almost covered both her blue eyes.

"Greetings, Trish! I would like for you to meet my new Captain, Eden," Joseph said enthusiastically.

The older woman and the girl turned around and looked at both of us with excitement in their eyes. The older woman, Trish, had long braided white hair that went halfway down her back. I could tell even from far away that she had crow's feet on the corners of her lovely blue eyes. She also had full lips, pierced ears, and long beautiful eyelashes. She was wearing a long, sleeveless, blue dress that was tight around her hips. She was the most beautiful older woman I had ever seen.

"Hello, Joe! And nice to meet you, Eden," she said.

Joseph smiled back at her and said to the younger one, "Greetings, Sarah! Could you show Eden around? He's new."

"Of course, Joe. Come on Eden!" Sarah agreed and sprang up cheerfully. She grabbed my hand and pulled me away until we got to a bookshelf with words on them I could not pronounce. She began talking but I was paying more attention to how many books there were.

"You must like books," she said.

"Well, where I came from we didn't have much. All I could do was read."

"That's cute," she smiled.

My eyebrows jumped up. "Flirting is a woman's trade. One must keep in practice."

She looked surprised. "I don't see you as a Jane Eyre fan,"

she replied, "and I'm assuming that you think I'm flirting with you, but I'm not. I'm just friendly."

I walked down the rows of books before I changed the subject. "So, can I read all these books?"

She followed me. "No, but you will read a lot of books."

I looked back at her over my shoulder. "How long have you been here?"

She giggled and then said, "Three years. Trish is my grandma. My mom was not talented at anything, so my grandma never pushed her. When I was born though, grandma said she saw that I was extremely talented so she asked if I would like to do what she does. I said yes and then she asked my mom and she agreed as well."

I nodded my head in understanding. *That made sense.* "So, that's all have you've done since you've been here?" I asked her.

She put her left hand on her chin. "Well, mostly I've been training. We have to learn a lot about history and how history books in schools are wrong. We learn different languages, math, biology, and anatomy. I have been on three missions, but nothing too dangerous."

I turned away from her and thought to myself that this was going to be really hard. I was about to ask Sarah one more question but I was interrupted by Joseph.

"Eden, it's time for us to go."

Sarah hugged me and said, "I can't wait to be friends. Bye, Eden." She released me and, with a dull look, I approached Joseph. He put his hand on my shoulder and guided me to leave the room. I saw Trish still at the table reading a book with what looked like weird words in it. I couldn't tell if it was early or late out.

"Come with me. We're going to my chambers." We walked down the hall up and up a few stairs. I was amazed that I didn't see anyone.

"Judges don't always live on the Gate. We're allowed to

have families and most of us go live with our families. However, if there is a mission, we have to return to the Gate and prepare. For young Captains, most live on the Gate until they're about eighteen. If they have families, they're allowed to visit them."

I shoved my hands in my pockets.

"I'm assuming that I'm never leaving here because I don't have a family."

Joseph stared straight ahead. "Indeed. You will stay here, prepare, and train. When the time is right, you will become a Judge."

We continued walking and, once again, it all seemed to become a little clearer to me. My purpose was to bring death.

We went up some stairs and entered another hallway. We walked past eight doors before finally arriving at a door on the left. The sign to the right of it read: *Judge Joseph Cain*.

Then under the sign, there was a small, round, black scanner. Joseph stood completely still as the black scanner shot a laser up and through his eyes. I heard it beep and the door opened. Joseph walked forward and I followed.

His room was large, about the size of a two-bedroom apartment. It looked empty and plain. There was a bookshelf on one wall and guns and ancient weapons on the other. Some words caught my eye: swords, spears, shields, and axes.

He pulled out a metal chair, sat in it, and placed his right arm on the square, black metal table. Following his lead, I pulled out the chair near him and sat down.

There were books on the table. Some looked old and some looked new.

"Eden, I know this is soon, but in two days I'm taking you on a mission to take down this fanatic group in London. I will give you a mission brief the day before. You don't have any training, but I think with you, you'll learn best through experience, anyway. In the meantime, I want you to read all these books." He placed four books on the table. "You have until the day of the mission brief to finish them."

Joseph reached for them one by one and handed them to me. One book was the Bible, another a history book, an anatomy book, and the last was a book on the history of Judges.

"You will also have weapons training until the day of the mission. You must learn how to shoot a gun and how to kill precisely with a knife," he continued.

I looked down at the books and said to Joseph, "Do you really expect me to finish reading all these books? There are more than two thousand pages here."

He stood up from his chair and held the door open for me. "Yes, I do expect you to finish them. Now, begin."

I got up cradling the books and, as I started for the door, I heard him say one more thing.

"Don't fail me." Then he shut the door behind me.

I headed to my room and all I could think about was the mission. I passed two people and I didn't see who they were because I was looking down the whole time. I could hear them whispering to each other as I walked by.

"That must be Joseph's Captain . . . Looks rough around the edges."

Whatever they were saying to me didn't matter, though. Joseph gave me a purpose and I wanted to succeed. Once I got back to my room, I read for about six hours until I fell asleep.

Later, I was awakened by a bang. I popped my head up and saw a man opening my door. He had long, stringy, black hair and a huge grin on his face.

"Eden Dowler, I presume!" he said with a voice that sounded like he had something in his throat. His black eyes were wide open and he was dressed in a black dress shirt, dark pants, and dark shoes. He also had on a military green trench coat with black fingerless gloves.

"Yes," I replied.

"I'm Judge Judah Kosner, and I will be your weapons teacher. Come with me to the shooting range."

I wiped my face and followed Judah down the hallway and up three stories of stairs, down another hallway past what looks like a classroom. He had a slim body and stooped when he walked. He also was considerably shorter than me.

He finally opened the door and I followed him into the classroom. Inside there was a target carrier, ceiling baffles, and a bullet trap in front of me. There were twelve stations inside and more guns in one room than you could ever imagine. As I counted in my head, I figured there were at least 300 different types of guns varying in size, ability, and purpose.

"I already set you up in station three. Let's head there now," he said.

We walked to the station where I saw a headset and a semiautomatic gun on the table.

"Pick up the gun and show me what you got, Kid. Hit the target ahead," he instructed, his arms crossed.

I picked up the gun with my left hand and aimed it at the target, but before I could shoot he hit me on the head and said, "Now, if you're not careful, the gun will recoil on you. You're holding it too loosely. The proper gun grip for this type of gun is this." He reached over my shoulder and adjusted how I was holding it.

"Place the gun between your thumb and index finger. Both of your thumbs should be on the same side. Your thumbs need to be high and pointing forward to give you more strength on your grip. Now, your right hand will be your support hand. Your support hand's thumb needs to be along the side and pointing away. Place your trigger finger on the trigger guard until you are on target and ready to shoot."

I placed the headphones on my head, aimed at the target,

and pulled the trigger five times. Immediately after, the target carrier brought my target up to me. I had hit it only three times.

"We have a lot of work ahead before you can go out in the field. Can't believe Joseph wants you out there this soon," he said.

"I can do better."

"Very well. We'll stay here for four more hours until you're able to hit the target every single time."

I was there for three hours. Once I finished, I went back to my room and continued my reading. I read for eight hours straight. What I learned was that the history books didn't match what the House of David's history books stated. So many things were different—the real reason why the World Wars all started, the Vietnam War, the Crusades, Muhammed was led by the belief that these artifacts, these holy artifacts, could help the enemies gain more power. I learned that many people believed that these artifacts had special powers, but according to the books, there was always a scientific reason why the artifacts would work or not work.

That night, I wasn't able to sleep. Judah came in to tell me it was time for weapons training again. For two hours we shot different types of guns. With every minute, I became more proficient. Judah even said, "Eden, you have a certain knack for weapons." Except when he said that, I was more certain that I had a knack for death.

When I came back to my room later that day, Joseph was standing there waiting for me.

"Follow me," he said.

We went to the fourth floor into the War Prep room. Monitors surrounded the entire back wall and there was a round table right in the center with twelve seats around it. It really looked like Arthur's round table.

Joseph sat down and pulled up a chair next to him for me to sit.

"Judah said that your shooting has gotten incredibly better. I guess you will be able to become the House of David's Reaper."

"What's the mission?" The screens on the wall changed and showed pictures of Earth. Then they narrowed down to a singular point in California around Dublin City.

"Mission: Blood Mary. It is located in the city of Dublin where someone is claiming to hold the blood of Mary in a tube. This 'someone' is Marco Hale. Marco claims that while he was visiting Rome three years ago, the Mother of God came to him and gave him a vial."

The computer screens rapidly changed images that corresponded to his story.

"So, Marco brought it back with him and has used it to generate a following of radicals. We would have taken this lightly, except we learned that Marco was plotting to spike the alcohol supply at an event in California called Coachella with the liquid in the vial. We don't know what's in the vial. But we think that it could be a poison that would kill anyone who drinks it. We're not sure of his motives, but when reading his Twitter posts he would complain about how the government is getting rid of jobs, and also how people have lost their faith and how the church needs to bring faith back. Trish has been following this for a while and I think this would be a good mission for you to go on. It should be a simple extraction."

I nodded in agreement and felt a flutter of excitement.

"Captain Sarah Bradley, Judge Trish Bowden, myself Judge Joseph Cain, and you, Captain Eden Dowler, will go on this mission. We will take a helicopter at 0800 tomorrow and we will land ten miles north of Dublin. From there, we will work our way down to the house. Our mission is to sweep the house, find Marco, and take him in. We will survey the property at noon and hit the house later at night. Trish and Sarah will be the ones surveying the house and in 2000, we'll be the ones hitting it. We will not engage

64

unless we have to."

I nodded at Joseph to let him know I understood.

"Now go get some sleep. Your outfit will be given to you in a briefcase before the mission. Be up at 0700. You're dismissed."

I headed towards the door, paused, then looked at him over my shoulder. "I know this is my first mission. I'll do my best."

He just nodded, then turned his attention back to the monitor.

I hardly slept that night. Eventually, the morning came. I found a briefcase with my new clothes at my door. Inside were a blue polo, khakis, and brown shoes. I put them on and headed towards the deck where the helicopter was. Joseph, Trish, and Sarah were standing right next to it, talking. Joseph and Trish nodded at me. Sarah smiled and waved.

We all got into the helicopter; Joseph sat next to Trish and Sarah sat next to me. As we ascended, Joseph talked to us through the headphones we were wearing, but I couldn't hear a thing; I was extremely focused on the task.

The flight only took a few hours and there were already two cars waiting for us at the local airport where we landed. Joseph and I got into one car and the others got into the other. On the passenger side floor, there was another briefcase.

"Open the briefcase," Joseph said.

Inside there was a black vest, black pants, and black boots.

"That is a long-sleeved, shear-thickening fluid (STF) armor, ballistic leggings, shin guards level IA, black Kevlar 3A pants, and Damascus steel-toed boots," he explained. "When a weapon strikes or penetrates the armor you're wearing, the shear-thickening fluid immediately hardens. Once it hardens, it becomes ten times stronger than Kevlar. This happens instantly and the STF becomes flexible again afterward so you can continue to move," he continued.

I gave him a quizzical look. "What does that mean?"

He kept his eyes on the road. "The only thing that would possibly hurt you is getting shot by a shotgun at point blank range."

We arrived at a cheap, rundown hotel.

"Let me guess, all of the shittier hotels were booked already?" I said to Joseph as he walked in to talk to the clerk.

"We won't be here long. We just need to get in and out."

After paying the clerk and receiving the room key, we walked to the room. As soon as we entered, Joseph said, "You need to get this right. This should be an easy mission, but you must be prepared for everything. If something goes wrong, you must be willing to take a life. They don't know who we are, so if you kill, leave no witnesses. The House of David must not be jeopardized by this mission."

I was a little nervous but I didn't want to let Joseph down. I was determined to do my best to succeed at any cost.

Trish and Sarah arrived at the hotel a couple of hours after us. I had already changed into the mission attire, but Joseph hadn't changed into anything and was still wearing his blue suit. Trish was wearing casual clothes, too. It was only Sarah and me who were wearing the mission gear.

We got into one car this time; Sarah and I in the backseat with Joseph and Trish in the front. We arrived in the neighborhood where the house from the computer screens was. Joseph drove by it twice before stopping.

"We know the dimensions of the house so we know the risk. We just need to get in and get Marco," Trish said.

Joseph gave out instructions. "Eden, you will be going through the front and, Sarah, you will be going through the back."

"Aren't you two coming with us?" Sarah asked.

"This is your and Eden's mission," Trish responded.

I looked at Sarah and back at Joseph.

"What are you talking about? I've only been in this group for, like, four days. I'm not ready for this!"

"Sarah has been on multiple missions with me. This is just a get in and get out. You should be fine and if something breaks out, then we will step in immediately. We want you to do this," Joseph said. "If you read the books I gave you and worked hard in your training, then you will not fail."

Knowing my luck, I might get Sarah killed.

Trish handed Sarah and me black athletic sunglasses with a little screen on the right side next to the lens.

"Those glasses have a camera in them which will allow us to see what you see," Trish said, pulling out a computer pad. Then, Joseph handed us little black earpieces.

"These earpieces will allow us to communicate with you. You can talk to us and we can talk to you," he said. We put the earpieces in and tested them out. "Under our seats, there are two medium-sized glass cases."

Sarah and I reached underneath the seats in front of us and grabbed the cases. I opened my case to see a handgun, three clips, and a black, eleven-inch tactical knife.

Sarah's cases contained only a dual semiautomatic handgun and six clips.

As we got out of the car, I could see that Sarah didn't seem as nervous as I was. I didn't think that I would be this nervous but I could feel my heart racing. I had only been learning for four days and for him to think that I would be ready for this seemed absurd.

The car drove away. It was a cold, windy night, and it was giving me a creepy feeling. Maybe it was because it was my first mission or maybe because I was about to experience something new.

"Let's go, Eden," Sarah demanded. "I will sneak in from the back. Check out the front and try to find a way in. Hopefully, everyone in the house is asleep. Remember, this is a fanatic group.

Don't underestimate them and don't lose your cool. You must be calm and focused." She sounded so confident and I was thankful.

I nodded in understanding.

She headed towards the back and to the right while I headed straight down the street until I got to the front of the house where I snuck in slowly. It was a ranch-style home, and the yard was empty. As I approached the side of the window, I took a quick look inside. I couldn't see anything because the windows had blinds.

"Hold. Do you want me to get in, Joseph?" I asked my tiny earpiece.

I didn't receive a response. *Maybe this was all a test to see my worth*.

"Fuck it. I used to rob people on the streets of New York. I'll just break into this place," I said out loud. I made it around the house and found a side door with a window. I jammed my knife in between the lock and the door frame and pushed the door open. I was surprised to hear no alarms.

There wasn't anything that surprised me about the kitchen: gray granite countertops, white cabinets that looked recently updated, and standard black appliances.

"Sarah, how does the back check out?" I asked into my earpiece once again. I continued to survey the kitchen and couldn't hear any signs of people in the house.

"I'm going to check this shed and the garage and I will meet you inside. Examine the second and first floors," she responded.

"Roger that." I've heard in the movies that you have to respond with that, though I wasn't really sure, and I didn't know what else to say, anyway.

Eventually, I headed out of the kitchen into the living room with pictures of a loving family hanging up on the wall. I grabbed a frame off the wall. It was a picture of Marco, a short thicker woman, and a beautiful little girl. I studied it for a minute, then I heard a noise coming from upstairs.

I put the picture down and made my way upstairs quietly. I moved one foot at a time, slow as a turtle, making sure I didn't make a sound. I wanted to contact Sarah, but it would blow my cover. I raised my gun. There was a noise from a room two doors down from the right.

I approached the room and slowly opened the door. It looked like a field of colorful flowers like the ones you see at Skagit Valley. But I caught a whiff of something I was very familiar with. It was a cherry smell masking the scent of decaying rot. There was a man inside; he turned around, and it was Marco.

The flowers turned into bodies and I saw the candles burning in a circle around him. He was in a black coat, barefoot, and his head was shaved bald.

"Sarah, I found Marco, and all his followers are dead," I said confidently, never taking my eyes off him. Then my gaze darted to the corner of the room to a little girl. It was the little girl from the picture. She was sitting on a chair with scabs, lesions, and blisters all over her. She looked like a diseased, flea-infested dog you normally would find on the streets. Anger filled my body.

"What did you do to her?"

He looked at me with a smile on his face like he hasn't lost anything. "This is God's will. He wants to cleanse this world of the impurities that have fallen. These insects weren't as pure as I."

I raised my gun, pointed it at him, and yelled, "What did you do to her?"

I heard approaching footsteps from behind. Sarah walked up beside me.

"Marco, where is the vial?" she asked. But Marco had a confused look on his face.

"Vial? Or do you mean the pure blood of Mary? I was given this by Mary herself when I was lost in the tunnels."

Sarah approached him slowly. "Wrong. You were given that vial by a member of an organization called Seditio."

"No, NO, NO! Mary gave me this herself! She was the mother of God and chose me to deliver justice."

He was yelling. He reached out his hand to his daughter and urged, "Come, Child."

His daughter approached him slowly. I can see blood dripping from her inner thighs.

"You didn't? Did you rape your own daughter? How could you?" I shrieked, my voice trembling with anger.

Marco held her hand and she dropped to her knees. She was coughing blood and yellow puss. "She isn't my daughter anymore. She is a vessel for the new world," he said creepily.

My blood was boiling. *How in the world is someone like this allowed to live?* A monster like him doesn't deserve to live.

"The vial contains a deadly virus, Marco. If you drink it then you will surely die. We can't allow you to give that to anyone," Sarah said.

But Marco completely ignored Sarah. Instead, he picked up his little girl and began to kiss her on the lips. "You guys can watch while I finish my duty to Mary," he said.

I couldn't take it anymore. I punched him in the face. I hit him so hard I felt his face mold across my fist. He dropped the girl and stumbled back. I grabbed his throat and punched him again. He dropped to the floor, and I climbed on top of him and continued to punch him over and over and over. His two front teeth came flying off. Finally, I grabbed his collar, lifted him up, and snarled, "I don't give a damn about you or your fucking followers. But your own daughter? How could you do that to her? How could you hurt her? How?"

He just grinned. I grabbed my knife off my side and raised it to finish him off.

"Wait, Eden! We don't know where the vial is!"

70

I didn't care, though. All I could see was red, but someone grabbed my arm again.

"Please don't kill my daddy. He doesn't know what he's doing."

It was the little girl. She was bleeding and barely alive. I got off the man and faced her.

"Mister, I wanna go now. It hurts too much," she said to me.

I could tell she wasn't going to make it. The best thing for this girl was death. She sank to her knees, coughing and bleeding in pain, and all I could think about was Dusty. I wanted to give this little girl peace.

I got on one knee and grabbed her close to me. "May you rest," I whispered, then I grabbed the knife and slowly pushed it into her heart. Her eyes closed slowly and her head tilted to the side as if all of her muscles had loosened up.

She fell limply to the floor. I could see a hint of a smile on her face even as she laid there dead.

Sarah surveyed the room and approached Marco, forced him down to his knees, yanked his hands behind his back, and zip tied his wrists.

Joseph and Trish shuffled into the room, looking proud. Trish approached a painting on the back of the room. It was a painting of the Mother Mary. Below the painting, there was a bowl containing a clear liquid.

"Don't touch her blood!" Marco yelled.

Trish turned her gaze to Joseph. "This is the sample. Call the Gate and tell them to isolate the area."

Joseph approached me. "You did well. You killed her out of mercy. Don't let this define you."

"This doesn't define me. I am who I am. Death."

Sarah looked at me with sad eyes. I knew she was sad about the girl dying, but she was sad for me, too.

Then, out of the corner of my eye, I saw one of the dead bodies move.

"DO IT FOR MARY," Marco yelled.

A black-haired man with blood all over him stood up, aimed his pistol at me, and took a shot. Joseph darted in front of me. The man fired another four shots into Joseph's chest.

I stared at Joseph with shock and awe. *Why would he do that for me?*

"Are you okay?" I yelled in concern but he didn't even look hurt. He stood up tall. The man looked at him in horror and backed up until he stumbled against the wall.

"Here's another lesson, Eden. Show no remorse to your enemies. Kill that man."

So, I shot the man in the head. His body hit the wall and slid down like a sack of potatoes.

Joseph stared at Marco so intensely. His presence was so powerful that I was overwhelmed to the point where I couldn't move.

"You don't scare me! Mary will save me!" Marco cried at Joseph.

"Mary can save you from Death. Death comes to us all," Joseph muttered ominously. Then he pulled a thirteen-inch knife from inside his suit jacket and swiped at Marco's head.

"Eden, we're leaving now. Trish and Sarah will handle this from here on."

I followed him to the door and, one last time, looked back at Marco's body. His eyes were wide open and his throat was still oozing out blood. I've seen death so much that this was the norm for me.

As Joseph and I left the house, at least ten people wearing black leather suits and gas masks came in. Joseph and I drove off in a black Nissan Altima.

"How did you survive being shot?" I asked Joseph.

He stared straight ahead at the road and responded as calmly as always. "Each Judge is given the previous Judge's Finger of God. The Finger of God is a piece of blood-stained wood said to be from the cross Jesus was crucified on. The founder of the House of David found twelve separate pieces of it scattered in a white cloth and discovered its great powers. If the Finger of God (FOG) is touching your body, any wound you suffer will heal in a matter of minutes."

I looked at him in shock. "Is the wood holy? Blessed? How does it heal you so quickly?"

Joseph chuckled. "Around 1902, Judge Jonathan Hubbard tested the Finger of God to see what property it possessed. He discovered that the wood had bacteria in it. Once it touches the skin of a human, the bacteria has a reaction that allows the human body to produce red and white blood cells at an accelerated pace which helps create collagen—a tough, white fiber that forms the foundation for new tissue. The collagen forms immediately once the skin has been pierced and fills it with new tissue, called granulation tissue. If the Finger of God is on your skin, then the holder will be able to regenerate and heal. However, if the holder is shot or stabbed through the heart then the person will die."

I was so amazed at what I was hearing. I didn't know anything like that existed.

"So why don't I have one? How many pieces of it do we have?" I asked.

"Miraculously enough, we only have twelve pieces. That is why it was decided that only the twelve Judges can hold a FOG," he said.

"But if it has the ability to heal people then why don't we share it with the world? Why not make more pieces?" I asked.

Joseph looked at me, sighed, stopped the car, and started to unbutton his shirt. He opened it and showed me a scar on his upper right pectoral. It looked like a little piece of wood was stitched into his skin.

"The problem is that, when studying the pieces of wood, Jonathan found out that breaking them into smaller pieces would kill the bacteria and taking the bacteria from the wood would kill it as well. He concluded that there was something about those twelve particular pieces of wood that keeps the virus alive and tampering with those existing pieces would eliminate the powers of it entirely. To this day, no one knows why, and no one knows how to recreate the bacteria. Some people even say the bacteria could contain traces of the blood of Jesus. But what we do know is that having our twelve Judges protected with the FOG has made us even more strong in protecting humanity. I told you, Kid. Twelve is an important number at the House." He looked at me with a comforting smile.

This time, I was satisfied with the answer he gave me. There were so many things in this world that I still didn't know. Being a Judge would help me understand more.

"Does it bother you that you killed Marco?" Joseph asked.

"No. He deserved to die. I would do it again if I could."

He looked at me with the same stoic smile. "Good. You are my weapon of death. You need to be faster on the attack, though. You were .05 seconds off. Don't hesitate. You are letting your emotions control you. I'm okay with that because you're using your instincts. However, don't let anger consume your judgment."

"That knife of yours . . . is it an ordinary knife? The metal looks different," I asked with extreme interest.

"Judges usually carry a weapon that we like to call a Tool. Each Tool is either found or made. Usually, the Tool represents something significant to the Judge. Mine is this 13-inch knife. Growing up, I've always liked knives and I've always been good with them. Only Judges can have tools," he added.

"What Tool do you think Death would wield?" I looked out the window. I could feel Joseph's eyes on me.

"A death scythe."

"Yes. A death scythe seems suitable for Death."

Chapter 4: You Must

AS I LAY IN my king bed, I hear the rain hit the window of my room. I study my blank walls. I never really liked having pictures up. I've always felt like wall art does nothing but clutter up a room. I'm a simple human. I don't need a whole lot to live, really, just the essentials.

My room has only that, the essentials. A bed, a brown single-drawer bedside table, a desk, a computer that I designed myself, a brown six-drawer dresser, and a black and white striped rectangle rug. My room is spacious enough to hold everything I need. It is on the top floor of a two-story house. It has two windows, one in front of the room and another one on the right side. My room's walls are painted navy blue with white accent trimmings. The most meaningful part of my room is the six pictures of my family which I have spread out on my dresser, bed, and bedside table.

My computer is a custom workstation desktop that is fully prepared to handle multiple resource-intensive tasks such as software development, 3D modeling, video rendering, VR development and more. I customized it with the latest in workstation technology from NVIDIA, Intel, and AMD. It holds six different motherboard mounting orientations, a dual-hinge carbon fiber front door, support for up to 40 total system hard drives, and 1mllimeter tempered glass side panels. My workstation is everything, especially since beginning to work at my parents' bakeshop. It has become my only connection to software and technology—which was my favorite component of engineering school.

All I can think about is what a weird person Eden is. I want to figure out his secrets. How can murder be so normal to someone? He just killed a man without any remorse. And how was he able to survive being beaten like that? He was shot multiple times and his skull was bashed in. Anyone who was shot that many times and beaten like he was should be dead and not be able to walk or even defend himself. I don't know why this is bothering me so much. It doesn't make any sense to me. What is a Judge? I don't understand. I want to know what's going on. I need to figure this out.

Knowing that sleep isn't an option at this point, I get out of bed and get onto my computer. I log in and type into the browser "Judge." The only thing that pops up is information on standard court judges.

This isn't right. I must be missing something. "Wait." I need more information. I know that Eden is going to be here for a while. Maybe, if I locate where he's staying, I can follow him.

I pause. Why would I do that? Why am I so curious about this man? Is it because he was able to do something that I've never thought about doing? Killing isn't something that usually comes naturally to people, or is it?

Murder is something I'm not sure I'm capable of comprehending, but at the same time, I want to understand. If someone that cold could exist, then there must be someone who has the warmth this world needs. I want to save him and show him there's another way than murder. But do I need to save him? Why would I save somebody like that? I barely know him. Maybe it's an excuse I'm telling myself.

I can't help but keep coming back to the truth that I know: Killing is never the right way to go by things. However, Eden makes me think there's more to it than that; I want to know his mindset to understand his point of view. It's almost like I want the power he has, in some way. But that might be a lie, too. I think my curiosity about death and suffering is why I want to see things through his eyes.

Nothing is wrong with being curious, though. Most human beings are curious by nature. As children, we are born as little scientists, endlessly curious about this world and everything that lives in it. I'm a prime example of a curious individual. I want to understand everything and come up with solutions that help better situations and better people's lives. But I need the power, experience, and knowledge to fulfill this goal.

I check my phone and I notice that Mary has texted me five times.

11:00 pm DUDE! I can't believe that all happened yesterday
11:01 pm I'm glad we left before the police got there we would be in some junk!
11:02 pm Orion??
11:03 pm Answer!!!
11:03 pm Fine bye

I don't respond because I just want to be alone with my thoughts. I want to better understand what happened today.

"I'll text her tomorrow," I mumble.

I roll over on top of my covers. The clock says 12:00 am. I grab my pillow and doze off.

I wake up to Carly Rae Jepsen's "Call Me Maybe." I look at the screen of my phone and it is 5:00 am. I turn off the alarm, rub my eyes, and head to my bedroom door.

"I can't believe that I slept in my work clothes," I say under my breath after looking down at my shirt. I walk down the hallway past my mom's room to the bathroom. I usually go to work early on Thursdays to start prepping fresh bread, mixing up cookie dough, and baking cakes. I always take a shower, brush my teeth, and wash my face.

I head back to my room and everyone is still asleep. I head to my closet and pick out my outfit. I grab dark blue jeans and my dark brown, size thirteen boots off the floor. Then I head to the dresser and fish out a t-shirt from the top drawer and socks out of the bottom drawer. Then, I head out the door for work.

Usually, my mom and my grandparents arrive at the bakery around 9:00 am and our four employees arrive around 10:00 am. We usually hire college or high school students to do the rest of the work, and they are highly skilled and very intelligent. They are good kids and are willing to learn and help out.

Jake Lewis is twenty-one years old, goes to the University of South Alabama, and is majoring in marketing. Jake works as our local delivery driver. He has brown hair, a smooth face, blue eyes, an oval-shaped head, dimples, and pencil thin eyebrows.

Johnathan Bennett is thirty years old. He's in the Air Force but is going to school at Spring Hill College and trying to get his graduate degree in business. He's 6'7" with a slim build. He has a bald round head, a beard shadow, strong jaw features, green eyes, small ears, and a high-pitched voice that you can't mistake for anyone else. He isn't as outgoing as the others but he's a fine baker. In fact, his specialty is baking lemon pies and devil's food cake.

Rebecca Courtier is eighteen years old and works as our cashier. She's 5'2" with short black hair, a small nose ring, brown eyes, and freckles. She wears dark makeup and has a raspy voice. She goes to a private school in Baldwin Country, which is all the way across Mobile Bay.

Jamal England is twenty-one years old. Jamal goes to the University of Mobile and is majoring in music. He's a very talented trumpet player and he plays in parades during Mardi Gras I can see him making it big one day. He's six feet tall with a muscular build. He has brown skin, a temple-faded haircut, and a trimmed beard. Jamal's most defining feature though is his half-sleeve on his right arm that included images from his life. On his arm, he has a cross, an image of his mom and dad hugging one another, his grandparents' names, musical notes, and a trumpet. He's very kind, caring, and loves to listen to others and understand their lives. He works as our website developer and online salesperson. He's been doing a good job of expanding our business while keeping it within the region.

I leave the house, making sure I don't wake anyone, lock the door, and head to my car. I drive a 1999 green Honda Civic. It isn't the greatest car in the world, but it gets me from point A to point B. Also, the gas mileage on it is amazing, which saves me a ton of money.

I get in my car and head down to the store. It's still dark out, but it still looks surprisingly peaceful. Driving through Mobile is therapeutic and calming. I like to listen to music and go into my own world. Usually, I opt for the classics: Wolfgang, Beethoven, Brahms, and Vivaldi. Their music makes me feel alive. It sends me to another world. It's like, I'm able to see the world they're creating. I can feel their emotions, their pain, suffering, joy, and happiness.

I arrive at the store and see someone leaning against the door. He's dressed in all black with a hoodie. I can't make out his face but I can tell that he's average height and muscularly built. I cruise by but still can't get a better look, so I drive by and park my car at the back of the store.

Before I get out, I grab my baseball bat from the backseat, then I call 911 and tell them that there's a suspicious man at the front of the store and to send a cop immediately. After I hang up, I walk to the front cautiously.

"Nice to meet you again, Orion," I hear as I turn around the corner. The man standing there pulls his hoodie back and, to my surprise, it's the guy from the wine bar. Eden. He has light brown skin, a dark 5 o'clock shadow, and his stringy long hair that he has pulled back into a man bun behind his small ears looks like he hasn't showered in a while. His eyes are either green or hazel. He has light freckles on both cheeks, pretty thick eyebrows that seem to be kept up. I also notice his strong facial features. He also has a defined chin line, a deep dimple on the left side of his face, and high cheekbones. He gives off a somber, but confident vibe. I wouldn't have expected that from someone who could kill a man so easily.

I give him a guarded look and demand, "Why are you here? This is a strange time to be lurking around someone else's workplace." I tighten my grip on my bat just in case I need to use it.

He looks at the bat, smirks, and says, "I heard you guys make the best devil's food cake." I can tell he's been drinking and he smelled like dead meat.

I see Mobile's sheriff's car pull up. Then, the sheriff steps out and asks, "Are we having any problems here?"

He was a bigger gentleman, 5'11", bald, and he was wearing the traditional all beige uniform.

"It's okay," I say. "Just an old friend who just arrived back in town wanting some cake."

"Would you like for me to go in with you?" he asks with a cautious look.

I think about it for a moment, then decide to give Eden the benefit of the doubt. "That won't be necessary. He's about to leave."

The sheriff nods, gets back in his car, and drives away. I unlock the front door and turn my attention back to Eden. "Well, you should come back when we're open."

He begins to walk away, whistles and says, "Fine. You don't have to be all uptight. I'll be back when you guys open up."

I enter the store and when I turn around he isn't there. "That guy is really creepy," I mumble.

Then I hear someone yell. "ORIONNNNNNNN!" Mary is running full speed from across the street into the store, then stops in front of me. She smells unusual like she has been dumpster diving.

"What are you doing here, Mary?" I ask.

"Well, I was just running and I noticed you were talking to that guy from the wine bar last night," she explains, panting.

"It was nothing. He said he wanted devil's food cake and I told him to come back when we're open," I say. "I'm going to start prepping for today. You can either stay and help out or go home and we can get something to eat later."

She whips around and heads to the front door. "Yeah… I'm totally not going to help you bake. I'll just head home."

As I walk away, I hear her say, "If he bothers you again, Orion, I'll take care of it. By take care I mean punch him in his Egyptian-looking face."

I smile at her. "You're one of a kind, Mary. Thanks."

She smiles back at me then leaves the store.

As I head to the backroom, something keeps nagging at me. Mary lives twenty minutes away from the store and that's by driving. Why would she run here? I'm going to have to ask her about that later. I need to focus on baking cookies, brownies, and bread. Baking calms me down and helps me think. These two unexpected visits have already wasted forty minutes of my time. I need to get back on track.

I begin prepping and getting the bread and cookies in the oven. My mom and grandpa arrive at 8:30 am and they start making chocolate chip cookies, M&M cookies, sugar cookies, and peanut butter cookies. Then, just like the usual, Jake, Jonathan, and Rebecca arrive at 9:00 am and they begin getting ready for the day.

The day goes by fast. A lot of cookies sell out today. Usually, during the fall, we don't get as much business from outside of Mobile, but today we receive a lot of tourists wanting to try our cookies. They're from all over. We even have some from New York, California, Germany, France, and Australia. I've never left the country before so I'm fascinated whenever I meet people from different parts of the world.

Later in the evening, I'm in the back cleaning up. Rebecca calls me to the front of the store. I put the broom down in the corner of the kitchen and then I go see what she wants. "Hey, do you need anything?" To my surprise, I see the guy from the wine bar standing at the counter.

Rebecca approaches me and mutters, "Orion. This guy says he would like for you to help him."

He looks at me with this sadistic smile. He's now wearing a long black coat, black combat boots, and black gloves.

"Rebecca, go bring some more chocolate chip cookies from the back," I say to her firmly.

"He's hot! Give him my number, O," Rebecca whispers as she heads to the back.

I just look at her and roll my eyes. *If you only knew that this guy is a cold-blooded killer you wouldn't be saying that.*

"I would like some fudge brownies and a bottle of milk. Also, I would like to chat," he says.

"What do you want to chat about?" I ask reluctantly.

"I just have a few questions to ask you. We can do this the easy way or I can break the bones in your body. Either way I'll get the answer I'm looking for," he says, smiling with both hands on the counter.

It's not a stretch to say that this guy isn't afraid of getting into trouble. I'm inclined to believe he's part of a group that is either untouchable or has the means to do what they do without being detected. I don't know if I can win this. If I don't talk to him he'll hurt me. But then again, if I do and say something wrong he could hurt me, too. What's the right thing to do? I don't want to fight back because it'll cause a scene. I don't want others to get hurt. After what I saw last night, I know this guy can kill us all without any hesitation. He can kill me easily. I'm not a fighter but I can figure out a good solution.

If I call the police, it might cause an even bigger problem and he would still be able to kill all of us. We would lose a life or many lives. Also, I don't know what organization he's with. If he can kill someone in broad daylight and not suffer any consequence, then he must be connected to very powerful people.

I can get the gun from under the counter and shoot him in the leg. But then again, I've seen him get shot multiple times, and he was still able to kill a man and heal from his injuries almost instantly. I don't even know what to make of that. Is he a demon? An angel? He referred to himself as Death earlier. Is he really Death? Is he immortal? What is this power? I'll talk to him, it's my only choice.

I reach for two brownies and grab a bottle of milk and say, "That will be six dollars and thirty-two cents. Take a seat at the table by the window and I'll talk with you."

He reaches into his pocket and fishes out a wrinkled twenty-dollar bill, puts it on the counter, and says, "Okay. Oh, and you can keep the change."

He grabs the brownies and milk and walks to the table as directed. I follow him and sit right in front of him.

"So, what do you want to talk about?" I prompt.

He begins to stuff one brownie in his mouth and with three bites swallows it and grabs the milk and chugs it until it's almost empty. He wipes the crumbs off his mouth. I've never seen anyone inhale a brownie before.

"Wow. That was actually a pretty good brownie. You're a good baker," he says with a surprised look on his face. He reaches into his coat and pulls out rolled sheets of paper. Then, he rubs his chin with his left hand almost like he is thinking. "By the way let me reintroduce myself. I'm Eden. I'm the man that killed a guy right in front of another guy, right in front of you. It's no big deal."

This guy has to be crazy. I squint at him.

He lifts the rolled-up papers in his hand and starts reading them.

"Okay, so your name is Orion Carter Bachman," he read from the piece of paper.

"Where did you get that information?" I respond immediately.

"From the internet, stupid," he says in a sarcastic tone. "For a guy with two bachelor's degrees, a masters in engineering, and a PhD in the works, you seem kind of dumb."

"Well, I never would have thought that someone I met at a bar would kill someone in front of me and then look me up on the internet. Oh, wait—and track me down in person," I snap back.

He studies me, his demeanor becoming more serious and straightforward.

"Well, let's just cut to the chase. Looking at the data I have on you, you seem like a solid kid. Smart, athletic, intuitive, genuine, self-aware, cautious of others, and you think things through. At the counter a minute ago, when I basically threatened you, I can tell you played the situation out in your head accordingly to figure out the best solution," he says.

I don't understand what he's getting at.

"Yes," I reply carefully. "I knew that if I grabbed the gun under the counter and shot you in the leg, you would just heal and attack me. I remember last night how you were able to recover so I didn't want to take the risk. I didn't want any casualties, either, if you and I would have ended up fighting."

"Trust me, Kid. The only person that would have died would have been you. I wanted you to give me a reason to kill you but since you're smart I guess I'll have to go with option two," he says.

I tilt my head to the side and ask, "What's option two?"

He sits back, grabs the bottle of milk, and finishes the rest of it. Then he wipes his mouth off and says, "Do you want to change the world? Do you want to be able to save lives? Only the people whose lives you save will know. Do you believe in God? Miracles? Free will?"

Now he really has me baffled. "What are you getting at?"

He interlocks his fingers on the table, stares at them, and answers, "I'll give you this choice: You can either keep working in this bakery, continue to pursue your PhD in engineering at South Alabama, and influence the lives of people in this region. Or you can come with me and fuck some shit up."

Usually, people cater to me. They try to follow my lead, and for the most part, do whatever I say. This guy is different, though—he's in control. He knows he has the power in this situation and knows that I have no choice. However, I feel as if he wants something else from me.

"I can also tell you what I do blah, blah, blah and why I'm in Mobile," he says lackadaisically. "If you accept, I will tell you what I do, who I am, and how you can become what I am, but your own version."

Do I want to live this life? My dad said you should always live life to the fullest. Am I living my life to the fullest? He killed a man with ease like he was trained to do that. If I had that experience I could use it to do so much more in the world. I could bring hope and save so many people. I could be the hero my dad was to me, but to millions. I could gain the power necessary to achieve any goal I want.

My mind continues to play this out. This could be my only chance to fully live this life. I've never taken a risk in my life; I usually live my life cautiously. So, the urge to try something out of my comfort zone is strong. But is it stupid to follow this man, this murderer? I barely know him and I don't know what trouble he might be in.

I take a deep breath and deduce the situation thoroughly, going back through all of the facts. The main question is: Can I trust him? Can I obtain this power? I've been in Mobile helping my family store for too long. Maybe it's time to live my life and live it to its fullest potential. I could die, or this could be an amazing adventure but I'll never know unless I try. I need to take this risk.

"I accept," I finally say.

Eden smiles. "Let's begin, shall we?"

"What do you mean by 'begin?'"

He springs up from his chair and gives me a weird smile. "I'll be in contact." He shuffles towards the door with his hands in his pockets.

"I don't know what that even means!" I call out to him.

He pauses, looks at me over his shoulder, and walks back towards me. "I have to lay low for a little bit. I have killed too many men and my presence here in this city is becoming known. If I associate with you too much right now, then your family, friends, and other people you care about will be in danger. And I believe your family has something I need. So, I cannot have you or them dead before I get this thing," he explains. "You hear?"

"What's going on? Is my family in danger now?" I stand up and glower at him.

"I don't like to repeat myself. Nothing will happen to you or your family before I get what I'm looking for. I will answer all questions in due time," he says firmly, then grins. "Don't worry, dumbass, you'll be fine. You just accepted my offer so I can tell you this—you remind me of a colleague of mine and if you're anything like her, then you'll make a great employee."

"What?"

"I'll be leaving Aiden here to watch you. He's quiet, but he's extremely good at what he does. So, you'll be safe until it's time for me to get that thing from you."

After he leaves, a guy about seventeen walks in, around 5'9" slim, medium-length messy, black hair, big blue eyes, a short nose, a round-shaped head, and milk-honey colored skin. He was wearing a long, black oversized jacket, brown military pants, black military boots, a blue shirt, and a silver locket necklace. At first glance, he seems mysteriously emotionless.

He reaches his hand out to me for a handshake. "Hey, I'm Aiden Jager. I'll be protecting you."

Protecting me? There's no way this kid is older than sixteen.

His voice is gentle. It sounds wise, like he has been through some intense life experiences. It still doesn't make sense to me, though. He looks too young to sound this wise. I decide not to question him. "Thank you," I say, shaking his hand. Then he exits the store.

What a weird kid. Why would a kid so young be sent to protect me? Is everyone in this organization that mysterious?

I go back to the kitchen to finish cleaning up for the day. Rebecca walks past me and asks if everything is okay. I assure her that everything is alright and there's no need for her to worry. My grandpa and mother leave the store around 6:00 pm and Rebecca leaves soon after that.

I close the store at around 8:00 pm. Locking the door, I see that Aiden kid sitting on top of a yellow 2017 Camaro. *How subtle.* I exit through the back door. I get into my car, roll the windows down, and turn the radio on. I want to feel the cool air against my face. We aren't usually this lucky with the weather in Mobile. Having lived here all my life, I'm accustomed to extreme humidity and dramatic rain showers. After it rained all week, the temperature is around fifty degrees right now and it feels extraordinary.

When I arrive at my house, I see my mom in the front yard checking the mailbox. I take a second to look at my house – my relatively normal house. *Why did Eden want someone so, normal?* We live in the Oakleigh Garden Historic District which is a historic area of Mobile, Alabama on Government street—one of the main streets of Mobile. One of those streets where we constantly hear cars go by. My family has been in Mobile since the city was founded. So, we have accumulated a significant amount of money over time. Bachman House was built in 1906. Our home has four bedrooms and five bathrooms and is 5,227 square feet. It features a gourmet chef's kitchen with commercial-grade luxury appliances, four second-floor bedrooms and a luxurious master suite that overlooks the beautiful oak trees with Spanish moss.

I park my car in the driveway behind my mom's black Tesla model X.

"Hey, O! I have dinner on the table," my mom says, approaching me as I exit my car.

"Oh, thanks! Yeah, I'm just going to go shower, then do some studying," I say.

"O, you study way too much! Go hang out with your friends." She always sounds so proud of me.

As I walk past her, I pause to put my hands on her shoulders. "Okay, okay!. I'll see if anyone wants to go out."

She kisses me on the cheek. "Good boy!"

I enter the side door of the house into our kitchen. My grandpa is in there getting something out of the fridge. He asks me if I want anything.

"No, sir," I respond quickly. I continue to walk past him and up the stairs until I get to my room. I fall on my bed and I think. *Maybe mom is right. I have been working too hard lately. It would be nice to just get a drink with a couple of my friends.*

What Eden said is still troubling me. *What if there are more men like that guy outside the bar? What if they are going to come after me too?* I don't want my friends to be in danger. But he did say that Aiden will watch over me and he seems like a trustworthy person—creepy, but he seems to be on top of his job.

"Screw it! I need to go out and get a beer." I take off all of my clothes, except my underwear, and toss them in the hamper in the corner of the room.

After showering, I wrap the towel around my waist and brush my teeth. On the walk back to my room, the scent of rich cinnamon fills my nostrils. I'm assuming my mother is baking cinnamon rolls. *She must have gotten a sweet tooth.* They smell so delicious.

I get to my room, grab my phone, and start texting Joseph, Matt, and Jacob.

9:00 pm, Me: Hey! Do you guys want to get a beer at the wine bar?

9:05 pm, Jacob: Sure! Be there at 10. I'm not drinking so I can be DD. Does anyone need a ride?

9:06 pm, Matt: Count me out on this one tonight

9:06 pm, Joseph: I'm in! See ya at 10. I'll just get a taxi.

9:07pm, Me: Jacob pick me up

9:08pm, Jacob: I got you O! Be at your place in 30.

9:11 pm, Me: Bet

I throw my phone on the bed and head to my closet to pick out some clothes. My whole closet is pretty simple: button-downs, jeans, two black suits, and my work clothes.

I grab a pink collared shirt and a pair of jeans. I comb my hair to the left and I head downstairs. I check my phone and see a text from Jacob telling me he's here.

I yell goodbye to my family and head outside to Jacob's blue Jeep Wrangler parked outside my house.

"So, the almighty Orion finally has time to hang out with the peasants!" he yells out at me as soon as I walk out the front door.

I roll my eyes. "Yeah, yeah!" I get in the car and buckle up. Jacob is about 5'11 with a little belly. He's black, has a round face, medium-sized ears, brown eyes, a thick beard, pierced ears, and a mini afro. He's wearing a black polo and khaki pants. As we pull off my driveway, Jacob turns on the radio. "Jesus Walks" by Kanye instantly comes on. Jacob says something to me, but I can't hear a word he's saying because the music is so loud. I just nod and smile instead of asking him to talk louder.

I can see the yellow Camaro three cars behind us. I'm pretty sure it's Aiden trailing us.

We arrive at the wine bar and Jacob parks right in front of it. I have always loved the laid-back atmosphere of this bar. The Picasso pictures on the wall make it feel trendy, yet the variety of the crowd gives off a welcoming sense to everyone who walks in. Everyone is just living a normal life without any worries in the world. *This is what it looks like to live life.*

We take a seat at one of those oddly designed barstools. I always wondered why they included such outdated looking chairs in the bar, but decided they help give the bar a stylish and fancy look. Jacob calls the bartender. To my surprise, it isn't the usual Mary but someone else.

She is an attractive girl who seems to be in her late twenties. She has bob-length brown hair and long bangs, but what strikes me the most about are her bright, ocean blue eyes.

She greets us right away with a genuine smile and a cheery voice. "Hey! Would you like to try out our specials for today?"

Jacob responds jokingly with her, mimicking her outwardly happy voice. "Hey! Are you new here?"

She catches on right away. "Yes. Today is my first day."

Then I hear the door open and Joseph's bright orange shirt catches the corner of my eye as he walks in. He is a 6'4" athletic guy with messy, blond hair and olive eyes.

As Joseph approaches, I catch a glimpse of Aiden sitting at

the table by the window. He doesn't acknowledge me at all, he just continues to look at one of the Picasso paintings on the wall.

"So, the anti-social Orion finally comes out to play," Joseph says happily.

"I know, right! He never wants to do anything." Jacob laughs.

"Whoa! Unlike you two losers, I have stuff I have to do," I say.

"Calm down, Mr. Sensitive," Jacob replies.

I laugh. I really am lucky to have friends like them. I have known Joseph, Jacob, and Matt since I was eight and even though I know a lot of people in Mobile, these are the few who I actually consider close enough to be my family. They have been with me through my father dying and everything.

What I have found is that many people tend to use me because I'm smart, attractive, and have a family that is well-off. But these three guys always tell me the truth and whenever I need guidance, they're there for me. Mary is my family too, but she never really hangs out with me and the boys. She isn't as close to them as I am.

Joseph pats me on the back. I look back at the waitress curiously. "I'm sorry about that. We would like to have three Coors Lights on me."

She smiles at me and asks, "Bottle or glass?"

Jacob chimes in with the biggest smile, "Glass, please, beautiful."

She chuckles and gets three beers out of the fridge and pours them into glasses for us.

I grab the beer in front of me, take a sip, and tell her, "Thank you! I know that this is cheap beer, but it tastes so good to me."

Joseph grabs his beer and, before he takes a sip, says, "I didn't want Coors but I do like free beer." Jacob just laughs and begins drinking. As soon as I put my beer down I realize I forgot to ask the waitress her name.

"Hey, sorry, it was rude of me not to ask this, but what is your name?"

She smiles at me. "My name is Sarah."

Jacob chugs the rest of his beer and puts the glass down. "Well, pleased to meet you, Sarah. You are now my favorite bartender. If you don't mind, can I have your number?"

To our surprise, she looks at Jacob and laughs. "I would love to go on a date with you, but I'm not going to be here long. I'm just working here temporarily."

"Aww!" we drawl.

Jacob puts his head down. "My sweet angel turns me down and now is just going to leave me here in this city with you losers."

Joseph frowns at him. "Who are you calling losers, you dork?"

Sarah just chuckles and affectionately calls us dumb. Jacob orders another beer.

Why is Mary not working today? I want to text her but, usually, Mary finds her way to me.

"Why isn't Mary working today?" I finally ask Sarah.

"The owner wanted me to start as soon as possible so she gave Mary the day off."

"Oh, okay." I nod. I look back at the spot where Aiden was and he isn't there anymore. I just need to enjoy the night and my friends. We continue drinking, have a good time, and chat with Sarah. I don't know what it is about this girl but she reminds me of me. The only difference between us is that she is sure of herself and I'm still trying to figure out what I want.

Joseph and Jacob head to the bathroom and leave me and Sarah to ourselves.

"Can I talk to you for a little bit?" I ask her. "You seem so self-confident. You know who you are and what you want. How did you figure out what you wanted out of this life?"

She gives me a reassuring look, like what a mother gives their child when the child asks her a question about something so simple.

"Well, I knew at a young age that I wanted to help people. To put a smile on their face. I have seen a lot of sad people in this world and there is this one person who has been through so much hell that he sees the world differently than a normal person does. I want to be his light and show him the brightest in the world. I was given an amazing life and a loving family. Knowing that not everyone in this world has that and seeing it firsthand has given me a new perspective in life. I want to be the person that can put a smile on everyone's faces and give them hope. That's why I'm always smiling. Sorry for babbling. But, to answer your question, once I stepped out of my comfort zone, I was able to figure out what I want. Sometimes you have to take a chance to find what you want if that makes sense."

I can't help but smile. "Yes, that makes a lot of sense."

She laughs. "I'm glad you understand. Sometimes I have trouble explaining things."

What do I want for myself? I want power and the only way I can get what I need to protect the people I love is to learn from Eden. Jacob and Joseph get back from the bathroom.

"All right, ladies and gentlemen! It's time for me to go to bed," Jacob declares.

This makes me think. Jacob usually likes to stay out until five in the morning, but the fact that he wants to leave this early usually means he didn't have money to go out with in the first place.

"You must be broke, and I'm not paying for you, so I'm going to head out too," Joseph chimes in as he finished the last of his beer. *I knew he didn't have any money.*

"Okay. I have to go to the bakery tomorrow morning,

94

anyway," I say, getting up from my seat and, just before I leave with Jacob, I wave at Sarah. "Hope to see you around."

"We'll meet again very soon, Orion."

Jacob and I wave goodbye to Joseph as we both get into Jacob's car. He turns on some more Kanye, but it only takes a few minutes to reach my house. We pull into my driveway. Someone is sitting on my porch. It's Aiden.

"Hey, O, do you know that guy, yo?" Jacob asks.

"Yeah, I know him," I reply. "Don't worry about it."

Jacob throws me a concerned look. "Okay, but it's like, one o'clock in the morning and there's a guy sitting on your porch."

I put my hand on his shoulder and assure him, "Jacob, it's alright. Trust me."

He nods. "Alright. See you later, Bro. Don't be a stranger!"

I open the door and laugh. "I'll try not to."

He drives away and I walk up to Aiden. He has his arms on his knees and he's eating Skittles.

"So, what are you doing here?"

Without looking at me, he says, "Eden, told me to give this to you." He hands me an old black Razr flip phone. "He said he will call you within the next two weeks, so be ready." He stands up and begins to walk towards the street.

I look at the phone. "Okay."

As I lay down, all I can think about is what Sarah said to me. She's right, and it becomes clear to me what I want to do. I grab the flip phone and look at it. *When is he going to call? What if I don't answer?* There is nothing for me to do now but wait for him to call.

***

Days go by, and I haven't received a call. I haven't seen Aiden or heard from Eden, either. Life goes back to normal. I go to the bakery, study, and get that occasional beer from the wine bar.

I've seen Sarah at the wine bar more and I feel as if we have become close. Mary hasn't been around lately, but Mary usually does this. She goes days without talking to me, so I'm not really worried. She does her thing but she eventually comes around.

After closing the bakery one Tuesday night, I'm sitting in my car getting ready to go home and I hear a ring. It's the cell phone Aiden gave me. I flip it open, and it's a blocked number calling. I answer it.

"Hey, fucker."

"Whoa! You don't greet someone like that," I respond.

Then there's silence and he follows with, "Everything has quieted down. Aiden reported that no one is following you. So, it's a good time for us to meet. I can tell you who I am and who I work for now. And most importantly though, I can also tell you about the artifact that I'm pretty sure your damn family is hiding here."

"Okay," I hesitate. "Where do you want to meet then?"

I have no idea what this guy wants with my family but I can't explain the adrenaline I feel at the same time. It almost feels like I'm another step closer towards gaining the power I want.

"I haven't really thought about that," he admits.

Something I've noticed about Eden from only knowing him a short period of time is that he isn't a very prepared person. It always seems as though he does things off of instinct instead of thinking things through.

"Well?" I prompt.

"Meet me at the Deck. We should be safe there and they have amazing drinks to boot. Just be there tomorrow, cunt."

Really? A bar? Right before I'm about to say something he hangs up the phone. I close the phone, drop it to my side and ponder over how this is going to go. *What we are going to talk about? Is it magic? Is he actually a dead body? Does the government know about this organization?*

96

The Deck is a bar in downtown Mobile that boasts they have the biggest deck. I haven't been to that bar since I was twenty-one years old. I have noticed, though, that Eden likes to drink quite a bit. I don't know if he has a drinking problem or if he just likes the buzz.

I go about my normal day at work. Once I finish cleaning up and shutting down the store, I go home and change into blue jeans, a white t-shirt, and a black leather jacket. Eden didn't tell me what time he was going to get there so I decide to go with my gut and show up at about 9:00 pm. I can't miss family dinner with my mom and grandparents. We have stuffed chicken with mashed potatoes, carrots, and corn.

Right as I'm about to leave the house, my mom says to me, "Orion, the store is doing amazing. I know it's because of your dedication and the time you've been putting into making everything run perfectly."

"Mom, it's not because of me that the store is doing so well. It's because of you. You hired great employees and the work that you, me, and grandpa put into it has really made it succeed. If Dad was here he would be so happy to see the store prosper," I say, smiling.

Tears start to flow down her cheeks, and then she hugs me.

"'Rion, thank you for being an amazing son and human," she says while hugging me. I embrace her.

"I love you, Mom."

I head towards the front door and I look over my shoulder to tell the rest of my family goodbye and that I'll see them soon.

I arrive at the Deck at 9:00 pm. I hate being late; one thing that I always hold myself to is being on time. I head in through the front door and, to my surprise, I see Eden right away.

He is wearing the same thing he was wearing earlier and sitting at the bar with five shot glasses in front of him and a bottle of Coors Light in his hand. On the wall beyond the bar are four televisions and bottles of all kinds of cheap liquor. He is talking with the bartender who is a short girl with brown hair and S-shaped eyebrows. Her black t-shirt hangs down to her thighs so you can barely see her running shorts.

Without hesitating, I walk up to Eden. He notices me and says right away, "HEY! You made it. I actually didn't think you were going to show." I can tell that he's drunk just by the way his breath reeked of liquor.

"What would you like, Dear?" The bartender looks at me and bends over on the bar as she asks. I order a Corona.

"So, you're a Corona man. You fancy," Eden says to me. He stares at me while I take the first gulp.

The bar smells like smoke and is very dark, in fact, I can barely see a thing. I don't understand why he would want to meet here, of all places to go to Mobile. Normally only drunk college students go here. It's a good place to meet because it's so dark and known as a college bar, which makes "criminals" not even consider looking at this place.

"So, what do you want to tell me, Eden," I say with the bottle close to my face. He turns in his chair.

"Huh?"

I utter, "What do you mean 'huh?' You invited me here after I accepted your offer."

He puts his left hand to the back of his head, scratches it, and cries out, "OHHHH! I remember now!"

What did I get myself into? What a loser. He takes another sip of his beer.

"Okay. Here it is. I'm a part of an organization called the House of David. The purpose of the House of David is to find ancient artifacts or mythical treasures so they that don't get into the hands of evil people who would use them to push their own agendas. Basically, people are stupid and if someone says that this artifact saved them, they could easily start a cult that could cause

98

mayhem, and we don't want that to happen. Any questions?"

With a shocked look on my face, I ask, "What do you want with me? Why are you even in Mobile? I'm assuming there must be an artifact in Mobile. Am I correct?"

He sips on his beer again and looks at me with a raised eyebrow. "You're very perceptive. That's why I like you. I'm here looking for an artifact that was brought here when Mobile was founded. The artifact is called the Chains of Peter. These chains were used to keep the apostle, Peter, locked up while in Rome. We have information that the artifact is with one of these four families and your family is one of them."

Shit. I sit back in the chair, stumped.

"So that's why you've been following me? Because you think I know where this artifact is? To be honest with you, I have no clue where this thing would even be. We have a bunch of stuff in my garage if you want to come and look. We do have an old trunk that has a lock on it."

Suddenly, there's an alert on the television.

"This is a special announcement. There have been eight murders in the past twenty-four hours. These were home invasions. Only one family has been identified so far and it is the Helton family. The Mobile police are stating that they were all shot to death and their home raided. There are no suspects," the broadcaster states.

I look at the screen with horror and I turn to Eden who maintains the same calm demeanor he has had since I met him.

"Were those the other families? And did you kill them?" I wonder if he can hear the anger in my voice. "If I didn't accept would you have killed me and my family as well?" I continue.

His face changes more. I can't tell if he is just as shocked, or if he knew this was going to happen. "No. I didn't kill them. I've been laying low for a few days now, hardly even left the hotel actually. I thought that, maybe, they would show. But now I'm

99

wondering if they got the same information about the families as I have."

He suddenly stands up so quickly that his chair falls to the floor. He grabs the back of my shirt. "Take me to your house now. I'll explain everything on the way. If you don't, your family will die, Boy."

I leave twenty dollars on the bar. We run out of the door and get into my car.

"Hey! Don't forget to put your seatbelt on!" I say to him as I start my car.

"Idiot. You're worried about me wearing a seatbelt when someone is on the way to kill your fucking family? Just fucking drive."

"Well if you get hurt, it's not my fault." I start to drive. "So, who's coming to my house? Are they looking for the artifact, too?"

He continues to look straight ahead. "Throughout history, you get these factions that start because they believe that these artifacts have power. The Nazis in Germany, the Crusades, and Charlemagne's Holy Roman Empire are the biggest, but lately, there have also been many small ones. The small ones usually die out quickly, or we step in and put an end to it right away. Recently there has been a new faction that is on the rise called Seditio. They are in search of the remaining artifacts; however, we already are in possession of many of them. We don't know their goals or agenda. All we know is that they have been searching for the artifacts and are tied to many crimes around the world. The fact that yesterday I was attacked by a member of their organization should have been more of a reason to panic." He shakes his head and pauses. "I should've killed them all. I was sloppy and stupid. I won't make that mistake again."

I'm becoming more interested in this organization Eden is speaking about. *I have to join this. I have to understand all of this.*

This is the knowledge and adventure I need to be able to understand to change the world. Then quickly, the worry for my family's lives starts to kick back in. I tried to be calm earlier, but now I can feel the pressure on me.

"So, all of that being said, I came to you to find out information about the artifact and also, I'm recruiting you to be my pupil. As my pupil, you would be under me and you will come with me to the Gate to be trained and go on missions. The offer still stands." he adds hastily.

"We can worry about that later. We need to save my family first."

"Let's get this straight. I don't give a damn about your family. I'm not worried about your family. The only thing that concerns me is retrieving the artifact before they do. Anything else is collateral damage."

I look at him, disgusted. "Well, you don't need to worry about them. I'll save them myself." We arrive at my house and I park my car in the driveway. I bolt up to my house to see my family sitting there watching television.

"Orion! Why did you barge in the house like that?" my grandpa asks, looking at me with confusion, along with my mom.

"Y'all are in danger. We need to leave right now!" I yell.

Without any hesitation, they stand up and head towards the front door.

"Where do you guys think you're going?" a man says from the dark. He walks into the house wearing a blue t-shirt, brown khakis, military boots, and a black backward baseball cap. He has green eyes and a scar across his eyebrow.

"Obviously, someone tipped you guys off that we were coming. I just would like to know who. Was it that Judge? It really doesn't matter. Here's the thing, you either tell me where the Chains of Peter are, or you die. I was gonna kill ya and destroy your house looking for it, but it would be so much easier if you just tell me," he says. His voice is raspy and his face looks like a drug dealer when smoking his own drugs—extremely aged with spots all over.

"What on earth are a Chains of Peter?" my grandpa stutters.

He points a gun directly at her. "Sir, you've lived a long life. I'm just gonna kill you now."

I dash in front of him. "Let them go! Just kill me."

He rolls his eyes. "Are you stupid? They would run to the police and tell them. They've also seen my face. There's no way any of you are going to leave here alive."

Suddenly, I hear a swoosh. The man's eyes open wide and I see a line run across his neck. His head begins to slide down, falling from his body, and his body collapses. Behind him, I see Eden with a 13-inch knife in his hand and blood splattered across his face. He looks so intense. He reeks of death—a foul, pungent odor.

Everyone is speechless and unable to move. My mom and grandpa have their mouths wide open. Not acknowledging them, Eden pulls out a phone, dials a number, and says "Confirmed: 6 killed. I need someone to come and clean the area ASAP. I'll pin my coordinates. Come within two hours."

He walks towards us. "Could you take me to this old box you said you have?"

How did this guy kill six men and act so nonchalantly about it? My mom and grandpa look at each other then at me. There is so much fear in their eyes.

Eden gets right in my face. He points his knife at my family.

"Okay, I'll ask again. Where is this box that you told me about earlier? Either you take me to that or I'll kill your whole family. Got it?" The crimson blood from the blade drips on the floor.

I can barely look at him. He is threatening my family. "Just get that blade out of their faces, okay? Follow me," I say.

"Good idea. See, all it takes is a little threatening to get the job done with you."

I walk past him and into the kitchen. I reach the side door.

"Hey! This is a pretty nice kitchen. I like the granite and ivory counters," Eden utters.

"How can you compliment my kitchen while literally threatening to kill my family?"

"I'm just saying that it is a lovely kitchen. Geez." He shrugs.

I walk into the garage to find five dead bodies scattered all around the backyard, but it is so dark outside that I can't distinguish what they are wearing or what their faces look like. But what I can see is that three of them are missing heads and the other two are missing their hands and have their throats slashed.

"How were you able to kill these guys so fast?" I ask in awe of what he had done. "I was inside for at least ten minutes and you did all this without a sound."

"I've trained for many years, Kid. I have gotten extremely efficient at killing," he says.

I look down and I can see the blood drip onto the grass, covering the entire path.

"Beautiful isn't it," he says calmly.

"What do you mean 'beautiful?'" I respond.

He continues to stare at the bodies. "Can you not see the flowers? Can you not smell the white roses? There is beauty in death. It's kind of relaxing when you think about it."

"Are you completely mad? All I can see are bodies and limbs everywhere. If you didn't notice, that smell is blood." I'm almost yelling now.

He turns his gaze to his knife. "You wouldn't understand," he speaks calmly. "You haven't suffered in your life so you can't appreciate the beauty in death. One day, you will."

After making it to the garage side door, I unlock it and reach to the right side to turn the lights on. The overhead lights flicker on and we see my mom's 2020 SUV and my grandpa's 2017 van.

"So where is this box?" Eden says as he scans the room. I go to the back of the garage. My dad's workstation is there along with an old rusty washing machine and a bunch of old boxes, one of them standing out because it's noticeably older than the others. Eden spots that one right away.

"Is that it right there? Please don't tell me you guys were keeping something so legendary and old under a bunch of boxes."

"Dude. No one even knew my dad had something like this. Are you sure this is it? I think my dad would have mentioned it to someone." I spoke to him with raised eyebrows.

Eden reaches for the box, knocking over the three boxes that are sitting on top of it. He puts the box on the workstation.

"That's not the box I was talking about. I've never seen that one before," I say. "Maybe someone put that here."

It is an old wooden box the size of which would hold size thirteen shoes. It has water damage and scratches on the lid. He lifts the lid slowly.

I'm secretly eager to see what's in the box that I had no knowledge existed until now. I actually never even went in the garage; it was usually my grandparents or parents who did.

He sets the lid aside, peers in, then looks at me and says, "You gotta be kidding me."

"What?" I ask with anticipation, not really taking him seriously.

He points at the box and tells me to look for myself. I walk over to the box to see two old, corroded, brown metal shackles and two beer cans in between the shackles. That isn't all of it, though. With the shackles are two old crawfish tails, some candy wrappers, and two pairs of holey brown socks that look like they used to be

104

white.

"You guys literally used one of Christianity's prized artifacts as a trashcan."

"Literally, I had no clue this was even here."

He grabs the box anyway with a sigh. "At least, we didn't have to go through some drawn-out scheme or look through some secret hiding spot to find it."

I nod in agreement and then he pulls out his phone.

"I found it, and I'm on my way back to the Gate," he quickly says into the phone. Then he stops right as he gets to the garage side door. "I heard you back there when that guy threatened you. You told him to kill you instead of your family."

"I would trade my life for my family or anyone else," I answer.

"Do you not care about your own life?"

"I do care about my life, but I care about all lives. No one has the right to take the life of someone else. I want to live, but if I can save someone else's life in exchange for my own, I'd gladly do it."

"Yeah, well, one day you will be put in a situation where you don't get that choice. You will have to choose to kill someone. You can't just say 'Kill me.' Things don't work like that."

I look him straight in the eyes. "To me, that will always be a choice. I'd rather risk my life to protect someone than let them get killed."

"We'll be in touch," he says as he opens the door. "Remember, you accepted my offer and I will hold you to it."

"So, like when? Are you going to call me or something?" I find myself yelling in a panic, but he just waves.

"See you soon, Orion."

I don't understand what's going on. "Eden! Is that it? What's next?"

He reaches the street.

"I said I'll be in contact, Kid." And just like that, a black truck pulls up with eight guys in black jumpsuits and huge goggles covering their whole faces and white hair nets over their heads. The men begin wrapping the bodies in some type of saran wrap. An Asian girl in a red leather jacket and white tank top starts talking to my family. She tells them that they cannot go to the police because they don't know if the men that attacked them had people inside the police department. She also told them they will watch over them until they know they're safe.

Right as I'm thinking about how pretty the Asian girl is, I see another girl approach her and this girl is someone I know. It is Sarah from the wine bar. I'm taken back at first by her outfit. She is wearing an all-black military outfit with heavy military boots, and she's carrying a clipboard in her hand and a semiautomatic gun in the holster of her pants. She smiles at me and waves. I want to talk to her mostly because I want to know what's going on.

Instead, I stand there thinking to myself. *What on earth is going on? Why is this happening to me? So many dead bodies. Is this what it means to be in this organization?*

The men gather up the bodies and put them in the truck. Once everyone leaves, my family doesn't talk about what just happened. Maybe they are afraid of what they saw and what the woman said, or maybe they just want to forget it.

I move my car from the street to the driveway, and find Mary walking on the side of the road. I wave at her, but she acts like she doesn't see me. I don't know if she's lost in thought or if she maybe saw what had just happened.

As I sit inside my car, I want to drive away, but all I can do is think about whether I should contact Eden or wait for him to contact me. I want to do something. My family is in danger and I feel helpless. I don't have the strength to stop anyone from hurting my family—I will have to let someone else do it for me. *Am I that weak?* I walk inside and go to bed.

***

Days go by. I don't hear from Eden. Eventually, days turn into weeks and weeks turn into months and, still, not a word. I go on with my everyday life and see Mary regularly. Sarah isn't working at the wine bar anymore but I would occasionally see her ordering donuts at the bakery. Even though she never talks to me, she always throws me a smile.

***

Three months pass since my encounter with Eden. It's December 15, the day I graduate with a PhD in engineering. Even though this will be my third time wearing a cap and gown, it still feels unreal.

The graduation is being held at the basketball stadium. Our colors are red, white, and blue so the stadium seats are blue and the railing is white. The stage where we receive the hooding is four feet off the ground and is covered in banners from all the different colleges behind it. On the stage are all the deans and the president of the whole school.

My whole family and friends came to my graduation. Even Mary showed up to support me. I'm primed and ready, but it still bothers me not hearing from Eden for this long. I figure, the fact that I still see Sarah around must mean that I still hold some importance. Maybe they want to make sure that my family and I don't go around talking about the organization and what happened at my house that night. Either way, it unsettles me not hearing from Eden.

As I'm in line to get my doctoral hood, I get this weird feeling. It's the feeling when someone is watching you, but you don't know where they are. You can feel that person's presence near you. Even throughout my excitement of finally receiving my doctorate, I'm distracted by the feeling of someone being near me.

Eventually, they call my name and I march across the stage. The president puts my hood on and my family claps. I walk off the stage and go back to where I'm sitting.

Once the ceremony concludes, I head outside and take pictures with my family.

"You ready to go?" I hear from behind me. I turn around and it's Eden wearing his normal all-black attire. My family looks at him with fear in their eyes.

"Orion! What is he doing here?" my mom instantly asks. Matt, Jacob, and Joseph look at each other, confused about what is going on. They don't know because I haven't told even my closest friends about what happened that night.

We take a few steps away from my family and Mary slaps Eden on the butt. "Uh huh! You're still a tight ass, I see," she speaks to him like she'd known him for years.

Eden looks like he doesn't buy into her joke. "You're still a weirdo. Who greets someone like that?"

I'm distracted at this point and can't tell if I'm happy or scared to see him. "Where are we going?" I finally ask.

He smirks. "That, my friend, I cannot tell you. You accepted my offer and you must come with me now."

My grandpa steps in front of me. "He isn't going anywhere with you."

Eden begins to laugh. It's an incredibly sadistic laugh. "It was his choice. Either you're coming with me now, or I'm leaving."

I grab my grandpa's shoulder and reassure him. "It's fine, Grandpa. I want this. I'll go, Eden."

My mom comes up from behind me and hugs me. Then, I see a tear roll down my grandpa's face and he hugs me too.

"I love you, O. You're a grown man. I can't stop you from making choices even though I wish you would stay here. Just promise me you'll be back," he tells me.

I walk up to Mary. "Hey, look after my family for a while, okay?" She pinches my left cheek, grabs my face, and kisses me.

"What was that?" I pull back, surprised.

"I was just curious." Then she laughs. "You know I'll take care of your family. Bye, Orion."

Next, Joseph, Jacob, and Matt come up to me. I can see the sadness in their eyes. Joseph hugs me, then walks past Eden, throwing him a cold stare. Jacob shakes my hand.

"I'm not going to ask you what's going on with her, but I trust you. Just come back." I nod at him pat him on the shoulder.

Finally, it's Matt's turn. "I don't know what shit you've gotten yourself into, but I want in." Eden looks at him like he's an idiot.

"No, you don't want to go where he's going."

"I'll miss you, Matt. Don't worry."

Then Eden and I walk away. "So, where we are walking to? Do I need clothes?"

He just puts his arm around me.

"You don't need anything. From this point on, in fact, you are nothing. But you will become something."

Eventually, we reach a parking lot where there's a black duffel bag in the middle of the lot. Eden opens the bag, pulls out a bottle, then says, "Drink this fast and don't ask questions. Just do it."

I grab the bottle and examine it. It's a regular metal water container. I peer inside, and it looks just like water so I drink it.

"You're about to be asleep in t-minus two minutes. Also, I hope you're not scared of water."

"What?"

Then he punches me in the face and I must have blacked out. I'm not sure how much time went by but eventually, I hear someone say, "Wakey! Wakey!"

For a split second, I'm not sure if I can open my eyes. I squint them open and find myself in the backseat of a car. I sit up carefully and make out two people. If my vision isn't so blurry I can maybe figure out who they are, but I can't tell. I blink several times before muttering. "Where are we? Who are you two?"

It's at this moment I suddenly feel apprehensive about my decision to join Eden's organization.

"You don't need to worry, Orion," I hear someone say. "Everything is going to be okay."

That voice sounds so familiar.

"Sarah?" I say, confused. I feel some comfort from hearing her voice that I was able to calm myself down a little bit.

"Eden, you didn't have to punch him!" Sarah exclaims. I assume that the driver was Eden at this point. "If you would have just given him the drink, he would've fallen asleep on his own."

"Wait, why did you punch me?" I ask Eden.

"I didn't know if the drug would work. Thought it would be quicker just to knock him out," Eden says. He's always unconcerned. He becomes a bigger mystery to me each time I meet him. I don't know if he's just crazy, or hates me, or is like this with everyone.

"Hey, Orion. Don't worry about it," Sarah chimes in. "He's an ass to everyone."

Then I notice my vision getting clearer and I see Eden turn his head. "Am I being the asshole? Can you tell me?"

"YES!" Sarah and I yell at the same time. Part of me got a little chuckle out of that. I turn my focus out of the windows and all I can see is nothing. Just darkness and grass fields. *Where are we?* I lean forward and ask, "How long have I been out for? Where are we going?"

"You have been asleep for about eight hours," Eden answers. "We are going to the drop spot for the helicopter to pick us up and take us to the Gate."

"What is the Gate?"

Sarah responds this time. "The Gate is a ship that never stays in the same location. It sails the seas, constantly moving. The

Gate is a 610-foot, 15,000-ton behemoth. The ship was built of 520 airtight steel cells and is powered by two A1B nuclear reactors offering 250% more electrical capacity than the Nimitz Class Battleship."

Then Eden interrupts her with an awkward stare. "Sorry about that knowledge dump coming out of her mouth. Basically, the Gate is where the House of David is headquartered. We don't have any other outpost except the place where the House of David was founded, and only the head of the House knows where that is. Not even Judges know. We will only be given the location if there is an event that devasted the organization or we have been compromised."

Was I really asleep for eight hours? This organization is very mysterious. Did I make a mistake? I can't think that way. I wanted this. I want to be able to protect the ones I care about. I want an adventure. I want to live with no regrets. I want to live.

Then Sarah looks at Eden. "The House has never had a Captain nominee so old. You think he'll make it?"

"He has the education so he doesn't need to worry about that. He only needs to learn to fight and use weapons," Eden responds. "He has a wrestling background so it should be easy for him to pick up those skills."

"That's not the point I'm getting at Eden," Sarah continues. "You and Aiden were brought in young and you both saw things that no ordinary child should see. I was lucky that my grandmother hid me from those horrors, but you were raised in it. Do you think someone this late in the game can deal with this life?"

What are they talking about? It's like Sarah doesn't think I'm ready for this.

"I didn't choose him for his smarts or potential," Eden says to her. "I saw you inside of him. He has a good family, a great outlook on life, smart, dominant, analytical, and kind. He isn't like me at all and that's what the organization needs. More people like the both of you. You both are soldiers raised to be death dealers."

I can see that Sarah really cares about Eden by the way she looks at him. It's a look of love and understanding. But I can also see the massive wall that Eden puts up, though. He's damaged and you can see it by how he lives his life and how he talks. Sarah just keeps looking at him with caring eyes.

"I understand," she mutters, then she looks at me. "Well, since you're about to be part of the House of David and Eden's Captain, you should know a little more about this man."

I can't wait to hear more about Eden. "Let's hear it."

"Well, Eden was brought to the Gate at the age of fourteen. His Judge was Joseph Cain. Joseph has a very calm personality, he remains unperturbed and composed even when surrounded by enemies that could kill him. He's an overly strict mentor. When Eden was off on his attack by 0.6 seconds, he would scold Eden. He had a very cold and calculating approach to doing his job."

"If you don't know already, Eden likes to read. I'm pretty sure he picked it up from Joseph, who is now named the King of Hearts. The King of Hearts is the CEO of the House of David. You only become the King of Hearts after completing over thirty successful missions and being voted on by the twelve Judges. Once Joseph got promoted, Eden moved up to a Judge. Eden became a Judge at the age of twenty-one. Eden, by then, had completed twenty missions and found ten artifacts."

I'm learning so much about this organization and Eden.

"So even if you complete a mission, do you always find artifacts?" I asked.

"When you go on a mission, you are going on them based on leads. Usually, you do find something. However, you have to prove the significance of the artifact. Basically, we go see if it really has the power that it's rumored to have or not."

I just nod at her. I'm getting a better understanding.

"You'll learn more about the House in your training." She

must have seen the astonishment in my eyes. "But Eden is known as the Death Reaper. He got this name because he kills a lot."

That makes sense.

"Your predecessor was Aiden. I think you've met him? Short guy, messy hair, big round blue eyes, looks lost a lot," Sarah says to me.

"Yeah! I remember him very well. He's kind of creepy?"

Sarah laughs. "Aiden is a sweetheart. He was the youngest Judge in the history of the House of David. He became a Judge at the age of sixteen. Eden found him on one of his missions in South Africa when Aiden was just ten years old. He was actually living on the street with a black cat. Eden felt bad for the kid and took him. Personally, I think that Eden saw himself in Aiden and that's why he took him in. Little did he know that that little boy would become one of the best Judges ever."

"So, you should be kind of happy, Orion. You're being added to a tree of great Judges."

I didn't know that Eden's teacher is the King of Hearts or the head of the organization. He's not just a crazy killer. He has the pedigree to teach me things that I would have never dreamt I would be able to learn.

"So why is he like he is? What made Eden the way he is?" I probe Sarah. She always has an amazing smile on her and it brings a warmth to her presence. But she looks at Eden as he continues to keep his eyes on the road.

"Eden? He has had a hard life. Joseph hasn't had it all that easy, either. Even though he doesn't think this, Eden isn't as bad as he seems."

Then, with a sarcastic grunt, Eden chimes in. "Listen, Orion. You're going to have to work hard and push yourself or you will fail. You might see things that will change you completely. Stay strong to your conviction."

A sudden ambition comes over me. *I must not fail.* I want

to become strong. I need to.

"Eden? How did you survive getting shot so many times? The damage that you obtained should have killed you, how did you recover so quickly?"

Eden laughs before he responds. "I told you already, I'm already dead. You can't kill someone that is already dead."

Then Sarah jumps in, giving Eden a strange look. "He isn't dead. You'll find out about this in your training as well. All Judges have this ability. Eden is not that special, so do not let him try to freak you out. Don't get me wrong, he is a murderous asshole but he isn't dead."

Sarah and Eden seem like they have known each other for a very long time. I don't think Eden himself realizes how much Sarah cares about him. Looking at him, I begin to wonder if this is a man that someone should even want to follow. *What is so great about him? What makes him someone that people look up to? Is he worthy of this power or knowledge? Why is he a Judge to begin with?*

As I'm lost in thought, Eden says to me, "Yo, are you good with computers?"

Snapping out of it instantly, I respond, "Yes, I really like computers. My dad was big into gaming so I got into it big time. Why do you ask?"

He throws a computer into my lap. "Your first assignment will be to tell me what's wrong with this computer."

"So, what's the problem with it? Hard drive issues? Coding problems? You want me to hack it?" I ask while examining it.

"It won't turn on." He is very serious.

I hold the power button and there is a blinking battery on the screen. The battery is saying that the computer is dead and needs to be charged. *Is this guy computer illiterate? How wouldn't you know this?*

"The battery is dead, Eden."

He looks at me and says, "No way! Wait, I did leave my charger at the Gate. Makes sense." He laughs and Sarah calls him an idiot.

"Orion, on a serious note, you must be willing to take a life in this job. I'm just letting you know."

"You may believe that, but if there is another way I will try to find it."

Before Eden can respond, Sarah says, "That's the opening. I see the helicopter there."

"Time to go!" Eden unbuckles his seatbelt. As he turns to me, Sarah says, "Eden, do not do it."

"Do what?" I ask.

But Eden responds, "Time to go night, night."

"What?" As soon as I say that, Eden punches me in the face and everything fades to black.

Chapter 5: Live

ORION AND I are headed to the Gate to begin his training to become my Captain.

Every Judge has a Captain; Orion will be my second one. Before Orion, Aiden Jaeger was my Captain and I always valued him. He has an easygoing personality and is devoted to his comrades, despite appearing emotionless most of the time. He's an extremely focused individual when he wishes to learn something. Most importantly, he's devoted to me and would do whatever I want without question. It's almost like he sees me as an older brother or even a father figure. He can be cold-blooded especially towards his enemies and he shows no sense of honor or mercy— part of what made him an excellent Captain. He's ruthless, inciting fear among all who oppose him. Members of the organization have even said he is crueler than me, some referring to him by the name "Death's Seeker." Because of his aloof personality and difficult childhood, Aiden often has trouble interacting with others about topics that don't directly involve fighting. Even as he works to be more open about his emotions and get to know the world better, it is a struggle for him.

I met Aiden on a mission in Cape Town, South Africa when he was just a small boy. It was said that the helmet of Joan of Arc was brought there in 1300 by a French immigrant, so I was on a mission looking for it. All the information I had throughout the mission pointed to it being a false claim, but I went there to make sure.

When I first arrived in Cape Town, I noticed him, this small child standing on the corner eating a lollipop. He was an orphan who had lost his parents. I remembered him in an alleyway with what looked like his friend—a cat—when they had an encounter with an extremely drunk and disoriented man. The man had tried to take the lollipop from Aiden at first, and then pulled out a knife and cut the cat.

It was then that I approached the man and he grabbed my throat and threatened to cut me too. Little did the man know, I could have killed him in that very moment, but I didn't. The man actually stabbed me and I laughed, so he beat me up. Meanwhile, Aiden saw the gun in the man's pocket, grabbed it, and fired it at the man. He killed him before he could harm me any further.

While the recoil made this tiny child fall on his back, I approached him and said, "Nice shot."

Being so eager, the next thing he asked me was, "What do I do next?"

"Let me take you away from this." That was the day that Aidan became my first Captain.

As I sit in the helicopter, reminiscing on the day I met Aidan, I gaze out the window and see nothing except the blue ocean for miles and miles. It looks so peaceful and calming out at sea; nothing but an endless, dark blue plain that stretches into the sky. Hopefully Orion is able to live up to Aidan's same standards. All of the sudden, I hear him stir as he slowly regains consciousness.

"Where am I?" Orion utters, his voice picking up as more confusion sets in. "Why can't I see anything? Where are you taking me? And why did you punch me again?"

He's squirming around like a worm.

"I don't know why you're moving like that, but you aren't tied up. You know you can take the bag off your head," I state.

He sits up cross-legged and takes off the brown potato sack off his head.

"Are we flying?" he asks, looking around.

I sigh and continue to look out the window. "Yes, Orion,

you dumb shit."

He crawls to the window to see the endless blue ocean. Then he grabs the seat next to me, sits down, puts his seatbelt on, continues to look out of the window. He is much calmer.

"Where are we going? Will I see my family again? And where is Sarah?"

"We are going to the Gate," I reply with a steady voice. "I told you that in the car. As far as seeing your family, it depends on how long it takes you to complete your training. Even after you finish, though, you will still need to limit your contact with them if you want them to be safe. Sarah had to go do another mission. We will not see her for a while."

He stares at me with worry and uncertainty in his eyes.

"There is no going back now, you know. This is what you wanted. If you accept that fact, then you will be able to succeed here. If you don't, then you will either lose yourself or die. Stay true to yourself and you'll be fine," I say to him, but I can see a hint of fear in his eyes. "Are you afraid to die?"

"Yes and no. What I'm more afraid of is taking the life of another."

"Let me make this clear to you again. This training isn't something to make you feel self-righteous. I need a new Captain. You are analytic enough, perceptive enough, athletic enough, and smart enough to get the job done. Also, you know about Judges and how we work. I expect you to do your job no matter what it is. Got it?"

He nods. We fly for about two hours in dead silence before the pilot interrupts us to tell us that the Gate is open.

Orion and I look at the window to see a ship in the distance.

"So, this 'Gate,' the headquarters of the House of David, is a ship?"

I sit back in my seat and nod. "Yes. What Sarah explained

118

in the car was true. The Gate is a ship that never stays in the same location, it sails the seas constantly moving. It houses 1,000 employees, has twelve classrooms, a gym, a weapons shop, a swimming pool, and a gymnasium, a weight room, a shooting range, and a dining area. That is where you will be living," I explain.

"How long does the training take? When will I be ready for the field?"

"Depends on you." I rest my head on the window. "You already graduated from school so education isn't a must for you. However, you don't know how to fight and your physical prowess isn't up to par. I would assume it will take you four years to achieve a good Captain level."

This shocks Orion. The truth is that being in his twenties, Orion is much older than usual Captains. They usually get recruited at a young age and spend over ten years developing the skills necessary to complete missions. I was fourteen when I was recruited into the field and I was one of the older Captains at that point. Aiden was even younger than me when I brought him in and trained him.

I hope that Orion is a quick learner. I don't need him in the field as badly as I need his mind. Aiden is an excellent fighter and quick-minded in the field, but he lacks the natural ability to deduce a situation before it happens. Orion, on the other hand, has great reasoning and a calm inner self which should help him greatly.

We begin our descent to the helipad on the deck of the ship. I see two Judges standing on the deck waiting for us. I'm guessing they're here to welcome me and meet the new recruit.

The helicopter lands safely. I slide the door and immediately hear a voice call out to me.

"You've come back, Eden! Hmm, and you brought a cute friend."

Before replying, I take in the familiarity of my

119

surroundings. The wind is blowing extremely hard and the smell of salt water is everywhere. I exit the copter first and Orion follows me.

"So, who is he?" Ying Yue asks. She's a short Asian girl with hair as black as the night put in a ponytail with her bangs in the front. From what I know about her, she's from Shenzhen, China, and her parents moved to Paris, France when she was just four years old. She comes from a very wealthy Chinese family. I also know that, unlike me, she was brought into the House of David due to her father's ties to the organization at the age of twelve. She has plenty of talents, though. She is highly intelligent with an IQ of 169. She also speaks four languages, plays the violin, and is extremely skilled with swords.

I keep walking, ignoring her. Orion gives me a confused look, but I tell him we aren't here to make friends.

"You're such a huge prick," Ying mutters after us.

"Ah, yes, Ying. I do have a huge prick."

Then another voice chimes in. "Well, I haven't been back in three years and I can still tell that Eden is an asshole," Luka says. Next to Ying is Luka Raines, a thirty-three-year-old British guy with short light brown hair and a scruffy beard. Luka was brought into the organization at the age of seventeen and is a highly regarded marksman. He grew up as an only child with both parents living what most would consider a mediocre life. But Luka's story is that, at a young age, his father saw that Luka was very good at hunting, particularly with a bow and arrow. He would win bow tournaments against pros.

One day, he was in a tournament and was shooting against who would later become the Judge that he would follow as Captain. The Judge was so impressed at his skill in the competition that he not only recruited him but also personally paid for his parents' new house.

Just seven years after this competition, Luka replaced his

Judge, earned the nickname of the Artemis's Archer, after the respective Greek goddess of the hunt.

Luka is very outgoing and likes to have a lot of fun with the other Judges. He's a genuinely good person at heart and does the best he can to make sure he's able to complete the task at hand and also protect his comrades.

Orion and I enter the ship and walk down a long hallway with doors on both sides. We eventually arrive at a small room with only one window, white walls, one twin-sized bed with white sheets, and one pillow.

I point to the brown dresser in the corner of the box-shaped room. "In the top drawer, you will find your training shirts, in the second drawer, you should have your underwear, and in the bottom, you have your training pants. They are all grey and there should be a set of seven each. At the end of each day you will put your dirty clothes in a basket that will be outside your door at 7:00 pm every day." We stepped outside the room. "The bathroom is straight down the hallway. In there you'll find soap, a toothbrush, toothpaste, towels, and a brush." Orion looked as if he was analyzing every word I told him, but I continued, anyway, taking minimal breaks for questions.

"In your room, I left you three books. One on weaponry, one on fighting, and one on the history of the House of David."

"What time do I need to be up? Who will be training me?"

"You will be trained by Judge Judah. He has been here a long time. He's good at training people in shooting. Your fight training will be with Judge Wilburforce Amanor and his Captain Joshua Honore."

"Okay, that is all great but . . . what time do I need to wake up?"

"0700! Be ready. Judah is really old and has the tendency to go overboard." Before he can ask me anything else, I leave his room and go to the library.

Finally, peace within the books. I head right away to the section of fantasy novels and I see Joseph holding *Don Quixote*. He is wearing his usual blue stripe suit and a white button-down, but his hair has greyed a lot more since I've seen him last.

"I really like this book," he starts, still staring at the cover of it. "It always amazes me how writers are able to create these worlds."

I lean up against the bookshelf and cross my arms in contentment. "You look more stressed than usual. Is Sarah looking at the Chains of Peter?" Joseph knows I'm not the type to make small talk for too long.

He puts the book back on the shelf. "I'm stressed, Eden. There was something off about that artifact. It turned out that the Chains contained something that was very similar to that bacteria from the liquid we obtained from the Marco mission years ago. I don't know if there is a connection or it's just coincidence, but we will still be on the lookout for any traces of this bacteria."

I try to analyze what Joseph is saying but I don't see how these two artifacts would be similar in any way. "That is very interesting," I reply curiously. Joseph just nods.

"Don't worry about it, Eden. We have Sarah and Luka researching this. Anyway, do you think Orion is a good choice? He's much older than I would like, you know. We accepted Aiden before because of his young age and his killer instinct. But no one would have thought that he would turn out to be such a prodigy."

"I understand that, but I think we need to change things up around here. Orion has the intelligence and reasoning that Aiden lacked. I want to do things differently. I want to see how someone who was raised with a good foundation and never suffers does here."

Joseph walks close to me and lowers his voice. "I know you very well, Eden. I saved you, trained you, and taught you. I read this guy's file and the report on him. He and Sarah have very compatible features. Have you noticed this? Does he remind you of Sarah?"

"In ways, yes, but he's more tactical than she is. He also thinks about the situation as a whole and finds the best solution before acting on it. Sarah isn't that tactful, and she is one of the best Judges we have. So, you should be happy with my choice. She is way better than me and is able to sympathize more than me, we all know that."

"Yes," Joseph affirms as he puts his hand on my shoulder. "I wanted you to be my tool of Death and I can see that you don't look highly on yourself. But sooner or later, Eden, you need to realize who you are. I will approve your choice of this man but be careful. Not all pure men are great men. Sometimes the damaged are the ones that are able to understand the pain of others. Orion's upbringing might make him never able to empathize to the extent that you think he might be able to." Then he walks past me.

I still don't agree. I feel that Orion's never having experienced pain will help him bring joy to those in pain, which will make him understand them better.

Over the next two days, I monitor Orion's progress. He's making great improvements in his shooting and fighting, though I keep noticing one major flaw in the latter. He fights with reason and it's making him slow.

It's the third day of Orion's training when I run into Wilburforce on the way to the shooting range. Wilburforce is from Ghana and the oldest of three kids. He moved to the United States with his family when he was twelve and he became a Captain at seventeen. Like many Judges, Will is known for his intelligence and was recruited by his former Judge, Ja'Lisa Myers. Eventually, he became a Judge at age twenty-six. Many believe it was because Ja'Lisa was dying of old age, but he had plenty of accomplishments under his belt as Captain to justify it. He was able to find two artifacts and completed over twenty-five missions during his eleven years as a Captain, which is almost unheard of.

He specializes in hand-to-hand combat and close-range knife combat. He also gave himself the nickname Kwasi, which is some Ghanaian word that means a handsome, confident, intelligent, and well-rounded man. I don't think that Wilburforce is a Kwasi, to be honest.

"Greetings, Eden," he says in his normal serious and polite voice. "I noticed that you have been on the Gate a lot lately."

"Yeah, I have to make sure Orion is up to par. How is he doing, in your opinion?"

"He's coming along very well." Wilburforce looks at me confidently. "On testing, though, I've noticed that he's still showing reluctance to kill someone. He tries to find another solution and, sometimes, finding that other solution takes longer."

One thing about Orion that I'm starting to admire is his stubbornness to not kill.

"Keep me updated," I tell Wilburforce and walk away.

Now I can think of what drink I'm going to have. Then I hear a woman yelling my name. I see Sarah walking up to me.

"How are you, Eden? How is Orion doing?"

"Same old, same old. He's apparently doing quite well. However, he isn't to the standards that I would like for him to be." Sarah just smiles at me.

"He'll get there. I believe in him."

I roll my eyes. "I'm headed to the kitchen to get a beer. Do you want to go with me? Or do you just want to just keep holding me up?"

Sarah punches me in the shoulder. "I actually wanted to ask you if you want Orion to go on his first mission soon."

How soon? This makes me uneasy. "What is the mission?"

She crosses her arms. "We heard some rumors about a sword of Archangel Michael located in a region of lower Jerusalem by Rachel's Tomb. They are the same rumors as in the past, and

I've been doing all the research on it so it should be a nice starter mission for him."

"So, this will be soon? I think that should be good." With seriousness, she nods at me in affirmation and walks on.

I continue onto Orion's room. I knock on his door for a quick check in. I ask him how the training was and he responds that the training is going better than he had planned.

"Get some sleep. You'll be heading on the mission with Joshua," I say. I specifically chose Joshua Honore to be Orion's partner for his first mission. Joshua is an older Captain. He is a thirty-nine-year-old Caribbean man from Florida with long dreads, a trimmed goatee, and always smells like girl's deodorant. He has been a Captain for over twenty-three years. He has never been promoted because Joshua isn't good at tactical situations or the field. He's more the type of person that follows commands excellently, but isn't able to think on his own or be creative.

Matching Orion up with Joshua for the mission should work perfectly. Orion is a tactical thinker, and Joshua is the type of person who gets things done quickly and is able to follow a command.

"Also, you should get your mission brief tomorrow. Sarah is over this mission but you will be doing the mission with Joshua. I see that you two have been training together so you should be fine," I say.

"Yes. I have looked over the mission brief. Sarah met with me earlier about it so I'm aware of the details. Are you going to be involved in any way?"

Danmit, Sarah, I think to myself. *Why would you ask me to give him permission to be on this mission and then give him the details on it before I could?*

"No. I will hear details about what is going on, but I will be looking into other artifacts. Sarah will update me. Don't fail." I begin to walk away.

"Am I not allowed to call or speak to my family?" Orion calls out to me. "I know we're a secret organization, but I would really like it if I could check how they're doing."

I turn around, raise my left eyebrow. "No one said you couldn't call. You can call them anytime. You have a cell phone, don't you?"

Orion looks mortified. "I left it at home! I thought you told me I should forget my family and that I won't be seeing them for a while."

"Yeah, I meant you won't be seeing them a while because you're training and preparing. I never said anything about not being able to call them, Dumbass," I say with a smirk. He lingers there with the most bewildered expression. "Go ask someone to borrow their phone." He glances at me for a split second then dashes past me down the hall looking for someone.

I head to the library to do some research on the Blood of Mary—the artifact case Joseph and I had spoken about. I still don't understand why the same bacteria would be on the Chains and on the vial. I need to learn the connection between the two, if there is any connection at all. I walk to the far back where we keep all the mission logs of artifacts and, after a couple of hours of reading, I find that there isn't anything suspicious that would connect the two artifacts or cases. So, I leave and head to the Gift Room.

The Gift Room is a room on the Gate that is devoted to the continuous operation of computer servers installed into the floor and in the center of the room. It houses twelve computers that Judges or Captains can use to get into secret government files to find out more details on artifacts. We were able to get these servers because of a few missions that we completed that helped end World War II. What happened was, the House signed an agreement to stay neutral in all world affairs that do not have artifacts and, in return, the House received access to all government databases. This way, the House can browse and find information concerning artifacts to complete our missions.

Using the computers, I search the United States database first about the bacteria and I find nothing. So then, I search in France and Italy because most artifacts are found there. To my surprise, I find that over twenty years ago, the Denau family was killed in a home break-in and an unknown bacteria was found in their blood. I dig up information on the crime and the story.

They were a family of four: a mom, dad, son, and daughter. The police received a call about noise at the Denau home but when they arrived at the Denau's house, the door was already open. There was blood everywhere and bullet holes in the walls. The mom and dad were found shot in the head on the kitchen floor, the son shot in the head in the bathroom, and the daughter was said to be missing. It was recorded as a robbery, but nothing was stolen. However, from the reports, traces of an unknown bacteria were identified in the blood of the family members.

I pull up the pictures from the gruesome murders and the murder reports. I notice something that surprises me. The cops were unaware that the gunshots had to be fired by someone who was short. It also looks like the murderers shot into the wall after the crime in order to purposely make it look more like a robbery. *Was it the daughter that killed them? Or human traffickers?*

Reading more, I find that the Denau family has one single relative left, Meredith Scott. She is ninety years old and resides in Mobile, Alabama. This is the same Scott that is related to Panfilo de Narvaez. *Maybe this isn't so much of a coincidence after all.* I try to look for pictures of the daughter, but it seems like there are no traces of her. *Were they involved in Seditio? Is that why they're all dead?* I need to investigate Meredith Scott again. I feel like there's more to this story than I can see.

I look more into the bacteria and find that it's the same one that was found in Dublin. The Dublin tests from the Marco mission had proved to be inconclusive but it seems like there's more to this, though. I call Luka. It rings for a while, but Luka picks up eventually. I tell him to look into Meredith and that I will send him all the information needed—the information I had just found.

I leave the Gift Room. The only thing on my mind is the bacteria. *Were the Chains of Peter involved in the Denau murder? Is Orion's family involved?* They couldn't have been involved—the Bachman family has never left Mobile. Also, the box looked like it was maybe placed there on purpose because Orion told me he had never seen it before ever. There are so many puzzles that need to be figured out, but they will have to be dealt with when the information comes in.

Nighttime arrives and I can't sleep. All I can think about is the Chains of Peter. I keep thinking I'm missing something. I toss and turn all night and I finally get a little bit of sleep, but I wake up in the middle of the night thirsty.

One thing that the Gate always has is a good supply of booze. I grab a huge bottle of wine from the bar and chug it down. "This will help me go to sleep," I mutter. Then I look up to see Orion walking towards me with a book. He smiles at me.

"Go to bed, you drunk," he says and continues shuffling down the hall. I go on drinking until I pass out. I wake up to Trish throwing water at me.

"Eden, you've been laying here for over twelve hours. Luka has been looking for you," she says. I pull up to my feet and head to Luka's room.

"My head,'" I mutter to myself. I have never had a hangover this bad before.

On the way to Luka's, I see that Joseph has left a note on Orion's door. *Orion must have left for his mission.*

Eventually, I get to Luka's and knock on his door.

"Hey!" he says as he opens the door. "I got some bad news."

"What is it?" I ask. Luka shakes his head and proceeds to

tell me that Meredith died soon after I left Mobile with Orion.

"Was she murdered or something? It seems suspicious that she would die at this time, don't you think?"

"I don't know, Eden. She was ninety years old. These things happen to people who are that old. You're reading too much into this." I nod, but it's still bothering me. "Hey, Eden, you know what? Leave the Gate for a while. You need a vacation to chill. And you also need to lay off the booze."

"You're right. I should take some time. I'll be back when Orion finishes his mission." I say goodbye to Luka and head to my room. I pack up two sets of clothes in just a few minutes, and leave the Gate.

Chapter 6: Life

WALKING DOWN the halls on the Gate, I am stopped by Sarah. She smiles softly and says, "Hey Orion! Can we meet in the control room?"

I nod and follow her. I enter the room and I see Joshua sitting down in the chair in front of us. I pull out a chair and sit down right behind Joshua.

"Alright, guys! I have a mission for you lot," she says with her regular enthusiastic tone. I clutch my hands real tight with excitement. *This will be my first mission. I get to prove to myself that I belong here.* Sarah smiles at me and continues, "You will be heading to Israel tomorrow at 0800. There have been some rumblings about the Crown of Thorns located in lower Jerusalem by Rachel's Tomb. However, that is just a suspicion. What we're really after is the sword of Michael the Archangel. There is a group of fanatics that we believe is plotting to bomb Temple Mount which will cause massive amounts of tension to rise between Muslim and Jewish citizens. They want this because they are plotting for a war to take place so that they can show many people that the Jewish and Muslim religions are too violent and that their god is the one true God."

I shake my head and crack my knuckles. "Does the House of David usually deal with religious zealots like this a lot?"

Joshua turns his head and nods.

"Orion, please ask questions after I finish the brief," Sarah comments. I sit back into my chair and mutter, "Sorry."

Sarah giggles and continues. "After the destruction, the group planned to gain power by motivating the people, saying that Judaism and Islam are the wrong religions and this war would have happened because 'God wanted to destroy these false beliefs.' The leader of this group believes that possession of this sword would give them more courage to slay his enemies and carry through with their destruction plan."

I look down at my hands and they're shaking. I don't know if it's because I'm excited or scared.

The monitors behind us begin to show images of the location and pictures of the fanatic group. Sarah walks up to the table and places both hands on the edge. "It's amazing to me how someone's belief can be placed into an object and that this object can make them believe that they are superhuman or even a god."

Joshua stands up and walks to the monitor. He points at the center screen, then states, "The site has three openings, in front, at the back, and on the side. The hideout is located underground; the doors to the hideout are stone to match the walls. This group wears military clothes with a scarf over their mouths and goggles that block their eyes."

Sarah slides a folder in front of me. I open it up and find maps of the area. I frown and I begin reading from the folder. "According to the research we obtained, there's no military in that area so we assume they got these outfits from the black market."

"This file states that there are ten hostages. Is that correct?" I ask Sarah.

Sarah looks at the monitors seriously. "You're correct."

I figured there would be hostages but the one thing I don't want to happen is to get them killed; I need to help everyone stay alive at any cost.

Sarah puts her hand on my shoulder. "You're going to do great, Orion. Don't overthink this."

She gives me some sort of relief. I walk to the monitor. "People in this region speak Hebrew and Arabic. I know both so I should be able to understand and communicate with them. I can also tell you all what they're saying."

Sarah crosses her arms and says with a smirk. "When did you learn Hebrew and Arabic?"

I chuckle and continue to look at the monitor. "I learned them when I was a boy. My parents were strict about learning religion and made it so I would know these biblical languages."

Joshua pats me on the shoulder. "Well, I'm glad we have you on the team then."

Sarah continues. "We're also aware that they have bombs with them. Orion, you're good with coding and hacking, right?"

"I can pretty much hack anything. For this region, I doubt the technology or software they have would be any good. It will be like taking candy from a baby. Wait, how do you know I know how to hack and code?"

Sarah heads towards the door. "Unlike your Judge, I did my research about you." She stops at the doorway and tells us in a cheery tone, "You guys go to bed. We leave tomorrow at 0800. Orion, this is your first mission. You need all the sleep you can get." She exits the room followed by Joshua.

I look at the monitors in awe of what I have gotten myself into. *Is this what I truly want? Will I die? What's going to happen?* I exit the room and head down to my bedroom. I lie in my bed and all I can think about is the mission. *Am I trained enough? Do I have the combat skills to success? What if I die? I don't want to die.*

I wake up at 6:00 am in the morning. I open my door and find a briefcase outside my room. I bring the briefcase inside and set it on my bed. When I open it, I find a black vest, gray Kevlar pants, and black boots. I put them on and proceed to the landing strip of the Gate. There I see Sarah looking out at the sky with her hair flowing in the wind, untied, just free.

"Good morning," I say.

She turns her head, smiling. "You have to take in every moment, you know."

She looks so at peace and calm. *How can someone like her be in this organization?* I stop and soak in the cool air, the smell of salt. The warmth of the sun hits my skin. She's right, it's extremely peaceful. I stare into the distance, seeing nothing but the ocean and ask, "Where are we?"

She closes her eyes. "Did you know that the Gate never stays in one place? It continuously moves. One minute you're in the Gulf of Mexico and the next you're in the Indian Ocean. If you live on her long enough you can see the world. However, to answer your question, we are in the Mediterranean Sea. South of Croatia."

As we stand on the deck I can see some land in the distance. "Are we flying there or taking a boat?"

"We're flying there. I should have given you more information on the brief but I didn't want to overwhelm you. I'll tell you more now. We're flying there but will be parachuting down fifty miles from the target. The drop zone is miles from people so no one will be too aware of us landing. Once we land we have walk three miles from the drop zone where there will be car waiting for us, and it won't be anything fancy. We want to seem like locals to not bring too much attention to us. We will drive until we are within ten miles of the target and then the mission will begin."

A big gust of wind blows up behind me. "Well, that is a lot to take in. I've never parachuted before."

Joshua walks up behind me. "Just pull the cord when we tell you to or you'll die. Pretty simple, to be honest."

I raise my eyebrows in shock. "But how do I glide down?"

Sarah and Joshua walk to the helicopter, ignoring my question. We all get in the helicopter. Ying Yue is in the pilot seat. "Hey, Orion, congrats on your first mission," she says.

"Thanks! Are you on this mission too?"

Sarah sits next to her and says, "Ying Yue is the best pilot and she's also here for backup."

133

We put our headsets on and begin to fly to the drop zone. Joshua tosses me my parachute, hands me some goggles, and I put them on.

"Are you ready? We're about to jump," Sarah says through the headset. Joshua opens the copter doors and jumps out. I move closer to the door and I can see clouds and the ground. My nerves begin to take over me and I slowly begin to freak out. I feel a hand on both my shoulders. Sarah is giving me a reassuring look. "Orion, you don't have anything to worry about. I believe in you. Just jump and when I say 'pull' tug on the cord on your left arm. Might take you a while to glide down but I trust that you'll catch on. Jump first and if I see any problems I'll jump and help you."

It doesn't quash my nerves but it appeases me a little bit. I get closer to the door, my hands on the holding bar above my head and my toes hanging off. Then I feel a sudden push in the center on my back and I fly forward, falling to the ground fast. I hear someone in the headset say 'pull.' I grab the cord and the chute comes and jerks my body. I cruise down to the ground following Joshua. Once everyone lands, Sarah debriefs us on the mission and grabs two pistols from the duffle bag on the ground, and hands them to us. Then Joshua passes me a combat knife. We get in the car and head to the site. Joshua and I survey the area and we communicate to Sarah the layout of the surroundings. Jacob and I notice two members of the group coming towards us. Our scouting report is right, the men are wearing military clothes, but they have a scarf that covers their mouths and goggles that block their eyes, which create blind spots for them at certain angles. I signal to Joshua to hide behind boulders. As the two men walk by, we sneak up behind them, choke them, and take their uniforms.

After we put on their uniforms, Joshua asks, "Orion, do you think this will work?"

I really don't know but I'm sure as hell going to try. I smile at him and say with a confident tone, "Yeah. We should be fine.

Just don't say a word. Let me do all the talking, okay?"

He nods and we move the bodies behind the boulder. "Sarah, we're going to infiltrate the hideout. Over."

As we're walking to the hideout, she responds, "I'm going to get in touch with the local government and bring help. Let's not take any lives, okay?"

Joshua immediately responds, "Roger that."

We proceed to the hideout and we see ten heavily armed men outside. We keep walking, then a man comes up to us. In Arabic, he asks, "Is the perimeter clear?" I look at Joshua and back at the man. I respond to him in Arabic, "Yes, the perimeter is clear." The man nods at us and waves us through.

The hideout is built into a hill. We walk to a stone door; there a man was guarding it. I nod at him and he opens the door for us. Once inside, I assess the environment. Based on the report descriptions, the hideout is very primitive just like I thought it would be. Everything inside is basic and made of stone and clay, the doors inside are wooden, and there are no windows. As we continue to progress, we notice that there are bedrooms with steel beds.

A few feet down the hall we see an open room. Inside of the room are ten people tied up with bombs strapped to them. From what I can tell the bombs are computer-activated.

"Sarah. There are hostages with bombs attached to them. I think they're going to be used as suicide bombers," I whisper through the headset.

"Oh, God. We have to get them out safely," Sarah says.

"Joshua, we need to split up. I need to find the control room," I whisper. Joshua nods and heads down the hall to my right. I walk forward and see a room on the left side. There are three monitors, a single keyboard, and a man sitting in a chair in front of it. I sneak up behind the man and begin to choke him. He starts to fight back but my grip is so tight he passes out in a matter of seconds. I drag his body to the wall and prop him against it. I pull the chair back, sit down, and begin typing. The tech is very outdated; the keyboard is from the early 2000s. There's an old flip phone and the monitors are dusty and bulky. Under the table are three small server boxes that make a lot of noise. The computer is already unlocked and getting the information I need is a piece of cake. "Sarah. I'm in their files. It seems they have a small cell arriving today at 0700. The leader is expected to arrive today in preparation for their bombing mission. It also seems as if the bombs are triggered by typing in something on the computer. I can hack the bomb's trigger and control them. You need to stay on the outskirts and when you see people pull up, wait twenty minutes then crash in and take them outside," I say through the headset.

"Great idea, Orion. I like that you're taking lead. Roger," Sarah replies.

Suddenly, I feel a hand on my shoulder. I jerk away and raise my pistol and, to my surprise, it's Joshua. "Calm down, Orion. It's just me," he says with his hands raised.

I drop my gun and kneel. "Joshua, here's the plan. The leader will be here in thirty minutes. We'll go outside and escort him inside. I'll hack the trigger of the bomb and have them remote-activated from the cell phone on the table. I'm pretty positive that the leader will have a trigger but looking at this I can rewire it to come from the phone we have. This is where you come in. You need to convince one of the guards watching the hostages to take a break."

Joshua looks confused. "How will I be able to do that? I don't speak Arabic," he says.

"The leader needs you," I say in Arabic "Just repeat those exact words and you'll be fine." His eyes grow wide. "Okay . . . "

I smile, trying to hold back my laughter, then we practiced the same Arabic phrase a few more times until Joshua had it down "Once the guard leaves, you need to take the bombs off of the hostages and put them in the corners of the room. Don't worry, they won't go off. You ready?"

Joshua sighs. "Ready as I'll ever be." Then he puts his hand on his chin and says, "Wait, you know how to deactivate a bomb?"

I look at the computer and the cellphone. "How they have the denotation set up, it's remote control. I just need to change the signal from the computer to the cellphone. Shouldn't be that hard."

"I'm going to trust you," Joshua says. "If it doesn't work then we are fucked so if you don't do it, let's just pretend that you did. Okay?"

I shake my head. "Once we bring the leader to the room, I'll put the gun to his head and tell the men to lower their weapons. I'll threaten him; I'll say I have the bomb trigger and that I'll blow up the room. The men will lower their guns and the leader will lead me to the sword. While I'm gone you need to tie the men up and empty the clips of the guns. Do that just in case we have any surprises." Joshua looks at me and gives me a thumbs up.

I begin to hack the computer and rewire the detonation of the bombs to come from the cellphone I have. Joshua gets the guard to leave his post and begins to remove the bombs from the hostages. Once I finish, we head outside to greet the leader. He pulls up in an old beige Hummer and exits the car with four men wearing military outfits. He walks to the door followed by twelve men and says to me in Arabic, "Show me the hostages."

I nod, opening the door. We walk to the room with the hostages. I stay within arm's length of him and when he enters the room, he instantly notices that the hostages are not wearing the bombs anymore. He yells at us, "Where are the bombs?"

I pull my gun out and aim it at his head. "Tell your men to drop their guns now," I order calmly.

He chuckles. "Are you stupid? There are thirteen of us and one of you. Kill this man," he says. The men point their guns at me, ready to fire.

I pull out the cellphone. "If you move an inch then I'll blow up this room killing all of us." His expression turns to confusion. "Yeah. This is the trigger to the bombs," I say with a smile.

As understanding sets in, a look of worry slowly appears across his face and glances at his men.

"Don't look at them. I hacked your system too easily, if I may say. So, tell your men to drop the weapons or die." He gives his men a look and they drop their weapons. Joshua points the hostages to the exit and they file out.

The leader asks me who I am.

"I'm Orion from the House of David."

He walks right up to my nose. "You are a devil and devils deserve to die." I tighten my grip on my phone and point it at his head. "Then kill me." The soldiers look around at the bombs and start to freak out but their leader laughs.

Sarah's voice comes on the headset. "We've taken the outside."

I train my sight on the leader. "The place is surrounded. Do you want to die for nothing? Take me to the sword."

He spits on my shoe. "Fuck you."

Josh shoves him which causes him to stumble forward.

"Joshua, you stay here and watch them."

He nods and instructs the men to get on the ground.

I follow the leader until we arrive at a stone wall. The leader pushes loose stone in the upper right corner and the walls open up to an empty room with one table in it. He walks inside first then I follow with the gun still pointed at him. The room was well lit due to there being only one hanging lightbulb, but I could still see. As we enter the room, I spot the sword on the table.

"Guys, I found the artifact," I announce through the headset.

I grab the sword and begin walking out with my gun in the other hand.

"Orion," Ying Yue says through the headset. "One of the hostages ran back inside to get a bracelet."

"She's coming back." I see a young Muslim girl wearing an all-black gown run through the hallway. The leader pushes me backward, grabs a gun off the ground, then grabs the girl.

"Drop the gun and hand over the bomb trigger," he barks.

He's oblivious to the fact that Joshua has emptied the clips. I throw him the cellphone and tell him to push the button to activate the bombs.

"I'll be seeing my Lord soon," he says, grinning, then pushes the button. Nothing happens and he tries to fire the gun but it's empty. This gives me enough time to charge him and take him down. I get him in a headlock and choke him out.

"The artifact is secure and the leader is subdued," I say into the headset.

Joshua runs into the room. "Bro, I saw you toss him the trigger. Didn't you configure that cellphone to activate the bombs?"

I stand up and dust myself off. "Man, I don't know how to disarm a bomb. At first, it seemed like easy coding and rerouting but when I looked into it more I had no clue what I was doing. I just told you I did because I needed you to believe it so we could pull this off."

Joshua's mouth drops and he starts laughing hysterically.

We exit the hideout with the artifact and the leader. "Nice work, Captain," Sarah says with a smile on her face. "No deaths, the hostages are safe, and the artifact is secure."

I look around and see Joshua herding the leader off to the officers. I also notice four patrolmen taking the hostage away and six others taking the fanatic group. "So, what's going to happen to them?"

"The local government will handle them," Sarah says. "We're only here for the artifact. We don't interfere with government affairs. Our job is to find out if artifacts are being used to manipulate people and lead them to do bad things. Once we secure the artifact or prove that the individuals are lying, we hand the criminals to their respective government. This is the deal we've made with many governments of the world."

I hold on to the sword and wonder if it will be my tool. Sarah studies it. "We will test it and see if the legends are true. But if they aren't then you can have it."

I give her my biggest smile, then I wonder if there was an easier way to save those people. "Would it have been better if I just killed that whole group?"

"You did the right thing. Killing isn't always the answer," Sarah replies.

I know that Eden would have done it differently.

"I like the way you did this. No bloodshed. Everyone has the right to live and we all make mistakes. They have the right to learn and grow, just like any other human."

I just nod at her and begin to walk towards the car. I get into the backseat. Ying Yue is in the driver's seat. "Congrats, Orion. You should be proud. You completed your first mission."

I take off the vest and place the sword at my foot, "Thank you. Are we heading back to the Gate now?"

She starts the car. "Yeah. You can take a nap. It's been a long day. Once Joshua gets in we'll leave."

"What about Sarah?" I ask.

"Sarah has to do paperwork with the government and debrief them," Ying Yue answers.

I close my eyes as I listen to the strong gust from outside, and drift away into my head.

I wake up once we arrive at the helicopter and it's about 1:00 am. Joshua, Ying Yue and I head to the Gate. Once we land, Joseph congratulates me and I head inside. I want to learn more about Tools so I go to the library. I'm looking over the history of Tools when someone interrupts me.

"I knew you were into computers, but I didn't know you could hack a control room."

It's Eden.

"That was the easy part. The code they had was so old school—one of the first ones I learned as a five-year-old when I started coding. I've always loved computers. My father was a big computer nerd so he got that instilled in me. When I got older, I used to take classes and from there, I taught myself the rest."

Eden pulls out a chair next to me and sits down. "So, you're pretty much a genius. Why stay in Mobile? You could've left and gone to different high-tech universities."

I laugh. "Going to those prestigious schools doesn't mean you're smart, Eden. Even college wouldn't let me do anything that would make a big difference on my own. So, I decided to help my family instead. In this world, it's about luck, money, and who you know. I don't know anyone, and I'd rather not be catered to."

With a confused look on his face, he asks, "Then, why did you accept my offer?"

"It was different. It wasn't fake. I saw an opportunity to make a difference and gain the knowledge and power I need to change and protect my family."

He just nods in some sort of agreement. *I don't think he knows what to say to me.*

"Eden, is there something I should expect?"

He sits back in his chair, puts his hands in his pockets and says with a subtle tone, "I don't know the exact answer to that, but I can tell you a story, though. It was about eight years ago. I was a newly named Judge. In one of our missions, we had a lead that there was a relic, an artifact in the black forest of Germany. So, I traveled to southern Stuttgart and I befriended a family there. I roamed through the forest for hours during the day and came back to the family's house to eat and sleep. I remember that they had a fat, little German boy there about twelve years old. I will never forget his name —it was Dirk. The father loved him more than he loved his wife. To most, it's natural for a father to love his only son that much, but this seemed like a sexual love to me at the time. I was so wrong, though. Little did I know; this family had a big secret. One day, I went to a pub in town with the father and we drank a whole lot. Those Germans can drink. He told me stories of his wife and how she hated the little boy. To be honest, I didn't care. I was on a mission to find the relic. Days went by and I became closer with the kid, Dirk. We would play, read stories, and I would even help put him to bed. It was the tail end of my mission, and I had concluded that all the evidence pointed out that the artifact wasn't real. I made travel plans and when I went to thank the family for the stay, I found out that the wife had killed the husband and the boy. I asked her why she did it, and she said because they didn't love her and all she ever wanted was to be loved."

Eden feels sad and lonely all the time even though he has people that care about him. I look at him worriedly. "Is being a Judge all about death?"

He leaves his seat. "No. Some of us haven't even seen death. Not all of us know what it looks like. I've just seen a lot of shit, Man, so I'm different. You must be ready for anything and everything. Humans are wild and complicated creatures."

I close the book and stand up as well. "I understand completely. However, everyone has the right to live. If there's a way to keep everyone alive then I want to do it."

"Yeah, well, sometimes it's better to just kill the person."

"Yeah, but that isn't me. All lives are precious."

"You need to get back to training. I'm going back on vacation. Be better when I get back," he says and walks away. I go to the bookshelf and pick out another book. I need to learn as much as possible.

It's been a month since my first mission and my skills keep progressing. About a week after we completed the mission, Sarah gifted me the sword of Michael the Archangel. I have been training with it against Joshua for over three weeks now. After eating breakfast, I head to the weapons room for another training session with Joshua. He tosses me my sword. Suddenly, Eden walks through the door.

"Orion, let's spar."

"Oh, hey, of course, this is a perfect opportunity for me to get better with this, the Heaven-Piercer." I hold up my sword.

"So, you decided to name your Tool?"

"When I found it, the hilt had its name scribed on it in Hebrew. So, I decided to keep the name. Sarah tested it. It's made out of a rare metal called rhodium and it dates back to 60 A.D. The metal wasn't truly discovered until 1803, so for someone to make it into a weapon like this is remarkable."

"Well, all right then." Eden shrugs. "Let's see how good you are with it."

"Yes!"

"We will be sparring with our Tools. You should be happy. Not all Captains get Tools. You're only the sixth one in House of David history to ever get one."

I look at Joshua with excitement and I tighten my grip on the handle. "Wow, that's amazing. Even with some sword training, I still am probably not at your level."

"Idiot. I don't fight with a sword." Joshua disappears into a room and comes back out with my Tool. "I wield the Deathscythe," Eden declares, taking it from Joshua's hands. "My weapon is basically like the weapon the grim reaper use in those cartoons, but deadlier. The blade is made of Damascus chromium steel and the shaft is made of carbon fiber and has a white tassel below the scythe." I've never seen Eden's Tool close up but I feel intimidated; there are bloodstains on the tassels. He takes off his shirt.

"Should I take mine off as well?"

"Actually, it would be a smart idea for you to put more armor on."

Eden turns to Joshua. "Hey, Dreads! Give him some more armor!"

Joshua heads back into the room and comes out carrying a body armor, knee pads, and a helmet.

"Is this necessary?"

"I'm coming at you with everything. Without those, you will die."

I put the armor on and Eden gets in a fighting stance.

"Are you ready to begin?" he asks.

I nod and hold the sword with two hands. Eden lunges at me furiously and swings his Tool horizontally, aiming the blade at my ribs. I block his attack.

"Whoa! You are much stronger than I thought," I exclaim.

I can tell that I have gotten stronger and my understanding of battle has improved. Eden plants his left foot under me and sweeps me off my feet. As I begin to fall, he elbows me in the gut. I hit the ground with a thunderous momentum. He flips backward and twirls the scythe over my head. I slowly pick myself up. I try to catch my breath. *What should I do? He has more experience.* I need to wait for the attacks and move to the side. He comes forward at me and I sidestep left. He hops behind me and hit me in the back with the staff. He flies forward and I roll on the ground. He walks towards me slowly, bloodthirst in his eyes.

"Why do you hesitate?" he asks. "Your thoughts aren't going to save you right now. When you fight, you fight to kill. You come to your opponent with unrelenting aggressiveness. You should be trying to crush me, beat me. If you don't come at me with all you've got, then it's simple, my friend. You will die."

I take in what he said. *He's right, I'm thinking too much. I need to attack.* I glower and come at him, swinging the sword wildly. I try an overhead swing, and he grabs my wrist and pulls it to the left. I try a punch with my left, but he ducks and punches me in the gut. I feel like I can't breathe. I drop the sword. *I have to get him to the ground, it's the only way.* I lunge and wrap my arms around him. *The only way I can win is to take advantage of my wrestling skills. I'm a way better wrestler than him.*

He judo flips me over his right hip and I hit the ground rolling to the side as I pick up the sword. He comes in quickly and stands before me with the blade pointing at me inches away from my face.

"You think way too much. You thought you could beat me with your wrestling, but you didn't consider that I'm stronger and have way more overall skills than you. In the beginning, you didn't block me. I let you block me. I could've killed you." He pulls his scythe back. "You fight with the fear of death. You shouldn't be afraid of death. Accept it as an old friend."

"What are you talking about? I was fighting to win. And I will never accept death to win."

I don't know what got a hold of him, but he begins yelling. "No. You were thinking! Thinking will get you killed. You may not see it but it was clear as day. If you hate death and love life so much, what about I let you live this life without your arm?"

He starts to swing and, all of a sudden, I hear, "Stand down. Eden!" He continues anyway and the blade flies down, hitting the ground next to me. I glare up at Eden with disgust.

"Why are you my Judge? I wish it was Sarah."

Joseph is in the doorway. Eden kneels. "You must understand, not all enemies are going to talk to you. They will just shoot first and ask for your corpse later. Get that through your thick skull. If you get in a situation and there's no other choice, what will you choose? To live or to die? Fight or not stand? Regardless of how hard that choice will be for you, you're going to have to make it," Eden spoke calmly.

We both stand up and I look at Eden right in the eye before responding.

"Sometimes there's another way," I told him. "You must find that other way. If you just accept the situation you're in, how will you ever move forward as a better person?"

He lifts his scythe and put it over his shoulder. "Live or die—what will you choose?"

"Live."

Chapter 7: To Fully

IT'S A THURSDAY afternoon and I am sitting in my room on the Gate reading some Edgar Allen Poe poems when I hear a knock on my door. "Come in."

Joseph walks in wearing a black suit with his usual white button-down. "Greetings, Eden. Your Captain, Orion, has been doing quite well, you know."

I close my book. "Told you he would be valuable. He's smart and has helped us find many members of Seditio."

"You were right," Joseph acknowledges as he leans against the door. "He's right on track to become a Judge. Judah has been wanting to retire for a while. The way Orion has completed these missions so quickly and without any casualties is quite impressive."

I look at him with uncertainty even though another part of me knows that Orion's work as a Captain truly is remarkable. It's been over seven months since bringing Orion to the Gate, and he's completed ten missions and discovered four artifacts.

"I don't know about being a Judge after only ten missions, Joseph. To be fair, these missions Orion's completed are relatively easy and his combat skills still aren't up to par. Yes, his intelligence is extremely high. But he's not willing to take a life yet. You know that in some situations he will need to choose to kill. Even in my career, I have failed in at least ten missions. He must be willing to fail and the fact is, he isn't used enough to losing yet. He hasn't had the experience of losing."

Joseph puts his hand on his chin in agreement. "Well, you have a point. Okay, let's test him out then. I'm sending you two to investigate an artifact—the sword of Joan of Arc. Ying Yue found out that Seditio has been extremely active in Paris, France. Ying Yue's early research has shown us that the criminal known as Whiteface has been particularly active in this area."

"What else do we currently know about Whiteface?" All I know about the name Whiteface is that he's on the Most Wanted list.

"Here's the information we currently have. Caldwell "Whiteface" Phillip is currently number four on the World's Most Wanted list. We know that he's a white German man with blond hair, a slightly thick red beard, and blue eyes. He's highly intelligent and has a civil engineering degree. He's high on the totem pole in Seditio and has also killed over thirty people that we know of. Whiteface is known for torturing and raping his captives. This guy is a psychopath who has no remorse for people. He's extremely dangerous and he has even killed one of our Captains before. If you and Orion run into him, we need you to capture him alive, if it's possible. He could be the key to finding the leader of Seditio."

"I don't know, Joseph. This seems like an extremely hard mission for him. If that Whiteface guy is in the city, we might have to engage. I've killed enough Seditio members that I know how this works. This guy seems like he could be looking for blood. If that situation arises then I will not be able to protect Orion and, quite frankly, I don't trust his judgment in battle yet."

"I know the risk, Eden, trust me. I think that when the situation arises, Orion will be able to understand what needs to happen and make the right choice."

I shake my head at him. "If you say so."

He puts his hands on my shoulder. "You leave tomorrow so get ready. I've already briefed Orion on the mission and he seems okay with it."

"You went to him before me? What the fuck, Joseph?"

"Don't ever curse at me, Eden. I'm your superior."

"Whatever," I mutter.

He walks towards the door to leave. "Yes, Eden I asked him about the mission first because I wanted to see what his choice would be. I thought he would say no due to the dangers. But he is driven by his desire for power and he wants experiences like this one so that he can gain that power. That's why he's so willing to take this mission. We can win from this as well as an organization. Plus, we eventually are going to need another Judge to take over. Judah wants to retire. Jamal is getting old and he can't contribute. Weren't you the one who said that Orion would make a good addition, anyway?"

"Yes, I did." I can't argue with Joseph. He's right. "Let's just see how he does. I want to see how his mind works, but if we get in a situation, hopefully, he can act. Also, I hope we don't run into a situation because I really don't want to fill out any more paperwork on him."

After my talk with Joseph, I go to the library to do some research on the Notre Dame Cathedral. While reading, Aiden approaches me.

"What's going on, Aiden?"

He looks at me with those clueless big eyes. "We're thinking about getting off the Gate to see a movie. Do you want to come?"

"No, I leave tomorrow for a mission."

"What type of mission? Do you need me?"

Maybe I do need him there. "Yes, I need you to be in France. This mission is very dangerous. There's a criminal that could cause problems and I feel like Orion is not going to do what needs to be done. I need you to be there in case things go awry."

"Then I'll prepare." He leaves the library and I continue reading about the Cathedral. Before heading back to get ready for bed, I stop at the kitchen on the Gate for a beer. As I'm about to take a sip, I hear a voice.

"Is anyone sitting here?" It's Orion.

"What's up?"

"I've been here for months, worked with many Captains, and been on multiple missions. I'm still wondering the same thing. How did you survive those gunshots when we first met? I asked other Captains and they said I'm too new to the organization to know yet. I have looked in the library to research it on my own and still can't find anything. I wanted to know from you personally, though. Why? Or how?"

I realize it's time to tell him. "Joseph told me about this when I was young after my first mission. The Finger of God was tested by Judge Hubbard in 1902 to see what property it possessed. In the wood, there was a bacteria. What makes the bacteria so surprising is that when it touches human skin, it has a reaction that allows the body to produce red and white blood cells which, in turn, causes the body to create collagen. The collagen then heals the wound and allows the body to keep fighting. Basically, with a Finger of God, your body will heal from any injury. The only exception is if you are shot or stabbed through the heart. Judges have their Finger of God stitched to their body. As you can see, mine is stitched on my side a little below my left armpit." I lift up my shirt and show Orion where my FOG is. He looks amazed.

"So only Judges are allowed to have these? How many are there? Why can't we give this to others?"

I get up and head to the door. "You're not a Judge, so you don't need to worry about that. Just know if you become a Judge, you will be able to learn all about the Finger of God. Until then, don't pay any mind to it because it doesn't concern you."

I leave the kitchen and I can hear Orion call out to me but I continue on my way to my room. As I lie in bed, I wonder again if Orion is ready. He's making a name for himself throughout the House of David. I don't know how I feel about taking Orion with me on this investigation of the Notre Dame Cathedral in Paris.

Then my mind jumps to my research and the details I know about this mission.

The Cathedral is known for the elaborately created stained glass windows, marble floors, and limestone exteriors. It was said originally that the artifact was lost forever, but we got a tip that the sword of Joan of Arc is located somewhere beneath the church. The sword would be 600 years old and legend has it that the sword can give the wielder the courage to go into any battle. Courage that is so overwhelming that the wielder can ignore the pain of any injury and continue fighting. Because of its incredible power, the Joan of Arc sword can be dangerous if it lands in the hands of someone looking to do evil, such as Seditio or any dictators.

The following day, Orion and I arrive at the Gare du Nord, which is known to be one of the busiest railroad stations in Europe. It's a cloudy and extremely humid day in August; it's around eighty-four degrees outside.

We get off the train and we take a taxi straight to Notre Dame.

"Eden, Notre Dame is a pretty popular place. Why hasn't anyone found the sword already? I don't see why we're investigating this sword when you don't have proof of it even being there. Maybe it's forever missing," Orion says to me.

"Maybe it isn't there or maybe it is," I reply. "Sometimes you don't need proof to go investigating and sometimes people look in the wrong places. The greatest found treasures are usually hiding in plain sight. You just need to have a little faith, my friend. Also, you should know Whiteface was spotted in this area and if he's here then there must be some truth to the rumor."

"Can I be honest with you? I feel like the House of David has become a group of treasure seekers. Yes, I've been on missions that involved tactical skills and fighting, but the other missions were relatively easy. I just disproved the rumors and legends and I was able to trick some members of Seditio, who I think weren't really that bright, anyway."

"Why do you think that?"

"Reading over old cases and the history of the Judges, we used to help in wars, stop events that could change the world, and collect artifacts that could change actual history. But since 1970, we haven't done any of that."

"If you read the code and the history of the House then you would also know that we don't interfere with national affairs. The House of David has always been what I told you before. Overall, the organization's goal is to collect biblical artifacts so that people with evil intent can't use them to manipulate people with faith. The House has only intervened in five wars: the American Revolution, French Revolution, the Napoleonic Wars, World War I, and World War II. And we only intervened because artifacts were being used in those wars. One of the most famous examples of our work was during the American Revolution when the British were using the Sword of Charlemagne the Great. King George the Third believed that the sword had the power to kill anyone with just one cut. So, we sent a Judge to investigate the authenticity of the artifact. After lots of research, our Judge, Oscar de Leon, believed this to be true. He claims he witnessed a man who was only nicked with the sword die instantly."

"Anyway, his mission was to retrieve the sword and end that war before the British could test the sword in battle. During the mission, Oscar infiltrated the British ranks and gave the American colonists the information needed to outsmart them. The Battle of Saratoga on September 19, 1777, was when all of this happened. Oscar received intel that British General John Burgoyne was leading a large invasion army southward from Canada in the Champlain Valley, hoping to join forces with two smaller British fleets: one marching northward from New York City and another one marching eastward from Lake Ontario. Oscar gave this information to the Americans, so later, when the British general thought that he was meeting up with two other armies, he ended up being surrounded by American forces instead. Oscar and four of our other Judges ended up killing him that night. So, thanks to Oscar's brilliant mind, the Americans won a decisive victory over the British and, in exchange, Oscar wanted the box from the British general—the box that carried the Sword of Charlemagne."

Orion frowns. "What are you getting at?"

I'm getting impatient. "What I'm trying to say is that we do not interfere unless we truly believe an artifact is involved. And nowadays people aren't as religious as they once were. So, they don't believe in using artifacts like they once did back in the old days. King George believed in the power of the sword and thought it could win the war for him. Little did he know; the sword was just an old rusty sword. The man who died from the cut probably just died from tetanus from being cut by a rusty blade. Our job isn't just to find the artifact but to also test and see if the legend is real. The piece of wood that I have heals me due to the bacteria in the wood. This bacteria isn't found anywhere else in the world. Maybe it's a miracle or maybe something else. I don't know. That's why you just have to have faith."

The taxi stops in front of Notre Dame. Orion gets out first and I follow. I pay the taxi driver and then we walk toward the Cathedral.

"By the way, your story on the history of the Judges made no sense to me. Didn't go with what I was asking at all," Orion says.

"Exactly."

"I don't know what the fuck that means."

I chuckle. The Cathedral is surprisingly packed with tourists. Orion walks up to the steps to the front doors.

"Hey, Dumbass!" I call out after him. "We aren't going inside."

"Then where would we be looking?"

"At the crowd."

"Why are we looking into the crowd? The artifact isn't in the crowd of tourists."

This is exactly why I asked Aiden to come as backup.

"We aren't looking for the artifact right now. I'm looking for someone who looks suspicious. Like you should've read in the brief, Whiteface has been seen in the area. They've been here longer than we have, meaning they've most likely already checked the inside. Also, I'm positive they know we're here, too. I've killed a lot of members of Seditio so most members would want to get revenge. Whiteface is very smart. Crazy, but smart. He would have members of Seditio around here to warn him of our presence. So right now, we're just going to walk around the building and be on the lookout."

Orion nods. "I understand that, but if we're uncertain that the artifact is here then why should we make ourselves known? We probably should have done more reconnaissance and read more about sightings. We're unprepared. This could end badly."

Why didn't I think of that? I keep forgetting that Orion tries to avoid confrontation.

"Yeah! You could be right. But I'm your boss so you'll do what I say."

Orion rolls his eyes. For over ten minutes, we both scan the crowd. I'm about to give up, thinking that they might not be in the region, after all, then I notice a strange look on Orion's face. I look in his line of sight and see a man with white paint on his face. He's extremely tall with flowing blond hair. It's Whiteface.

I grab Orion. "Let's go now!"

We sprint through a group of people. I see Whiteface heading for the street. He reaches a black sedan and gets in. Orion and I arrive at the same spot but it's too late.

"Fuck. That was fucking Whiteface. He thinks this is a game," I yell.

Orion looks around. "Eden, there!" He points at this guy at the corner staring at us. Then the man begins to run. I chase after him, bumping into people left and right. Orion speeds ahead of me. He has greatly improved; his stamina seems to be on point.

Within minutes, he tackles the guy on his stomach. "Why are you running?" He holds the man to the ground by the back of his neck and the man replies in French, which we both understand.

"He told me to tell you that he already has the artifact, but he wants to have fun with the Judge."

Orion grabs the back of his head and holds it to the ground; his knee is pushing his arm to the ground while his right hand holds down the other arm. Two cops approach him but I arrive in time to tell them that this is an investigation that doesn't concern them. I show them a fake United States Military badge. At first, they are hesitant but then eventually back away.

Once they leave, Orion asks, "What do you want to do with him, Eden? He's working with Whiteface." He's severely out of breath.

"I'll book us a hotel room. And then we can have some fun," I reply. Orion lifts his hand and I punch the new prisoner in the face so hard that he goes unconscious. We make our way to the hotel.

Once we arrive, Orion looks at the place with bulging eyes.

"Wow! Do you think we should be staying in a room so nice?"

"We aren't savages," I say. The prisoner squirms for a little bit and Orion hits him in the head. "Why did you do that?"

"I thought if you hit them in the head, they pass out."

"You know, for someone so fucking smart that was the stupidest thing you've ever said."

We walk through the lobby. We solicit stares from people because of the unconscious guy on my shoulders.

"Nothing to see here! He just had too much to drink," I

155

yell. Finally, I get to the front desk, and the attendee hands me the room key. I pretend that I don't notice her suspicious look and just smile at her.

"How in the world are we able to do this?" Orion asks on our way to the hotel room.

"Bro, we're in Europe, people here get drunk all the time. This isn't anything new."

Orion just laughs and we step inside the room. Immediately, I tie the man up to a chair. Then I slap him in the face so hard he wakes up. He looks lost for a second, then he gets his bearings.

He speaks in French. "Do what you want with me. I will not tell you anything. We will make the world believe again." His smug look is bothering me at this point and I can't help it so I punch him in the chest. Orion shoots me a glance, but I just shrug.

"What do you want the world to believe in?"

The man smiles. "Make them believe in God, of course."

"But most of the world already believes in God," Orion responds. "How will obtaining these artifacts help with this goal of yours?"

Now I'm angry. We're getting nowhere with this conversation.

"Blah! Blah! Blah! To be honest I don't give a damn about you or your fucking dumbass organization's goals. Where is Whiteface?"

He laughs and I start to laugh too. I pull out my knife and stab him on top of his thigh. He screams in pain, but I keep laughing.

"I'll ask again. WHERE IS WHITEFACE?"

He still doesn't respond so I slowly twist the knife clockwise and tears run down his face. After I make three rotations of the knife, he finally gives in.

"He is located three miles from the Eiffel Tower! He is in

an old abandoned coffee shop."

I pull the knife out. "See, that wasn't that hard."

Suddenly Orion's phone rings. I look at him as it continues to ring. "Are you going to answer that?"

Orion just looks at me. "We're doing something."

"Just answer the damn phone," I tell him as I let my forehead fall into my palm for a second. He rolls his eyes and answers it.

"Hey," he mutters. A look of excitement clouds his face. "Wait, really? Everyone is here? How did you know I was here? Oh, you saw me at the Cathedral . . . Okay, well, I can meet you later and we can get some food." He hangs up the phone.

"Who was that?"

"My friends and family are here in Paris. I'm thinking about meeting up with them later," he answers with an ecstatic look.

"How did they know you were here?"

He laughs like he's still in disbelief. "Two days ago, I told them I would be in France. I guess they thought I would be in the biggest city and wanted to surprise me."

Why would he tell his family?

"Why would you tell them where we would be when you know it's extremely dangerous if Whiteface sees you with them? If he gets his hands on them, they could be in some serious trouble, Orion."

"I understand that, but I didn't think they would show up."

I'm really glad I have Aiden here in case I need backup.

"Go have dinner with your family, but be careful. I'll deal with this guy."

Orion nods and leaves the room.

I look that the guy tied up on the chair and wonder what I'm going to do with him. "I guess I will just leave you here." I stuff his mouth with a sock and put duct tape over it. Then I leave the hotel and head to the abandoned coffee shop to find Whiteface.

While I was walking through the lobby, I see Orion with his mom, grandpa, Mary, Jacob, and Matthew. I walk past them but I hear someone running up behind me.

"Hey!" Orion calls out to me. "Do you want to have dinner with us? My mom wanted you to come."

I hesitate. I'm not sure if I should come or not. "No, I think I should handle the issue at hand. Enjoy your family."

"Dude, come! You're always working and you need a break. Even you, my friend, deserve a fun night out, even though you're an asshole sometimes. You're the reason I can explore the world and be a part of the House." He puts his arm over my shoulders and walks me towards his family.

"Thank you for taking good care of my son," Mrs. Bachman says. I feel a random punch on my left arm; it's Mary.

"So, we meet again," she tells me. "You all-black-wearing weirdo."

I just roll my eyes. I turn my attention to Orion's family, who are all staring at me in awe. "He has been a great addition and a valuable piece to the organization. We're very proud of him," I say.

"Ready to get some food?" Orion's grandpa asks. I try to object but Mary and Orion don't let me.

We eat dinner at L'Abeille, a restaurant named after Napoleon's favorite emblem. It is a two-Michelin-star restaurant with amazing dining and a great atmosphere. We get seated at the table and I can see how much Orion means to his friends and family. The love is so overbearing that I can feel it consume me. Everyone is happy and enjoying each other.

So, this is what it is like to have a family who loves you and supports you.

"Eden, tell me about your family," Mrs. Bachman says.

"Well, everyone in my family is dead. My master is the

only one I would consider my family. He's like my foster father."
Everyone looks at me with pity, but I try to smile. "Most of my
childhood, I was with him. I was training and learning so that was
a good thing for me." I can see the sadness in his mother's eyes
and I can see where Orion gets his kind heart from.

She interlocks her fingers and looks at me lovingly. "So
where did you grow up?"

I scratch my head for a bit. "Well, I've lived all over the
place. I've never lived at the same spot for too long. But my family
is Egyptian."

Jacob lets out a chuckle. "I thought you were Samoan or
something."

Matthew hits him on the back of the head. "You're a
jackass. Sorry about that, Eden."

I just shrug. "It's fine. Mary over here has called me much
worse," I say as I glance at Mary.

"Well, I'm just very honest." Everyone starts to laugh until
Mrs. Bachman chimes in.

"Where's Joseph? I haven't seen him since we did that tour
of Paris."

Jacob and Matthew take a sip of water and look thoughtful.

"The last time I saw him was when we were at the Eiffel
Tower and he was talking to this guy about football. Knowing
Joseph, he probably met a girl and hooked up with her," Jacob
says, smirking.

"Yeah. He told me he will meet up with us later," Mary
adds.

"Well, that sounds like him," Orion states.

"Well, if you ever want to you can celebrate the holidays
with us," Mrs. Bachman changed the topic. "You're a part of
Orion's life, so you're basically family now."

I don't know what's coming over me. No one has ever said
that to me. *A family huh?* I think to myself. Suddenly, I feel my

phone vibrate. Aiden is calling me. I glance at Orion and turn to his parents. "Excuse me, I have to take this." Orion nods. I leave the table, head outside, and I answer the phone.

"Yes, have you arrived?" I ask.

"I'm here and I also brought Sarah," Aiden says calmly.

"Why would you bring Sarah? I only needed you."

"Looking over the brief more, I felt like we would need more backup. There have been a lot of people going missing here in the last three weeks. An unusual amount, Eden. Seditio has been too active lately and, I don't know, I feel like we need this backup."

"Understood," I say. Sarah is a good person to bring along anyway. "I need you guys to find any abandoned coffee shops within a three-mile radius from the Eiffel Tower. Once you guys find one, send me the location. Orion and I will meet you there."

"Understood."

I head back inside and see that our food has arrived. I sit down and everyone begins to eat. Jacob orders four bottles of red wine and challenges Orion to a chugging contest but Mrs. Bachman asks the two of them to stop, reminding them that they're in public.

They both look at her and laugh. "I bet I could beat the both of you," Grandpa Bachman says with a smile. Orion's mother puts her hand on her face in shame and embarrassment.

"Well, I bet I can beat all three of you," I challenge.

They look at me with surprise. "You're on."

We each grab a bottle and start chugging the red wine. Mary, Mrs. Bachman, and Matthew stare at us in amazement. However, Orion, Jacob, and Grandpa Bachman are no match for me. I wipe the red wine off my face and Mary is the first one to comment on my victory.

"You are literally a drunk." Everyone starts to laugh.

"Sorry, but I do love drinking the nectar of the gods. It

160

gives me the energy I need." Now Orion shoots me a look while everyone continues to laugh.

This is my first time having fun like this with a family. I really like it. I feel loved. We hang out for two hours. Orion's mom pays for everything and everyone thanks her. We march out of the restaurant. She gives me a huge hug. "Glad to finally talk to you, Eden. We should do this again."

"Anytime," I say, hugging her back.

Next, his grandpa pats me on my shoulder. "We should drink sometime. Orion is not very good at it, and I need a drinking buddy."

"Anytime, old man," I reply with a laugh. Jacob, Matthew, and Mary wave at me and Orion as we leave.

"Don't be a weirdo!" Mary shouts.

"You have a lovely family, Orion," I say.

He waves bye to them as they get into a taxi. "Yeah, they're amazing, aren't they? I love them."

A couple of seconds later I feel my phone vibrate again. Aiden has texted me the location of an abandon coffee shop.

"Let's go! We have work to do."

We flag down a taxi and tell the man the address right away. In a couple of minutes, we arrive at the old abandoned coffee shop from Aiden's text. It's about 10:00 pm. The street lights illuminate Aiden and Sarah standing out front.

The coffee shop is an old, two-story building with white bricks. The windows are busted open and so are the big, red double doors. Orion and I approach them slowly.

"I scouted the area and I didn't see unusual people or activity. Maybe that guy was lying, Eden," Sarah says. Orion walks back and forth looking at the outside of the shop.

"Did y'all check the inside?"

Aiden grabs a piece of gum out of his pockets. "No. We wanted to wait until you got here, just in case there are men

161

inside."

We walk up to the big red doors. Sarah hands Orion the gun she had in her holster.

"Orion, stay behind us," I instruct him. "You don't have a Finger of God. If they have guns, you could be killed."

Orion scoots behind us. Aiden approaches the door and turns the knob. It's unlocked. He pushes it open and walks inside. Sarah flashes her flashlight quickly scanning the inside. There are broken chairs, tables, and glass everywhere. The shop looks like it's been abandoned for some time. We took a few minutes to check all around the shop, but nothing seems worthwhile.

"Let's split up. Sarah, you check the upstairs, Aiden you check the back, Orion and I will finish up here," I whisper.

"Roger."

"Eden! What if there isn't anything here? Maybe that guy lied," Orion says.

"I don't think so. He wanted us to be here. He wasn't afraid of me even though he knew about me, and knew about the House."

Orion continues to look around. "You're right. It was too easy to catch him. It was like he wanted to be caught. He wanted to tell us about this place, but why? What does he have to gain for doing this? What does Whiteface gain?" I hear footsteps running down the stairs towards us.

"Eden! You need to see this now." It's Sarah.

Orion and I make our way up the stairs. Orion is behind me and I'm behind Sarah. We walk past two doors and she opens a third rotten, wooden door at the end of the hallway. She enters first and I follow.

The smell of fresh blood hits my nose right away. A man is hanging from the ceiling with blood dripping from his mouth. He's missing his fingers and toes and a pool of blood is on the floor. The man is about 6'4" with dirty blond hair that is stained with blood. His face is so beaten up that he's unrecognizable and his

162

skin is so pale from being exsanguinated.

"No! Joseph!" Orion shouts. He runs up to him and hugs him.

"Orion, what are you doing?" Sarah shouts at him. "Who is that?" Tears are streaming down Orion's face now.

"This is my friend, Joseph. Oh my GOD. No!" He's barely able to talk in between sobs.

Sarah hugs him. "Orion, let him go, please."

He finally lets go of his friend's body and wraps his arms around Sarah. Then Aiden walks into the room.

"Eden! The back is clear."

"Call this in," I immediately say to Aiden. "Get the police here." Then I turn to the others. "Sarah, Orion, and I are going to pay a visit to the captive in the hotel room."

So much hurt is in Orion's eyes. I can feel the pain he's feeling, but anger takes over me. I want the Seditio captive.

We head back to the hotel room. Orion is still a mess. I don't know what to say to him. Sarah has her arms around him, comforting him.

I get back up to the room to see the captive there smiling at me through the duct tape. I rip off the tape and he instantly says, "Did you like the gift he left you?"

Orion runs up to him and smacks him over and over. I hear his cheekbones crack against his knuckles.

"I'll kill you! I will kill you," Orion shouts at the man in between punches.

I grab him by the shoulders. "Stop. This isn't you, Orion." Sarah pulls Orion away from me and hugs him tightly.

"Let's go, Orion," she says to him. They walk to the door together. The captive begins to laugh. This time, I walk up to him until I am only inches from him. I glare at him, then I pull out a knife from inside my jacket. He looks surprised.

"You're not going to kill me," he says with the same

163

derisive laugh. "I have valuable information. He said you would kill me." I grab the back of his head and pull it back as I smile at him.

"Yeah, well, I'm not him. You're in the presence of the God of Death. You made a big mistake and that mistake will never be forgiven. Before, I wasn't sure what to do with you, but now I do. I'm going to send you to your maker so you can fully understand. Not God. No, you're going to hell."

He can't hide the fear from his eyes this time. "You think that I am scared to di . . ." I swipe at his throat cutting it wide open.

"I don't care. Just die."

His blood gushes from his throat and he gags on his blood. I head to the door to check on Orion, leaving the corpse slumped over in the chair. Outside the hotel room, Orion and Sarah are sitting on the floor with their backs against the wall holding each other.

"Let's find Whiteface."

Orion stands up, wiping his face. "Okay." He begins to walk down the hallway.

"Where are you going, Orion?" Sarah calls after him.

"Someone needs to notify Joseph's family and I want to tell mine as well to warn them," he tells her.

"You do that. I'm sorry this happened to you, Orion. Whiteface will get what he deserves, I promise."

Orion looks inconsolable. I've felt this sorrow before.

"I wish I could help him," Sarah says to me. I tell her there isn't anything we can do right now besides be there for him. Sarah stands up and brushes off her pants.

"Want to get a drink?" I ask. She throws me a dagger look.

"You want to drink when your Captain's friend was just killed? What is wrong with you, Eden?"

"Well, drinking is my way of coping with loss," I say, throwing my hands up. "I don't know what to do, Sarah. I just

164

spent time with his family, and I also just killed the guy in there. Just get a drink with me."

"Okay." She sighs. We head downstairs to the hotel bar. We drink a few beers while pondering what to do next.

"I told him a little about my past," I mutter. "Not a lot but some things."

She smiles at me. "That's good, Eden. You're making friends."

I sip on the beer and continue, "I finally know how it feels to have a real family. Joseph raised me, but he never really gave me the same love I felt today at dinner. Then Orion lost his friend and I'm hurting from it, too. It felt like I lost someone."

Sarah puts her arms around me. "Nothing is wrong with having feelings, Eden. You can connect with people. We're humans, after all. We're genetically drawn to people. We all have this need to connect with others, so don't be ashamed to feel things."

I look at her with drunk eyes and wonder if she's right. Joseph never taught me how to connect with people. I always felt like I wasn't good at it. Sarah is the one who has always been able to make people feel comfortable and loved. *I'm really glad she's here helping*. I eye my drink and take another sip. "To fully understand, I must be able to connect. That's an interesting notion."

Chapter 8: Find

I ARRIVE BACK at the hotel where my friends and family are staying at around 1:00 am. I just got off the phone with Joseph's family and they are heartbroken to hear that their son was murdered.

My body is hurting, and my heart is in pieces. My friend is gone, and it's all my fault. Eden had even warned me. He made it clear that if Seditio were to find out who my family was that they could harm them, but I didn't listen. I didn't want to believe that my family was a target. I was so wrong. Nothing but ignorance on my end.

As soon as I walk in, I knock on my mother's door to tell her what had happened to Joseph. She can tell that I'm in pain and hugs me tightly. I tell her that I need to let the others know.

"Tell them, Orion. I'm so, so sorry. I love you, Son. We'll leave first thing in the morning." I hug her back extremely tight.

"I love you, Mom." Then I make my way to Jacob and Matthew's room to tell them the news. I knock on their door but no one answers.

"They decided to go to the club," Mary says from the doorway to her room. She was wearing a white robe.

"What's wrong, O? Hey." I can't find the words for a second or two, but her tone changes. She can tell something's wrong.

"Joseph was killed today."

Mary's jaw drops, her eyes widen, and she places her hands over her mouth.

"It'll be okay, Orion. Come in," she says.

I walk into her room and we sit at the end of her bed. I'm in

166

so much pain that I don't know what to do, but her arms around me are providing comfort at the moment. Joseph's beaten body is the most horrific scene I had ever seen in my life and I can't get the image to fade from my mind.

"It's going to be okay Orion," Mary repeats. "Everything is going to be okay." She starts rubbing her hand down my back. I start to relax. I see something else in Mary's eyes. She's biting her lips and I can feel the passion build up between us. I turn to face her and gaze into her eyes as I slowly move my hands down her neck. She sighs in anticipation. I drag the back of my right hand along her cheek and she breathes heavily. Her cheeks are warm and begin to get flush.

Then suddenly, I grab the back of her head, pull it back, and I kiss her neck. She moans as I lay her down on the bed. I trace my fingers from her lips, down her neck, until they arrive at where the robe covers her breasts. I open the robe up and kiss around her chest. I drag my tongue up from the middle of her chest to her lips then I start kissing her gently, grabbing her left breast with my right hand. Then I gently pinch her nipple.

I sit up and take my shirt off and she completely removes the robe. She sits up and we kiss again. I slowly push her back down to the bed. I suck on her bottom lip, then drag my tongue from her lips to her neck, down her chest until I reach the top of her vagina. I stop there and begin to kiss around it while tracing my right hand down her chest to her inner left thigh.

I begin to kiss up and down her left leg slowly. Then I drag my tongue from her knee to her vagina, then she grabs my head and pulls my head closer toward herself. I grab her arm and push it down to the side. I flick my tongue on her clitoris up and down. She moans louder and louder. I move my tongue left and right, savoring her taste. I trace my pointer finger from the side of her vagina to the opening, I push my finger inside of her and slide it in and out, faster and faster as I continue to lick her. I can feel her body tremble and tense up.

"Oh, my God," Mary screams and grabs my head to lift me. I pull my pants down and my penis is already fully erect. I slide the tip of my penis down her clit into her vagina; I can feel the warmth coming from her. I can hear her moan in pleasure. I slowly slide my penis in and she's extremely wet. Ecstasy takes over my body. I thrust slowly in and out. Then I start to speed up. Her hands begin to run down my back and nails begin to dig into my back. She pushes me off her to the side onto my back. She grabs my penis and sits on it, cowgirl. She begins to grind her clit on me while moving back and forth. She goes faster and faster than until her legs tighten up and shake. Her face turns red and I can feel the heat coming off of her. She grabs my face then kisses me. She gets off of me then gets on all fours. She turns over her left shoulder with her hair hanging over her face. I get on my knees, grab my penis, slide it into her, grab her hips and slowly penetrate her. I start moving in and out slowly, then I gradually speed up. I pound her harder and harder until I am almost there, then I pull out and ejaculate on her back. Mary falls to her stomach and I lay beside her. I can still feel her gazing at me.

"That was better than usual." She sighs.

I look up at the ceiling and smile, "I needed that. It's been a long few hours. Mary, do you mind if I sleep here?"

Mary grabs my head and kisses me once more. "You can sleep here, O. I'm leaving with your parents in the morning, though." I kiss her back to thank her. Feeling relieved, I roll over, close my eyes, and try to not think about what happened today. This is the life of a Judge, I remind myself. Incidents like this happen. Unlike Joseph, I get to move on. I have to live and be able to process all these things without succumbing to the pain and suffering of loss. Slowly, I fade off into sleep until I'm woken up by an alarm. I roll over to turn it off. The bed beside me is empty but I see a note on the pillow from her.

O,

Hope everything gets better. We did not want to wake you up since you have been going through a lot recently. The death of a friend can be extremely hard and challenging for anyone to ever have to go through. It's hard to lose someone that you care about. We will talk to you when we land back home. Take care. We love you.

P.S. Watch out for the Eden guy. He is a really strange character.

Mary

It's only a few words, but it appeases me. I put my clothes on and head downstairs for breakfast where I order a crepe and a coffee. I sit down at a table outside facing the street sipping my coffee when I feel someone standing behind me.

"So, this is what a Captain looks like," the voice behind me says. "I hope you like the gift I left you. It's so hard to get the House of David to notice someone these days unless you're looking for a fucking artifact."

I look up to see a man wearing a beige suit. His skin is very tan and his blond hair is messy. He pulls out the chair in front of me and, as he sits down, it hits me. This is Whiteface.

"It is nice to meet you," he says. "I am Cal Phil . . ."

"You're Whiteface," I interrupt.

He just smiles. "It is very rude to interrupt someone. Didn't your parents teach you manners?"

I know I should be afraid; anger fills my body instead. For knowing full well that I'm a Captain for the House of David, this man is extremely calm.

"What do you want with me? Why did you kill my friend?" I ask him through gritted teeth, being careful not to cause too big of a scene. He lets out a sadistic laugh.

"Our leader is very interested in you and wants you to join us. But your friend . . . I killed him because he wouldn't tell me where you were. He cared about you." He reaches across the table, grabs my fork, cuts up my crepe, and takes a bite of it. I reach into my pocket.

"I wouldn't do that if I was you," he speaks quietly. "If you do anything stupid, I will kill everyone here. So be a good boy and stay still."

I examine my surroundings. Men are surrounding the building and I begin to wonder how they all even knew I'm here.

He watches me scan the outside of the hotel. "Are you trying to figure out how we knew you were here? Well, you shouldn't trust everyone, but this will be a lesson that I have to teach you. You can either come with me now, or I can kill everyone in the vicinity."

I don't know how to react. If I call for help he will kill me along with several other innocent people. I can reach for my phone, but who knows if Eden will even get here on time.

"I'll go with you," I tell him.

"Smart move," he speaks coolly, dragging his hand across his face as he stands up from the table. I follow him out to where an old, black Ford Model-T pulls up in front of us.

"Where the fuck do you think you're going, Orion?"

I look behind me to see Eden running towards me. Without making any noise, I move my mouth to say "HELP ME." Eden takes the hint and pulls out a knife from his pocket, but one of Whiteface's men must have noticed, too, because all of a sudden, Whiteface is yelling, "Stop him!"

He grabs my collar and grins. "I gave you a choice and you're changing your mind now. I guess I'll have to teach you a lesson." He stabs me in my gut, and I feel my blood soak into my shirt. I fall to my knees, watching Eden butcher a couple of the other Seditio members.

"No, Orion! Get up. Shit!" Eden cries out to me. I put pressure against the wound and try to stand up, but Whiteface grabs my arm and drags me into the back of his car. He hops in the front, slams the door closed, and tells the driver to drive off.

I can taste blood start to flow out of my mouth. Whiteface pulls a cigarette out of his suit jacket, lights it up, and takes a few puffs.

"You'll be fine. I didn't hit an artery. This wouldn't have happened if you just would've listened to me. I just wanted to talk. But now I see that you have a lesson to learn, you can consider me your teacher," Whiteface says.

What will become of me? How will I get away? Will Eden find me? My body is too tired to answer the questions running through my mind and I feel myself slowly drift into sleep.

***

Splash! Water hits my face, and I wake up in a bedroom with my left wrist handcuffed to the bed. It's a small room with floral wallpaper. I'm lying in a twin bed across from a window that looks out into a grassy field. Standing on the doorway is an older man with long black hair, staring at me.

"Who are you?" I ask. I notice my wound has been stitched up. "Did you stitch me up?'

He kneels beside me. "Yes, I fixed you up." He has a Russian accent.

"Where am I?" I sit up in bed.

"You are in Whiteface's safe house. I am just the doctor for Seditio. He wanted me to stitch you up."

"I feel like I've been asleep for hours."

"You've been here for five hours if that is what you're wondering," the doctor says. "Our leader is very interested in you, but I don't think that Whiteface shares the same interest. He is a mad man."

Why did he sound so concerned if he works for Seditio?

"What does Seditio want?"

"Every member of Seditio wants something different." He walks towards the door. "We don't even know what our leader wants. But I have been in this organization for years. The previous leader said our goal was to bring a religious revolution. Bring back faith."

"Then why do you kill people?"

"Every revolution starts with blood." He twists the doorknob slowly. "He is ready."

As the doctor leaves, two men wearing black ski masks come into the room carrying a table and a chair.

"Well, well. Orion Carter Bachman from Mobile, Alabama. Let's talk," Whiteface says, coming in behind them. One of the men in the ski mask uncuffs me from the bed, ties my hands together, and places the chair in front of me so I can sit down. Then Whiteface approaches the table with an apple in his left hand and a knife in his right.

"Let me tell you a story about our leader. She's the child of our previous leader. Our leader killed her entire family, and no one knows why. She killed the previous leader of Seditio, who happened to be her father. Also, our leader killed a family in Dublin, California just because. What I'm getting at here, is that our leader does things without giving us a reason. But somehow, she was extremely interested in you, and it pisses me off. So, what is it about you that interests our leader, huh? Can you enlighten me?"

I watch him cut slices out of the apple and eat them one by one. "I don't know what your leader wants. I just thought that

Seditio is an organization that is looking for religious artifacts so that it can influence people's beliefs."

"Well, that's supposed to be our agenda, but I have another one. I'm trying to teach the world the power of choice and have a little fun on the side," he explains, apple pieces coming out of his mouth. "That guy back at the hotel killing my men? That was Judge Eden Dowler and you are his new Captain, aren't you? Maybe our leader wants you to get back at that Judge for killing so many Seditio members." He places his hand on his chin.

I scan my surroundings discreetly. *How am I going to get out of here?* One window and one door. And the only weapon I can see is the knife in Whiteface's hand. I'm outnumbered three to one and would lose this fight, anyway; I'm not that good yet. *What do I do? Will Eden find me?* I'm going to have to hold out until help comes. But how long?

Whiteface puts the apple core down and plants both hands on the table. "To be honest with you, Kid, I don't think that you would be a good addition to Seditio. You're not broken enough," he says. He sits back up and looks at me like he figured out a solution. "But you're in luck! I'm a great teacher." He turns to both of his men. "Take him down to the chamber. It's time for a lesson."

The men grab my arms and drag me to a kitchen. One of the men puts earmuffs on me first, and the other one puts a bag over my head. *Bang!* I feel someone crack me over the head with a solid object. As I'm processing the pain, I feel someone pick up both of my legs and someone else grabs my arms.

I hear people talking, but I can barely make out what they're saying. I finally feel myself being sat down in a chair. Each of my ankles is tied up to each leg and my arms are behind the chair, still handcuffed. Someone takes the bag off and I can feel blood running down my face.

I open my eyes and I see Jacob wearing a spiked collar that is chained to the wall. His mouth is taped and it looks like he's

173

been beaten up.

"Why are you doing this to me? I didn't do anything wrong. Why would you get my family involved? This cannot be what your leader wants. Do you think this will persuade me?"

Whiteface laughs violently. "Do you not understand? They said you were smart. You're with the House of David, too, which makes you an enemy. Do I trust my leader? No! Also, I want to have some fun. If you survive then you are worthy of being a part of Seditio. I want to teach you a lesson, but I also want to make you suffer. So, let's start with your friend here, who sadly was just at the wrong place at the wrong time."

I shake my head rapidly. "No!" I cry out. "No, that makes no sense! You had to have been watching me to know where to find Jacob!"

He looks at Jacob and kicks him in the head. "You're way more intuitive than your friend here. I'll tell you how I found them later."

I can see the fear in Jacob's eyes, but he still manages to not cower easily to Whiteface. "So, what are you going to do, torture me?" he barks at him.

Whiteface jams his hands in his pockets. "Let me tell you a story about my childhood. I was raised in a small town with only one church. Growing up, my father would travel offshore to work on the oil rigs for months at a time, so I was always at home with my mother. She was a lovely lady but very weak. Very weak."

Jacob and I exchange glances, not understanding what he's getting at. Whiteface walks up to Jacob and grabs his face tightly. "Like every small town, we had a pastor. Everyone loved him. But the problem was that he loved the children. Way too much. He would watch us shower at the school through a peephole he built in the locker room doors. Sick fuck. He had a favorite child." His face turned into a frown as he stood up.

"Me," he continues. "He loved my blond hair and said I

looked like a pretty girl. I loved being the favorite, you know. He would call me to his office after mass and teach me the difference between good and evil. And the things that he did to me were truly evil. For nine years this went on." Then his tone shifts. "But one day, he came to my house for one of his 'teaching' sessions. He walked into my room and right away told me to take my shirt off. He started to feel up my chest. What he didn't know was I had my baseball bat in the corner and my eyes flickered on it every few minutes until eventually, I told him I had something for him. I went to get the bat from the corner. While he was turned around taking off his clothes, *BAM*, I smashed him right on the back of his head. I tied him to the bed and when he woke up, I did to him what he had done to me for revenge. When it was over, I stood in the corner and all I could do was cry until my mom walked in. She saw the priest and she instantly knew what this grown man had done to me. So, she ran to the kitchen, grabbed the gun, and shot him." He lets out a heavy sigh. "What I learned that day was that you never see a person's true colors until they experience pain, suffering, and death."

What is this man getting at? Why is he telling me this? Whiteface must have seen the disgust on my face.

"To explain it better, I realized that God put me here to bring out people's true selves through pain and suffering, which leads me to you two. I am going to see what your true selves are. So, let's test your friend here first. Let's see what his true character is."

He walks up to Jacob and right before he pulls the tape off his mouth, he speaks to him quietly. "You can scream, but no one can hear you. Plus, if you do, I'll kill you." Jacob nods, and Whiteface pulls off the tape. Jacob sucks in huge amounts of air; he must have had that tape on his mouth for hours.

Then, one of the Seditio men hands Whiteface a baseball bat. "It's Jacob, right?" Whiteface asks him. "Well, Jacob, I'll give you a choice. I can either beat the living shit out of you, or I can beat the living shit out of your friend here." Jacob looks at me confused but I know what Whiteface is capable of.

Whiteface aims the bat at my head and asks Jacob once again. "What is your choice?"

Jacob shakes his head. "Fuck you!"

Whiteface guffaws disdainfully. Gripping the baseball bat tightly, he swings it violently at Jacob's face over and over again. Teeth fly out of his mouth and blood spews everywhere.

"No, stop! He isn't involved in this," I yell in anger. I shake and try to break free from my confinement. I saw this happening before it did; Whiteface's file indicated that he's merciless. Jacob is groaning in pain. Eventually, his body tenses up and his eyes become heavy.

"Wrong answer! Let's do this again. Should I beat you or your friend? If you do not choose this time then I will remove your foot," Whiteface continues.

"Me," I say.

Bang! Bam! Blood is all of a sudden flying out of my mouth. Whiteface had hit me so fast that I didn't even know what was going on. I spit out a mouthful of blood and all of a sudden, I feel the pain in my face.

"Now," he says to me, "if you say another fucking word, I will rip out your tongue and burn it right in front of you. I'm talking to your friend Jacob here."

I start to feel woozy.

"Now then, Jacob, what do you choose?"

Jacob shakes his head and mouths to me "I'm sorry." Then he turns to Whiteface and says, "Beat him."

Whiteface grins. "Thank you for making a choice." He raises the bat and hits my body repeatedly. I can feel my ribs crack with every swing he takes and slowly I feel myself slipping into unconsciousness. Still, I can hear Whiteface's voice.

"Let's have a little fun, Jacob, while your friend is out."

And I black out.

It feels like hours later when I blink my eyes open. Jacob is lying on the ground in front of me holding his head in his hands.

"I'm so sorry, Orion. I got scared. I knew that you were training to be in that organization. So, I just thought you would be able to take his blows better than me."

I lower my head, coughing up blood. "I would have done the same thing. It was the most rational decision." Deep down, I feel kind of betrayed. "How long have we been in here?" I ask him.

"I don't know," he says as he sits up. "You were out for four hours, though."

I spit blood to the side of me. "How did he get you?"

"Matthew and I were out at a bar. Matthew went to the bathroom and while he was gone I was standing by myself at the bar. When he came back, he had this big bag of money. I asked him where he got it from and he said he won it in a bet."

Nothing is adding up. I need Eden to come here. I don't think we'll make it out alive. But before Jacob can finish his story, the metal door swings open and Whiteface walks in with white paint on his face and red lipstick.

"You know why they call me Whiteface?" he asks the two of us. "It's not because of the white paint on my face, or because of my Wayne Gacy style of killing. I'm called Whiteface because when every person I'm about to kill sees my face, he gets white in the face."

One of the Seditio members behind him chimes in. "Then why paint your face white?" But Whiteface turns around so quickly he hardly even looks at him and shoots him in the head. The Seditio member's body falls to the ground, his blood and brains scatter along the wall behind him. Jacob's face is horror-stricken, but the sight of death has been very common lately for

177

me.

I look down at the corpse. The smell is just so bland. Meanwhile, Whiteface kicks the body. "Hey!" he yells to one of his other members. "Get this useless piece of trash out of here." Within seconds, a Seditio member enters the room and drags the body out by the feet.

"Sorry about that guy. He doesn't have any manners. The paint is because Pennywise is my favorite villain, and to you two right now, well, I am the villain." He lets out another one of his sadistic chuckles.

"Just let Jacob go," I beg him. "I'm the one you want. He has nothing to do with this at all." Whiteface slaps me with the back of his hand.

"Who the hell said that you can tell me what to do? You have no rights here, Boy." Then he grabs his bat, walks up to Jacob, and starts beating his legs with it. Jacob growls in pain until he is helpless.

"Stop! Please stop!" I scream at Whiteface.

He stops and gazes at the blood dripping from his bat. "If you were wondering . . . Yes, this is the same bat that I used on the priest. Pretty cool, isn't it? Still in good condition, too." He smiles admiringly at the bat, then looks up at me with anger-filled eyes. "Now tell me, Orion! Why does our fearless leader want you so bad? Tell me!"

"I don't even know who the hell your leader is! How would I even know your leader?" My voice fills the entire room. Whiteface doesn't say anything, though. He walks up to a table to my right, grabs a pair of brass knuckles, and puts them on.

"If you don't tell me something I want to hear, Boy, I'm going to punch you in your face." His voice was chilling.

He grabs the back of my head. "Do you believe in God?"

"Yes." I look him straight in the eyes.

"Good. Me, too." He smiles. "And you know what? I think

God has a plan for us all. His plan for me is to teach you or kill you! I don't know yet. Have you slept with a man before? Have you ever wanted to?"

"No. I haven't ever thought about that. And I don't hate the idea of gay sexuality. I think we're all born this way."

"Well, good answer! Because you're cute so I wanted to know if you wanted to go on a date sometime."

"I don't know what you're getting at, but no, I don't want to date you. You just kidnapped me and you've been beating us up."

He looks at me with disappointment. "Well, I was going to take it lightly on you but maybe I'll . . . "

Bang! The brass metal hits my jaw and I can feel my teeth rattle in my skull. He punches me in the face not once, not twice, but four times.

He draws his knuckles back and slowly licks my dripping blood off of them. "I love the taste of blood. It's so sweet and so warm. Did I tell you what happened when my mother killed that priest? We chopped up his body and buried every piece of him throughout the town. Before we did that, though, I was able to taste his blood. It wasn't as bad as I dreamt. That's why I eat raw steak now."

I don't know why this sick-minded individual is telling me these things, but he's mentally damaged beyond repair. I look at him with disgust.

"Did what happen with this priest damage you this badly?"

"I don't know. I have an aerospace engineering degree, you know."

How does this psychopath have a degree?

"I apologize, where were we? I haven't talked to a non-Seditio member in quite some time now. Sometimes I tend to ramble."

Then it seems like a thought popped into his mind. "Ah,

179

yes, I remember. I need to make you suffer to see your true character." He turns his gaze to Jacob but speaks to me. "Now, Orion, if I saw off his foot, would his screams of pain break you? I'm just trying to be a good teacher, you know? And seeing extreme pain is such a great lesson to learn."

He walks to the table and grabs a hacksaw before walking up to Jacob with it.

"This is going to hurt a lot. Please scream." Jacob starts fighting him and kicking his legs. "Hold his feet down," he says to the surrounding Seditio members.

"Please don't. Don't do this! Please," I scream out to them. Whiteface begins sawing his left foot off. Back and forth. The screams from Jacob are so devastatingly loud that my eardrums feel like they will explode. Jacob blacks out but Whiteface keeps going until he had sawed it completely off.

"Wow! Didn't think he was going that fast," he mutters as he stands up. "So, Orion, you're a Captain. Aren't you? Should Captains be associating with such weak people?"

I want to kill him, but my father's words keep running through my head. *Should someone like this be allowed to live?*

"You're a hell of a baker, you know. I have had a piece of cake from your shop, and it was to die for. That cute cashier girl was very helpful, too. She was so pretty and sweet," he says, blood still dripping from his hands.

"You better not have done anything to her," I say angrily.

He smirks and cracks his neck. "Our leader told me that she was a delightful flower, so I couldn't resist."

I start trying to force my way out of the chair. "Liar! You didn't kill her."

"Boy, she is long dead."

My heart begins to hurt. The pain shoots through my body. She was an innocent girl. *How could someone do this to another human being? How could he do this to someone? Who else has he*

180

Whiteface drags his bloody hand across his face, smudging the white paint. He approaches Jacob's unconscious body. "Pain is the only way you will learn." He laughs hysterically. "And learning is half the battle." Whiteface starts punching him over and over. "Wake up, you fat fuck!" But Jacob's body continues to lay there, limp. "Well, he's no fun."

Jacob's face is covered in blood. He's unrecognizable.

"Why would you do that to him?"

Whiteface walks up to me and grabs my chin aggressively. "Have you learned anything?"

I spit blood in his face. "Guess not."

He punches me in the skull three times and, after the third time, I begin to see black. *Am I going to die? I hope my family is okay. Eden, will you find me?* The memory of my father keeps me from losing consciousness. I mentally repeat the words he told me as many times as I can. I should cherish life and live it to the fullest.

I don't know if I will ever understand anything about the soul. I don't know if I'll be reborn. I don't know if I'll go to heaven. Maybe I've been lying to myself the whole time. Maybe I've been believing something that I don't even believe myself. *Do we get to see our dead loved ones when we die?* Questions continue to flood my brain before I fade into the dark.

Chapter 9: That In Living

WHEN I ARRIVE back at the Gate, it hits me that it's been a while since I've felt this pain. My heart is hurting and disappointment is filling my soul. How could I let this happen? I failed him and it all comes rushing back to me again: the memories of Dusty, the heartbreak, the sadness, the feelings of loss and anger. I punch the wall over and over again until I can't feel my fingers. Then I stare at my hand as I watch my blood flow out of the cuts on my knuckles. I'm lost.

"Eden, calm down. It's not your fault," Sarah says compassionately.

"It was my fault!" I yell. "I should've fucking killed that piece of shit. I let Orion cloud my judgment. Now, look at what happened. Orion was taken and it's all my fucking fault. I was fucking weak. I am Death." Rage fills me. I don't know it's because of guilt for failing or because I let myself believe Orion in that everyone deserves to live.

I smell cigarette smoke. I turn and see Joseph. He takes a big puff, blows out smoke coolly, and then says, "Are you going to sit here and complain? Or are you going to do something about this? What did I tell you when we first met?"

"I'm a weapon of the House of David. An instrument of Death."

Joseph pushes the burning end of the cigarette to the wall as he responds. "Then be that instrument of Death and kill all that gets in your way. Bring Orion back. He is a member of the House of David. You serve the House of David." His stern words calm me for a moment. Joseph has reminded me of who I am and what I need to do. I know that Sarah doesn't approve of Joseph saying those words to me, but they are words I need to hear. I look at Sarah and I see her face fall and then I turn back to Joseph.

"If a God of Death is what you want, then a God of Death I shall be. I will kill them all."

"Then let's do what we do and not leave one of our own," he says. "Let's kill Whiteface and Seditio once and for all." We head to the command room and Joseph explains the operation.

***

Wednesday, August 21, 2027. Mission: Whiteface

The mission is taking place 25 miles outside of Lyon, France near Maison Vidal-Fleury. Orion and thirteen other hostages are being held in an old, abandoned winery. As of now, two of the hostages are members of Orion's family and another two are his friends. Elise Bachman, Robert Bachman, Jacob Godbold, and Matthew Tyler were all in town visiting Orion when they were taken from their rooms at the Chateau de Runes.

The winery, where they are being held, is actually a disguise for one of Whiteface's torture sites. The winery is 43,000 sq. ft. and has a front entrance and back entrance. We have the layout of the inside; however, intel cannot be trusted right now because we don't know if Whiteface modified the inside.

In preparation for this mission, the French army has given us twenty troops to add to our three Judges. All commands will be coming from King of Hearts, Joseph Cain. Sarah, Aiden, and Eden will arrive in an armored bulletproof Mercedes G-Wagon and the French troops will arrive in six Pan hard VBL (Vehicle Blinde Leger). The mission will begin at 1800.

***

Promptly at 1800, the mission begins with Sarah, Aiden, and I arriving at the winery. The building is surrounded by French troops and two Seditio members who are guarding the front entrance.

"Eden!" Aiden says to me. "Everything is good to go. I'll go with you, and Sarah will take care of the troops at the back entrance." My heart is racing and the only thing on my mind is saving Orion. I don't know if he is safe or dead. Whiteface is

183

notorious for torturing and raping his captives. His kill count is in the thirties and many of those he let live have been reported to be so psychologically destroyed to the point that they kill themselves.

"Aiden, we will go through the front," I sternly said looking forward holding the Deathscythe. "And remember, Aiden—no survivors. Kill them all," I order.

"I will do whatever you ask of me, Eden."

The wind begins blowing and, in the earpiece, we hear Joseph's command. "Commence operation." Everyone begins to move at the same time. Aiden, a soldier, and I race to the front door, side by side. In front are five casement style windows, two on the left and three on the right, and the front door is made of steel.

"Aiden, throw a grenade in the second window to the left," I order. "Then jump through the first window and take them out." Meanwhile, I run to the door to draw the attention of the window shooters. They begin shooting at me, but no one is hitting me. Even if they are to hit me it would have done no damage. They do not know that I'm wearing long-sleeve STF (shear-thickening fluid) armor, ballistic leggings, level IIA shin guards, Kevlar 3A pants, and Damascus steel-toed boots. Wearing the STF armor and the Finger of God makes it almost impossible to kill a Judge.

Only Aiden, Luka, Ying Yue, and I have Damascus Chromium steel weapons. Aiden uses a Quiang, which is the Chinese term for a spear. Aiden's Quiang has a Damascus Chromium steel leaf-shaped blade, a red horsehair tassel lashed just below it, and a carbon fiber shaft. The tassel also serves a tactical purpose. When he attacks, the spear moves so quickly that it blurs the enemy's vision and makes it hard for them to grab the shaft of the spear. The tassel also stops any flow of blood from the blade getting to the shaft.

Luka wields a green PSE Carbon Air Stealth compound bow. The bow itself isn't made of Damascus Chromium steel, but

Luka altered the bow and made a few additions. At each end of the bow are two sickle-shaped blades that are seven inches long and three inches across. The blades look like a velociraptor claw at each end of the bow. These aren't just any blades, though, they are Damascus Chromium steel blades that Luka is able to use when he's in close combat. Luka calls his bow the "Speedy Thief," because it's quick to take your life.

Ying Yue wields a Damascus Chromium steel Khopesh, which is an Egyptian sickle-sword with a Shirasaya or "white scabbard." Ying Yue wanted to add a piece of her culture to her sword. The blade mount is made of Japanese wood with a hilt made of Nurizaya wood. The sickle blade of the sword is twenty-four inches long.

Finally, my weapon: the Deathscythe. I chose the Deathscythe to symbolize to my enemies that when they see it, they know that death is coming to them and that the God of Death is going to send them to the afterlife.

As we approach the front door, the soldiers stare at our weapons with astonishment and curiosity. One of them asks, "Why do you bring those to a war?"

"Because I am the God of Death. What do you think is the best thing for me to have? Wouldn't you think that a weapon of death that the Grim Reaper uses would be fitting? Don't worry, though, we do use guns, too."

He shakes his head with his gun pointed at the door of the house. With a quick hand signal, I order the shooters to take out the guys in the window. Aiden throws a grenade into the window. Members of Seditio scream.

Bang! I feel the warmth of blood on my face. The soldier who had just asked about our weapons is shot straight through his head. His lifeless body falls right in front of me.

"He should've been more careful," I mutter.

Aiden jumps through the window and all I can hear are

men getting stabbed with his dual-end Damascus Chromium steel spear. With the Deathscythe in my right hand, I use my left to grab a gun out of the inner holster of my jacket. I see two men with white masks poke their heads out the window and I shoot at them five times. One man, I hit in the chest three times and he stumbles out of the window sideways. I shoot the other in the head and he falls backwards.

I get to the door and, surprisingly, it's unlocked. I open it and slowly walk in. "Eden! How many men?" asks Joseph through the earpiece.

"Well, I killed two. I'm not sure about Aiden," I report. I continue to walk forward. I can't see anything, but I can feel the liquid at my feet. The lights turn on and I see Aiden in the corner by the light switch. I look down at my feet and all I see is blood. Aiden has blood all over his body and spear. He always has the same demeanor, though, even after slashing soldiers open. Aiden had cut the bodies up to a point that I can't recognize them at all. Sometimes I think he only finds joy in killing.

"Ten dead, Eden. I killed ten. There was another body that was covered in blood. He looked like he stabbed himself with the sword he had in his hand," Aiden says.

"You got that, Joseph?" I ask into the earpiece. "That makes thirteen dead. I know there are more men here. There's no way this is that easy."

Then suddenly I hear someone yell, "EDEN!" I turn and see Sarah. "You got to see this," she says.

We walk through a long hallway with wooden panels on either side. I glance in each room and, to my surprise, they're all empty. *How could every single room be empty?* I radio Joseph again on the headpiece.

"Is this a joke?" I can hear only static. "Sarah, where are their troops?"

"I don't know."

It's so quiet that you can hear the blood from Aiden's Quiang dripping off the tip.

I approach the window. I see that all of our troops are lined up in front aiming at the building.

"Well, well! Three judges in one place. Wow, I'm so lucky," says a voice through our headset. It sounds like a young woman with a raspy, weary voice.

"Who the hell is this?" I utter. I don't know what to do. I look over at the bodies and inspect them more closely.

"Aiden! These are the hostages. We killed the hostages," I yell.

"They were shooting at us," he says calmly. I thought they were the enemy." Sarah looks at the bodies in complete disgust.

"It was a trap, Eden," she says.

Then all of a sudden, the voice on the headset comes back. "Ha. Ha. Ha. So, you've figured it out. Yes, my loves, it was a trap. Don't worry, I killed Joseph quickly. Bullet to the skull," the mystery woman brags.

"How? Even the troops?" I ask.

"Let's just say not everybody in your organization cares."

"Traitors in the organization?" yells Sarah. I peek out the window and I see the woman sitting on top of the armored G-Wagon. She then slides in the driver seat.

"Don't worry, I hate traitors, too," she mutters back to us softly. Suddenly we hear the engine rev up and I see the tires spinning. She drives through the troops, hitting them with the front of the car, while the men shoot at her fruitlessly since the windows are bulletproof. One by one, she runs over them as she rolls the driver's side window down and shoots at them with a pistol.

"DIE! DIE! DIE! HA HA IIA HA," she yells viciously. She looks like a complete crazy woman fueled with some form of rage. I can't see her face because she's wearing a bike helmet. The truck stops. All the troops are dead, bodies everywhere. The field that was once so green now has blood splattered everywhere with pieces of armor, body parts, and clothing scattered around it.

"There. Ya' know, I killed some of your traitors now. Now I need you to kill someone for me," she says through the headset.

"Joseph wasn't a traitor! You had no—"

"You have no clue, Eden. I'll leave you with a gift, though. Whiteface is in a house three miles from here. Just head south, and you will see it. Hope you have a compass. That idiot Whiteface painted the house white."

"How do you know my fucking name?" I yell back.

She begins to drive away but suddenly she stops the G-Wagon. "So, are you going to take my gift? Because if you're not going to take it, why should I let all three of you live?"

Sarah looks at Aiden and me. "Eden. What is she going on about? Something doesn't add up," she says slowly. Then I hear a scream and see a sword go through her back and exit her chest, directly through her heart.

I quickly get behind Sarah and pull the sword out. Blood flows out of the wound like a water faucet and I spot a man covered in blood standing behind her.

"She said I had to do it if you didn't agree!" the black-haired man cries. "She would've killed my family." I raise my scythe. As I stare right through his eyes, all I see is a dead man. I swing down, piercing his gut. I pull the scythe, ripping through him.

"I don't care," I say after his ripped up body fell to the ground. Then I run over to Sarah and pick her up in my arms.

"Eden. I don't want to die." Tears are running down her face.

"You're not going to die, Sarah. I promise. Please don't die. Please," I beg. But blood starts running out her mouth and through her wound. I can feel the warmth of it as I grasp her tighter. *This isn't beautiful, this is sad. It hurts.*

Sarah grabs my face says "Hey! Hey, look at me. Take care of Aiden and find Orion. Okay?" I squeeze her tightly, looking over at Aiden. I have never seen him crying, but I swear I see a tear rolling down his face. I look back down at Sarah knowing that there are only a few moments left. With the last of her strength, she says, "Eden. I know your family hated you and you lost all of them and were alone. I have always felt your sadness. Please open up and live."

"Sarah! SARAH! No, Sarah, please don't go. Please." I beg, hoping my words would bring life back into her face.

"You aren't alone anymore," she continues. "You have a family now. You don't have to be al—" She exhales her last breath before she can finish.

"SARAH! PLEASE! I need you. I'm sorry. I'm sorry!"

Aiden sits next to me and grabs Sarah's hands. "May the winds of fall be at your back, as you walk through the patch of sunshine. Though I am not there to walk with you always look up into the sky and know that I will always see you," he whispers with his eyes closed.

Hot tears fall down my face uncontrollably. I haven't felt like this since Dusty died. Sarah was kind, loving, and always looked out for me. Her whole time alive, I pushed her away because I was scared that if she got too close to me, she would die as everyone else does. I never admitted that I saw her as a friend, but deep down I did. She was the closest thing to family that I ever had. My heart hurts. It hurts so bad. I loved her.

"Why! WHY! WHY . . . " I drop my head over her in agony. *This isn't how it's supposed to end for you. You have so much to live for. You have so much to do.* This life needs someone like her. I will protect those people like her, even if I have to give my own life.

I stand up, more determined than ever. I put my hand on Aiden's shoulder.

"Let's go, Aiden, we have work to do."

I will find you, Orion. This is my promise.

"Okay," Aiden replies in his typical cold tone. Sometimes I wonder what Aiden is thinking. However, I feel that Sarah's death has made both of us realize that this life shouldn't be taken for granted. We have to do whatever it takes to preserve it.

We walk to the nearest VBL and I see a black phone lying in the seat. I pick it up and call the House of David's command. "We have been compromised. Send reinforcements to my coordinates now. We have a Judge down. Sarah Bradley is dead," I announce. The keys are still in the ignition, so I crank the car.

I can hear the wind blowing so loudly from outside the car that I can't hear anything else.

Aiden grips his Quiang tightly. I can sense that the death of Sarah is affecting him more than I thought at first. I always forget that even though Aiden is a Judge, he's still just a young man. He has feelings and connects with people just like any other boy his age. I can see that during his time with us at the Gate, he has been learning a lot of lessons. He's growing slowly but surely.

"Eden?" Aiden says, looking out the window.

"Yeah?"

"Do you ever feel any remorse when you kill someone?"

I don't know where he's going with this, but it makes me think for a second. I think back to what Orion has been saying about life being precious.

"When I kill someone, I feel sad. I really don't like killing people. I do it because I want to protect the people I care about. But when I see you kill someone you never kill just to kill. You kill to protect other people and yourself."

I don't know how to respond to what he is saying. I don't know why I kill people. I thought it was because death has always been around me. However, I never killed for joy or pleasure. Just to protect the things I care about: Sarah, Joseph, Aiden, and my comrades. Due to my arrogance, I thought that death was always with me so I closed off my emotions. I never really embraced living life to the fullest.

"Eden," Aiden says. He must have noticed that I was too lost in thought. "There was nothing you could do with Sarah. We were both caught off guard. I should've been quicker. I wasn't efficient, but I won't fail you again."

When I look at Aiden, I see a person who says what he means and means what he says. He will not fail and he will give his life if it means completing the mission. And though Aiden has a hard time making friends and connecting with people, once he deems you as a friend, he will do whatever it takes to protect you. Even though he doesn't show it, I know he's hurting more than I'll ever know. It's my turn to reassure him.

"You're fine, Aiden. There was nothing we could have done. Let's just stick to the mission at hand and make sure that Sarah's death wasn't in vain." I floored it, jerking us forward. "I'm on the way, Orion." I will not lose another friend. I am mentally prepared for the battle at hand. In minutes, the house loomed in the distance.

It's a two-story white house. I get a message on our headset that Judges Ying Yue and Luka are in the area and will be arriving with Captain Joshua Honore. Five of us will be enough.

I park the car behind a tree line. "Aiden! Go scout the area." With a nod, Aiden disappears into the night to monitor the house and wait for the others to arrive. It's pitch black and the only thing I can see are the stars in the sky.

Eventually, I see a car pull up and Ying Yue, Luka, and Joshua all get out. They are battle-ready with determination on their faces.

"We heard about Sarah," Joshua remarks. I hold in the emotions that threaten to surge.

"She died trying to save a member of our family. We must

complete this mission because that is what she would want."

Then we hear movement in the bushes and Aiden appears.

"There are in total ten heavily-armed men guarding the house. As far as I can see, there are another ten inside the house with assault rifles, too," Aiden reports.

"I can take out all the men guarding the house with my bow," Luka responds. "Shouldn't be too hard depending on the type of armor they're wearing."

"I can't tell for sure, but I think they're only wearing Kevlar vests," Aiden replies.

Luka looks down at his bow and grabs an arrow. "Well, I'll just have to shoot them in the knees then."

I grab my scythe tightly and prepare to go to battle. "All right, Luka, you take on the guards. Ying Yue, take the front of the house. Aiden and I will take the back. Do not kill unless you have to. Just immobilize them so we can interrogate them later."

Aiden, Luka, Joshua, and Ying Yue look at me in surprise. "So, you don't want us to kill anyone? Who the hell are you? You're not Eden," Joshua says, still stunned.

"Shut up! It's for the mission. We need to keep some alive to get intel on Seditio. Only kill if it's needed," I reinforce.

Within a few seconds, Luka begins the assault. He heads to a tree and uses it for cover. He aims at the first man who's guarding the door of the house and shoots him in the legs. The man screams and the four guards guarding the front look around to see where it came from. Luka then shoots three other guards in the Achilles with such astonishing accuracy that he only used three arrows, one for each guard's ankle. It's no wonder he's the greatest marksman in the House of David.

Ying Yue rides her motorcycle past Luka into the fray. The crippled men that Luka shot start to fire at her. She is dodging the poorly aimed shots. Then she jumps off the motorcycle and lets it slide towards two of the men, badly injuring them. She then disarms the rest of the five men.

"Front is clear," she says without a hint of being tired. The men guarding the back begin moving in to cover the front, but Luka is able to take them down. As soon as he wounds them, they begin to shoot wildly.

"Shit! I've been hit in the arm," Joshua says through the headset. "A stray bullet got me while I was trying to sneak up to them from the side."

"Damn! I keep forgetting that you don't have a FOG," Luka answers through the headset. "There is a man approaching you from the left, Joshua. I'll take him out."

A couple of seconds later, an arrow flies through the air and hits the man on the side of the head.

"You know Eden just told us not to kill," Joshua says into the headset.

"Oops," Luka says back with a smile.

Aiden and I proceed to the house. We see shots fired at us from the second-story windows.

"Aiden, shoot at the window!" He follows commands and I continue until I get to the back door. I break the window next to the door and throw in a smoke grenade. Then Ying Yue and Aiden arrive beside me.

Once inside, I kick the doors open and shots instantly start firing. I roll to the left, flip a kitchen table over, and hide behind it. Ying Yue fires her guns killing three men.

"They have breached the house. Retreat!" we hear French voices say over their radios. Seconds later, Joshua comes through the front door wounding six more open men.

"I'm going upstairs," Aiden says in a monotone voice.

"Good, I'll finish up down here." I jump over the table and slice three other men in the chest, wounding them.

"Check in?" I yell to the others.

"The whole bottom floor is clear," Ying Yue says.

"Outside is clear," replies Luka.

I hear men yelling in pain and suddenly, silence. "Top floor is clear," Aiden says.

Bodies and wounded Seditio men cover the entire ground. "I don't see Orion here, Eden," Aiden concludes. "Were we lied to again?"

I don't think so. There has to be a hidden passage or door." I walk up to a wounded man and pierce my fingers in his wound deeper and deeper. "I'm only going to ask you once. Where is Orion?"

The man tears up, but he won't tell me what I need to know. Apparently, people under Whiteface are more terrified of him than anyone. They will not betray him because they're more afraid of what they'll do to him than death.

"We know who you are. The House of David's God of Death. We don't fear you," he adds with a smile. I want to kill him so bad, but I can't get myself to do it. I just shove him down to the ground and walk to another.

"Wait! Do you hear that, Eden? It sounds like someone is walking," Aiden says, straining to hear.

"Everyone stop moving!" I order.

Once the room is absolutely quiet, I hear the same footsteps. I walk into the next room until I get to the kitchen where I stand on the rug in the middle and figure out my next move. As soon as Aiden steps onto the rug beside me, we hear a slight crack from underneath. He drags his Quiang across the rug and moves it to the side.

"There's a door. There's an underground place in this house," Aiden said.

"Joshua and Luka, you stay up here and watch our back. Aiden, Ying Yue, and I will head down there. We are the best at closed-quarter combat."

"All right, I'll go first. My Quiang is very durable," Aiden says as he puts the tip of the Quiang in a crack then lifts the hatch up. Shots immediately fire and Aiden dashes down the stairs.

"Eden, go last. I'll head down now and clear after Aiden," Ying Yue yells over the screams of men getting attacked. As she disappears downward, I turn to Joshua. "Alert the House of David. We will be back with Orion."

I head down the stairs to see two men half-dead lying on the floor at the bottom of the stairs. Ying Yue is fiercely attacking a Seditio man. One after the other they continue to shoot at her but eventually fall. The looks on their faces say it all. It's like they know they're going to die but they continue to aimlessly shoot at her.

I continue to advance until I see a room to the right where Aiden is fighting five Seditio men. "I'll handle these guys, Eden, you keep going," he says.

I nod at him and keep moving forward down the long dark gray cement hallway. Every few steps, I climb over injured men that are bleeding out from Ying Yue's precise cuts.

The hallway lights flicker on and off. I open the door to the right and I see a room lined with metal shelves that are stacked with whips, scissors, knives, and other torture-like devices hanging up. After glancing inside, I keep walking to find Ying Yue standing over another dead body that she had cut up to pieces.

"Sorry, Eden. I know you said don't kill, but this guy tried to shoot me and he called me a Japanese cunt. You know that I don't like to be called Japanese. I am bloody Chinese. There absolutely is a difference."

I roll my eyes. "Wait, I thought you were Japanese."

She walks up to me and whispers an inch from my mouth. "If you ever say that again, I will kill you, you fucking douche."

I smirk at her and she smiles back.

"Head upstairs. I can take it from here," I say.

"Should I help Aiden?" she asks.

"He should be fine."

She heads upstairs to help Joshua and Luka. I continue until I reach the metal door with locks on it at the very end of the hallway. It's a heavy door with vertical bars. I tighten my grip on my scythe.

"The room is clear, Eden," Aiden says through the headset. "But there were bodies in the corner of the room. They look like civilians. I'm going to examine them. They look dead. I will alert the House."

"Roger that."

Right before I open the door, Aiden's voice came back through the headset. "Eden! Jesus. One of the bodies in the pile is from Bachman Bakery. It's the cashier."

I stop in my tracks, stunned by what I hear.

"The young one. Eden, she looks like he brutally tortured her or something. She's missing fingers. Rebecca—I believe her name was in the file."

"This was a planned attack. They never wanted the artifact. They wanted Orion this whole time. He had to have been watching for a good minute and this girl must have been kidnapped a while ago. Aiden, when we get back to the Gate we need to look up missing person entries. Everything about this keeps getting weirder and weirder. Nothing is making any sense whatsoever, but I will find out what's going on. One way or the other you can count on that."

"But why, though? Is it because his family had the artifact? This doesn't make any sense, Eden," Aiden says.

"I'll find out soon enough. Don't worry about it. We just need to complete the task at hand. Save our comrades, Aiden."

"Roger that."

I pause in front of the metal door. This is the only place Orion could be. *Is Whiteface behind this door? If he's not here then where else could he be?* I reach for the doorknob. I hear

196

talking and the grunts of terror. Blood crawls out underneath the door and pools around my boots. It's like someone had poured an entire bucket of blood on the ground in front of my feet. *What if this is Orion's blood?* I'm not scared but that thought makes me anxious. *What if I have failed him?* If he's dead then not only did I fail him, but Sarah as well, and I don't want that to happen. I slowly twist the doorknob, praying that I'll find Orion on the other side.

Chapter 10: You're Obligated

I TRY OPENING MY eyes, but it's like they're glued shut. I realize I have no feeling in my right leg. I can't move it at all. As my eyes slowly flutter open, I scan my surroundings. There is blood everywhere, but the smell is strangely that of sweet honeydew instead of a slaughterhouse. Something below me catches my eye. When I look down, I see piles and piles of white roses. They're so beautiful. It's the most pleasant thing I've seen in days.

I feel my muscles giving up one by one; my whole body is beginning to fail. I have been chained up against the wall for so long that I've forgotten how it feels to stand on solid ground. Then, I hear Jacob near me. He's wearing a spiked collar that is chained to the wall and his wrists are bound together. His left foot is missing and his face is a bloody swollen mess.

"Jacob! Jacob," I whisper.

His body does the slightest twitch. He has purple patches all over his body. He looks completely lifeless. All of a sudden there's banging close by, and I see Whiteface at a table to my right.

"Well, Well. You're awake I see," he says coldly. "Do you want to watch me finish off your friend? He hasn't been much fun."

I want to yell but I don't have the energy to shout words. My throat is hurting, and I can't speak. I want to help him, I want to save my friend. *How did Whiteface find us? Did someone betray me and the House of David?*

Whiteface ambles up to Jacob, bends over, grabs his face, and slaps him. Jacob still doesn't move.

"He's going to bleed out. I didn't think I would get to try

this out, but I guess this is the perfect time to use it," Whiteface mutters as he returns to the table.

"Please. Don't kill him. Please," I beg. I begin praying in my head.

"Excuse me?" Whiteface stops in front of me and smiles. I can see the fresh blood on his neck and the yellow in his teeth. His breath smells foul, like rotten meat. It's disgusting. I try to say something, but nothing forms.

"It seems as though you have nothing important to tell me. I wasn't going to kill your friend here, but since he has no more fight in him then what's the point of having a half-dead person in the room? Why don't we just make him completely dead?" His tone is chilling. He shuffles towards Jacob and laughs mockingly in his face. "I know what he's good for. Let's see how sharp this sword really is. His body will do perfectly as a cutting post."

My heart starts to pound in my chest.

"No!" I yell with all the energy I have left.

Slash! Blood spatters on my face. Whiteface pauses, grins, then, like a man possessed, resumes slashing in all directions like he's chopping a dead piece of meat. The blade slices through Jacob's body mercilessly, whipping his blood to every part of the room.

My friend's dying in front of my eyes. Finally, Whiteface stops, but he just stands to stare at what remained of Jacob as though admiring his handiwork. My friend is now completely dead. Slaughtered like a pig. Blood is gushing out of big gaping gashes, some of which are so big you can see flesh and bone.

Whiteface licks the blood and stumbles backward. "I just love the taste of swine."

My thoughts begin to race. Curiously, he would say that when I was just thinking about how my friend resembles a slaughtered pig. I will myself to stay relaxed for my own life, but how can I be calm? Jacob's dead. My heart hurts so fucking much that I don't know what emotions I'm feeling. I don't know what kind of monster would do this.

Whiteface throws the sword on the table and wipes his face with a towel that is soaked in blood. "He could have at least told me information about the House of David after all of that. He said he didn't know anything. What a pity to die like that. What a shame." He stands there glaring at Jacob's body lying in a pool of blood and pieces of human flesh. The sight is so horrific that I begin to fade. My vision darkens slowly and then . . .

***

Slowly but surely my eyes open as I begin to wake. Hours may have passed, but I'm not sure. *Why should I be punished? All I wanted was to help people, change the world, and be an influence.*

"Why? WHY? WHY?" Rage engulfs me. I did nothing wrong. "Why me? Why me?" I want to cry but there are no more tears left in me.

"Why you say?" I faintly hear a voice talking back to me. "Why you? Well, that's simple. Those who think they are innocent are the easiest to break."

Through the haze in my vision, I glimpse the white on his face and the blond in his hair. He never left the room.

"This whole thing," he says. "This whole world—it's just a shit show. You have those with power who want to keep the poor down but also who want the poor to serve them. Then you have the dumb fucks! They don't see that the government is only there for a certain few. They don't even elect people who have our best interest at heart. It's a fucking popularity contest if I'm being honest."

His voice is filled with hate. Then he grabs a wire speculum and with a calm tone tells me. "And then there are people like you.

The ones who think they're innocent, who think they're changing the world, but are doing nothing. They just watch and complain and say what they wish they could do. You're the worst sinners. People like you are disease and deserve to be taught a lesson." Still holding onto the wire speculum, he walks towards me. "And I want to be the teacher." He pulls my head back. "I want you to see this. Let's see if you really want to save everyone." He puts the wire speculum around my eye and cranks it open. "Let me ask you a question." My left eye is completely exposed. I look down at the floor and I see three people lying in front of me with bags over their heads. Whiteface pulls the bags off the first two heads to reveal my grandpa and my mom with duct tape on their mouths and their hands and legs tied behind them with rope. The third person still has the bag on her head, but I can tell it is a girl with strawberry blonde hair. I could also see black eyeliner is running down her neck from crying.

"Which one should I kill first?" Whiteface asks me. Tears are streaming down my mom's face. *How could he do this? How did he know who my parents are?*

"Please don't hurt them! Please! Do what you want with me, but don't hurt them!"

He looks at me and laughs. "This is my game, Boy! I want to see what you will choose to do," he says with a smirk. He grabs a gun out of his suit jacket and points it at the back of the girl's head. He stares at me, his gray eyes piercing through mine. "This girl has done a lot of bad in her life. She's a psycho piece of shit. She's going to kill a lot more people in the future too. So, kill her? Or let her live?"

My mom and my grandfather's words are muffled by the duct tape and I can't make out what they're saying.

"Life is dear. No one has the right to take it. She hasn't killed anyone yet. And I don't think she will," I say.

"My dear boy, there is a 50/50 chance she'll kill you. If

there is a possibility, shouldn't you try to take the best odds? Shouldn't you kill a murderer? If you have the slightest hint of danger, shouldn't you take the threat out of the equation?"

"But I don't know," I mumble. My head begins to hurt, and I feel like I'm about to pass out. "And you don't know, either."

"So, I'm assuming you're going to spare her, right?"

"Yes. No. I don't know. I won't choose."

"Very well," he says with an even bigger smile. Then he turns his gaze to my parents and laughs. "So, she lives. What about them?"

"Don't!" I cry out with what feels like my last bit of strength. "Please let them go. No more! Don't hurt them. Let them live."

He smirks at me and I can tell he's truly enjoying this.

"Come in," he says to the door. The door opens and Matthew walks in with blood dripping from his mouth. His left eye is so swollen that the left side of his face doesn't look like his. He walks until he's standing right beside Whiteface. Tears are visibly running down his face and he's shaking so badly that I can feel him trembling from where I'm standing. Then Whiteface speaks to Matthew.

"Since your friend, Orion, seems to be incompetent, I'll give you the same choice, but I'll make it a little sweeter. Pull the trigger at Mrs. Bachman in the head and you can leave this room. Or kill this girl and stay here," Whiteface tells him. He hands Matthew the gun and backs away.

I give Matthew a helpless look. "Matthew, don't do it. Please. Put the gun down. Don't kill my mom."

More tears roll down his face, and the pain in his eyes is agonizing to see. He aims the gun at my mom. He shakes his head at me and tries to say sorry but his tongue is cut out, which explains the blood trailing down his chin.

"Good choice," Whiteface says with an evil grin.

Matthew pulls the trigger, but nothing happens. There's a shocked look on his face. Whiteface guffaws with such force it bounces off the walls.

"You did it. I didn't say kill her, but you made the choice, too. You didn't know if there were bullets in there or not. You're free to go now—I'm a man of my word."

Relief is etched in Matthew's face. He locks eyes with me as he slowly backs up to the door.

"Leave!" Whiteface bellows. Matthew turns to open the door, and Whiteface pulls out another gun out of his suit jacket and aims it at Matthew's head. I want to tell him to run so badly but something keeps me from it. *He almost killed my mother. How could he just pull the trigger like that?* It's like he doesn't care at all. He would have killed my mother if the gun had been loaded. Anger sneaks into my heart and for a split second, I want Matthew to get what's coming to him. Death.

Whiteface shoots him in the head.

Blood and brains fly everywhere and his body drops on the floor with a loud thud. A dark river of red gushes out of his head. I know I should be heartbroken, but instead, I'm relieved. He almost killed my mom, and now he's dead. He got what he deserved. He's trash for even pulling that trigger.

Whiteface throws his right hand with the gun down in disgust. "Ouch! Did I do that?" He grabs my face. "I'm going to ask you again. You have two choices. Kill your parents, or kill the girl."

I spit in his face. "What does it matter? You're going to kill me, anyway, like you killed Matthew."

"I killed that man because he's the reason I found you and your family. All I did was offer him some money and he was more than willing to give you up. I'm not a bad guy, I just don't like people who betray their 'friends' for money."

"He wouldn't do that, he's my friend."

"What have I been trying to teach you this whole time? Let me make it clearer to you. People are trash and I'm here to be the teacher. So here I am, teaching you. Now choose!"

"No. I'm not a murderer."

He backs up from me and yells, "That not the right answer! You can't make the rules of this game. I gave you a choice on who dies. If you won't choose, I will."

Bang! Bang! He shoots both my mother and grandpa.

Something shatters in me.

"I gave you an out. You only had to kill the girl but you chose to let her live. That's the fucking problem! You don't make decisions. You think doing nothing is doing something and, well, it's not. But in doing that, you did choose."

"How? How did I choose for my family to die?" I yell in agony.

"In life, if you don't make a choice, someone else will make it for you. You not choosing was choosing. When people don't vote they are choosing because you're choosing to put your choice in someone else's hand. I'm trying to teach you. You will not learn unless you suffer." He lets out a laugh so sick and twisted, it sounds like that of a psych ward patient high on mushrooms. "You killed them, Orion, you know? All you had to do was pick one of the options given to you. It's a coward's way to not choose. You wanted me to decide. Yes, someone would have to die but it wouldn't have been your family. The sad thing is that when I shot your friend, I saw the relief on your face. You wanted me to kill him because you saw him as evil for pulling the trigger. You should see yourself as evil too because you killed your parents just like he did. I'll do you a solid."

He's about to open the door, but he stops and gives me an evil grin over his shoulder. "I have taken everything from you. Now you're nothing but a sack of flesh. The best thing for you now is death, and that will be my last lesson for you."

As he walks out, he tries to shut the door but Matthew's body is blocking it. It's like it reminded him of something. He looks at the lifeless body of Matthew and then turns to the girl.

"How could I leave a delicate monster like you behind?"

He shuts the door again and approaches the girl. She tries to roll away but she's already against the wall. He grabs her, throws her onto the corpse, pulls down her pants, and looks at me. "I just love fucking dead bodies." Then he gives out a demonic laugh.

I have no more strength left in me. I feel a void where my soul once was. I don't want to live. *Just kill me.*

"You don't need these anymore," he says as he takes the wire speculum off. Both of my eyes instantly shut.

***

Hours may have passed, but I'm not sure. My family's bodies are still there. The girl is in the corner rolled up like a used towel. I don't smell flowers anymore. *How did my life become this? I don't want this anymore. Who have I become?*

I must live. If there are people in the world like Whiteface, they must all die. I must clean up the mistakes. No more, no more, no more. This world created this monster and I'll make a new one. No, I'll kill them all. No more madness.

I chuckle a little out loud. Then my chuckle turns into a laugh. "I'll change the world," I mutter then feel myself drifting off again.

I woke up much later. I don't know how long I've been asleep. The girl is gone. I smell so putrid I want to throw up. Matthew and Jacob's bodies are in the corner of the room—both lifeless and drained of blood. I'm not disgusted by the dead bodies anymore. It's the way of life, even though this is not how life is supposed to be.

My father was wrong. Why should I cherish life and live it

to the fullest when some do not cherish the same life? Some people just want to destroy it and waste it away. I look around for the girl. *Where did she go?*

"Whiteface took the girl out, but couldn't take my family or my friends out," I say to myself. The man is trash and doesn't deserve to take another breath, but he doesn't deserve to die, though. No. Death would be too light for him.

I start to laugh out loud and lick my lips. I can taste dried blood on my lips. It tastes so salty. "I'll just have to make him suffer to the point where he wishes for death."

Nothing else matters right now but to get out and make Whiteface suffer. He wants to teach me a lesson, he said. The only thing he did was show me that my father was wrong. Whiteface isn't wrong about me. I wanted Matthew to die. Matthew was scum, just like him. People like him need to suffer more.

I want things to change. I want to believe that the world isn't filled with pain and suffering. My mind continues to wander. *Are you searching for me, Eden? I want you to stop searching for me. I don't want you to find me and see what I've become. I don't want Mary to see this monster. What's the point of living? The police can't fix monsters like this and the House of David can't fix monsters like this! Their mission is wrong. Finding artifacts is not enough. We can do more. I will do more. I have a new goal. I want to see my parents again. I want to see my family again. I can't handle living if there's nothing but pain and sadness. How are others able to live with such pain?*

Bang! Bam! I hear explosions outside, jolting me wide awake. The ground shakes. "What's going on?" I hear footsteps approaching.

There's a whisper in my ear. It's a girl's voice. "Don't make a sound and don't open your eyes." The straps on my wrist and ankles loosen up.

"Why are you helping me? Who are you? Why?" I whisper.

"Just helping a friend," the female voice says. I can hear screams from far away.

"What's going on?" I repeat.

The doorknob turns, I hear the door creak, and the mysterious person says, "Your friends are here. I want to see what you do now," she tells me. "There's a sword in the left corner in front of you. I will leave the door unlocked for you. You can either leave or get revenge. It's up to you." The door closes before I get to see who she is.

I should leave. Suddenly the image of my family's deaths come to mind. Whiteface is a disease and needs to be cleansed from this world. I know that I'm not a Judge but at this moment, in this instance, I will be his judge, his jury, and his executioner. I look at the white roses still on the floor.

"His blood will be delicious food for the flowers." I close my eyes. I know the sick bastard will come back. He wants to finish the job of teaching me a lesson and then killing me. He gets self-satisfaction from all of that, anyway.

I hear the door open. "Well, well, well," Whiteface says. "I guess our session has come to an end. I hate to say it, but you have been a horrible student and it hurts for me to believe that I'm a horrible teacher."

I can hear him licking his lips and grabbing the sword. I remain still so he can't tell that I had been untied. "Who put this in here? A little old-fashioned for my taste, but it'll be fun to cut you up with."

"So, are we done here?" I ask.

He looks shocked that I'm still able to move. Then, he laughs hysterically.

"You know what, fuck it. How about I cut your dick off and fuck you where it used to be?" He moves in closer with the sword lowered to his side. I spread my legs open.

"Eat my dick, Daddy."

"So, I'm your daddy now? Glad that you want to please me. Before I cut your dick off how about you suck mine? We're in a pretty dire situation in here, and the least a good student can do is give his teacher a treat." He drops the sword and pulls his pants down.

It's the only opening I need. I poke both his eyes with my left hand.

"You motherfucker!" he screams as he jumps back in pain. "How did you get loose? Who let you loose?" He swings his arms around in wild fury but he slips on the blood on the floor and crashes on his back.

I pick up the sword and slash both his Achilles' tendons. He cries in agony. "Fuck! FUCK! FUCK YOU."

"You did teach me something, you know, Whiteface? That monsters like you don't deserve to die. That would be too good for you. I have something much worse in mind."

He crawls until his fingers reach the lower end of the door. He tries to open it, but I walk over and smash the door while his fingers are still in between. The sound of bones breaking is even louder than the sound of the door slamming. As he yowls, I kick his hand out of the way and then I shut the door. I see the fear in his face now.

"Are you ready to have a little fun? I don't want people to hear you scream so what about we remove that tongue first? Oh, wait, no! I don't want you to crawl away, so let's break those legs and arms of yours first." I pick up the hammer from the table. With one windmill swing, I hit his left and right fibula, breaking them both. A deep guttural sound comes from him. I decide to break his arms next. I position myself next to his left humerus.

"Stop! Please! Stop!" he cries out.

"I'll give you a choice now. I can take your tongue out, or I can take out your eyes completely. Choose."

He shakes his head.

"Is that your answer?"

"No. Please! I'm sorry. I was doing what I was told. I'll tell you who my boss is. Please let me live."

He didn't let my family live. I pick up the sword again and point it at his eyes. "Is that your answer?"

"Please! I'll do anything."

All I feel is nothing. No sadness, no anger, no pity.

"Okay, that's your answer?" I speak calmly.

I realize that in life and death situations, you see what someone's true character is. You get to see their true selves. Whiteface's true self was a coward, a manipulator. A weak and pathetic human. Matthew was just as weak. He didn't truly see me as his friend. He saw me as someone who could help him. Once I was of no use to him, he decided that my life was worthless. The world is full of weak people like them both and it makes me so sick. As my anger boils over, I push the sword into Whiteface's left eye socket. Blood crawls down his cheek.

"Why! Why!" He covers his left eye with both hands.

"You chose by putting the choice in my hands. I gave you two options. You didn't decide, so I decided for you."

He tries to crawl away on his stomach but I grab his shoulder to turn him over and stab his other eye with the sword. As he lay crying and twisting with his hands over both eyes, I grab the hammer once again, and smash it into his open mouth, sending his teeth flying everywhere. Next, I pick up the medical knife from the table. I pry his tongue out until I get a good grip, then I cut it off. But I'm not done yet. Death is too good for him right now, and I want him to suffer. There's one more thing I had to do. Surgical scissors.

"You can't see now, Whiteface, but I know you can still hear me. You said you were going to make me suck your cock, right? Well, how about I feed you your cock instead? You can tell me how it tastes."

I pull his pants down, grab his cock, open the scissors, put his cock in between them, and snip it off. It fell to the floor limp. I pick it up, crank his deformed and smashed mouth open, and put his dick in between his lips.

He spits it out. I know the pain I had caused. *This is justice.* He deserves this and everything that has happened to him. This is justice for all the people he has killed. The women and men he has raped. All the pain he has inflicted.

"Death is only for those who are worthy and you are trash. You don't deserve relief," I spit out.

All of a sudden, the door opens.

"Orion? What the fuck?" I turn to see Eden standing in the doorway, covered in blood, holding his Deathscythe.

"This is Whiteface," I tell him. "You should probably get someone in here before he dies."

The fear that transfigures in Eden's eyes is something I've never seen before. I don't understand. Eden is known as the God of Death. He should be used to something of this magnitude.

"Let's go, Eden. I don't want to be here anymore," I say.

"Were there any civilian casualties?"

"My mom, my grandpa, and Jacob are all dead. There was another person, but he was a nobody."

"I'm sorry, Orion. I should've been here sooner. This is all my fault. Please forgive me."

I notice a gun in the holster of his belt. "Can I see that? The gun, I mean. Just to protect me if there are any members of Seditio still around."

He hands me his gun, and I look at Whiteface on the ground. He's nothing more than an insignificant piece of shit. I aim the gun at Whiteface's head and can feel Eden staring at me.

"Orion, what are you doing?"

I pull the trigger and Whiteface's brains scatter all across the floor.

"Orion! He was defeated already. There was no need for you to shoot him. You survived and you were the better man in the end."

"I know I was the better man." I hand him the gun back and walk past him.

I don't look back and all I can smell is honey. I walk past a room filled with bodies. Aiden is inside covered in blood.

We walk up several flights of stairs. I must have been underground. Eventually, we come upon a brown wooden door at the top of the stairwell. I twist the silver door handle and the door opens up to the kitchen of a small house. There's crimson spatters all over the white floral wallpaper.

There's a broken wooden table on the floor with three dead bodies surrounding it. The bodies are replete with bullet holes and cuts. Two are missing arms and legs, but I don't care. The dead bodies remind me of an art piece I just saw—something that Da Vinci would paint.

I move through the kitchen, stepping over broken glass and bullet casings, and I stop at a window that looks over a deep, modern, silver kitchen sink. Stepping over a severed arm, I edge up even closer to the window to see the bright sun peeking over the horizon.

The orange and yellow rays hit my skin as I splash water on my neck and face. Blood drips into the sink from my face and the stubble of my beard.

"Captain Orion! Are you okay?" It's Joshua.

"Never better."

But he looks at me like he's seen a ghost.

"I worried that all this would happen." He puts his hand on my shoulder.

"Did we lose anyone?"

Joshua sighs deeply. "Aiden, Eden, and Sarah went to a house where our intel said you were located but later found out it was a trap. And . . . " Joshua broke off and starts shaking his head.

"And what?"

". . . and Sarah was killed."

I feel like I should be heartbroken, but I'm so tired there's hardly any room to feel anything else. A small part of me blames myself for Sarah's death, but the other part of me thinks that maybe she needed to die. After all, Sarah was always the weak one. She didn't kill like Eden and the other Judges. She thought peace was the key, but she was wrong. This world doesn't need any more weak individuals in it.

Chapter 11: To Seek

BEING A Judge can be difficult, challenging, and rigorous but I was born into this lifestyle. I've been around death for so long that it has become normal to me. But this is not the case for Orion, who has led a much happier life than me. This is all new to him. I can see he's torn, broken, not the same man I met in that bar in Mobile.

"Eden," Orion says while looking at his blood-stained hands.

"Yes?"

"Why do you kill? Do you kill because it's your job?" I nod, although I'm kind of confused. "Why do people kill?"

"I don't understand where you're going with this, Orion."

He looks me straight in the eyes.

"Let's think about it this way. When I killed Whiteface, I did it because I was angry that he killed my entire family. It wasn't for duty, but revenge. I wouldn't have done it normally."

"I'm still confused."

"When I see you and Aiden fight, you both just know what to do. There's no doubt, no confusion."

Orion catches onto the frown of confusion across my face.

"Let me go into more detail. You and Aiden can kill without hesitation. Both of you are among the superior humans. I've been weak all my life. I've never had that instinct, drive, or decisiveness. I always questioned what I was doing. We need people like you in this world. We don't need weak humans," Orion explains, his voice intense.

Aiden has a bewildered look on his face.

Orion continues. "You and Aiden have this instinct, the

ability to be decisive. Most of you Judges were born with this instinct. That is why you became Judges. The first day we met, I watched you kill without batting an eyelash. I was at a loss for words. I couldn't understand what type of man could do that to someone. I thought you didn't see life as I saw it and that you were just evil. But I was wrong, and I see it now. You already had your mind made. You knew what to do. By knowing what to do you can fully embrace death".

Aiden grabs the back of Orion's seat. "Orion, stop."

Orion stares at Aiden.

"No. No. This system is wrong. All of it," Orion yells at Aiden. "I don't want to be this weak victim. This world lives on a basic principle. Survival of the strongest. Those who are killed by others are weak and don't deserve to live. If we work together we can stop all this pain and suffering. We have the means and power. Joseph is only worried about the fucking House. He doesn't care about this world or its people. If he truly cared; motherfuckers like Whiteface wouldn't exist and every member of Seditio would be wiped off this fucking planet."

I slam on the brakes and grab Orion by the collar of his bloody shirt. "You listen to me. I don't know what you're going through and I can't comprehend the emotional distress you've been suffering from these last four days. But I will not sit here and listen to you talk like this. You need to move forward."

Orion slaps my hands off. "Don't be weak, Eden. You're speaking like a loser. Don't be like Sarah."

I yank his collar harder, my face an inch from his. "Don't you ever speak about Sarah that way again. She was a beautiful person and a great Judge and I will not sit back and let you speak about her in such a disgusting manner. You fucking hear me?"

Orion huffs and brushes me off and I continue driving in silence until we arrive at the rendezvous point. Orion gets out of the car and walks up to Joseph Cain, who is in the distance. They exchange a few words, then Orion walks past Joseph and gets into the helicopter. Joseph walks up to the car and I roll the window down.

"Eden." Aiden sounds concerned. "I don't like what I see in Orion right now."

"He's broken," Joseph says. I hit the steering wheel with my palm.

"I don't like this, Joseph! He isn't the same."

"What do you mean?"

"The way he killed that man was vile like he wanted him to suffer. I don't think he's ready to go back in the field. He's too emotionally charged."

Joseph looks back at Orion in the helicopter.

"His whole family is gone, his life, Joseph. His whole life was taken from him. Do you think that someone can recover from that and still live a decent life? He isn't like me or Aiden. I don't know if he'll be able to make it," I say.

"He said he wants to get back to work, Eden. He doesn't have anything holding him back now. He could be an amazing addition to the House of David in his current state," Joseph disagrees.

"Joseph, I'm telling you, we need to give him the time he needs. This isn't about the House anymore, this is about his life." The more I talk about it, the angrier I get.

"Eden, it has always been about the House. I told you a long time ago that I will do anything to protect the House. I trained you to understand that it's the House before anything. You chose this man as your Captain and you've always had a good eye for picking people. I trust that you have picked a good Captain. You should trust him as well."

I just shake my head at Joseph and he starts to walk towards the other helicopter. "I'll see you back at the Gate," I call out to Joseph. "I'll also notify Trish of Sarah's death so we can arrange an honorable Judge funeral." I turn to Aiden. "We need to watch out for Orion. Keep an eye on him, okay? I'll do the same."

Aiden nods at me and gets out of the car.

***

It's been two days since returning from Mission: Whiteface, and Sarah's funeral is underway in Israel on the River Jordan. When a Judge dies, their Finger of God is removed from their body and placed in a tube until the replacement Judge is chosen. During the funeral, the deceased Judge is dressed up in a white robe, sandals, with a gold key placed in their left hand. This key symbolizes the key to the gate of Heavens.

Every Judge funeral takes place at the River Jordan because the founder of the House, David, believed this body of water was holy because it was where Jesus was baptized.

The Judge is placed in a rowboat on top of a bed of white flowers and then the Judge is blessed by the King of Hearts. Finally, the rowboat is lit on fire. The House believes that once the boat sinks and the water comes rushing in that the Judge's body is cleansed of the sins it has committed. Then, with the gold key in their left hand, they can open the gate of Heaven once they reach the afterlife.

Usually, only the Judge's family and friends come to the funeral, however, Sarah's funeral is different. So many more people came to see. I didn't know that she had touched so many lives, but it didn't surprise me at the same time.

Trish is there along with Sarah's mother and sister. I never met Sarah's family before but they have a striking resemblance to her. Her mom looks like a younger Trish and her sister has dark black hair.

Judges Luka, Ying Yue, Aiden, Joseph, Rebecca, and Jamal show up as well to pay their respects. A few Captains are there too. Joshua and Sarah's Captain, Olivia, arrived. Olivia is twenty-three years old and was originally recruited by Sarah for her computer skills.

I scan the crowd. "Where's Orion?" I whisper to Joseph, who's right next to me.

"He's on a mission right now. He's looking for an artifact."

"Why would you let him go on a mission at a time like this?"

Joseph moves his hands behind his back and whispers, "He said he didn't know Sarah very well and that finding the artifacts was more important. I can't force him to do something he doesn't want to do, Eden."

"We just lost a comrade, Joseph!" I'm disgusted, but I try not to raise my voice. "She fucking died trying to save his life. She died so he could live!" It hurt me to say it. Joseph doesn't say anything, but the look in his eyes tells me he knows I'm right.

The funeral continues and everyone says their final goodbyes to Sarah. I walk up to her pale corpse and kiss her on the forehead. I turn my attention to her family; they're not crying, but that doesn't surprise me. They understand the risk of being a Judge, and they're proud to see that their loved one made a difference.

After everyone had gotten the chance to approach Sarah's body, Trish, Sarah's mom, and her sister light the torch. Everyone begins to say the Irish Blessing. They throw the torch in the boat and, within seconds, it lights ablaze before Sarah's family pushes the flaming boat onto the river.

I've been to a lot of Judges' funerals but this one is the saddest one I have ever experienced. This is a funeral for someone I truly loved.

***

It's been six months since Sarah's death. We haven't had many Seditio incidents. They've been very quiet lately. I'm in the library on the Gate reading *The Great Gatsby* by F. Scott Fitzgerald. It's one of my favorite books of all time.

"Eden," I hear from a distance. Aiden's walking up to me.

"Hey. What's up?"

He sits down next to me and grabs a piece of candy out of his pocket. "Orion has been completing a lot of missions lately. I always thought that you left a lot of dead bodies during missions, but Orion has been making you look mellow."

"What do you making me look mellow? What's he doing different?"

"It's the way he's killing them. It's more brutal. A lot of hate in the kills."

I close my book and stand up. "Where is he now?"

"He's on a mission with Luka in Ethiopia. They're investigating rumors of the Arc of the Covenant." I walk towards the door. "What are you going to do?"

"I'm going to Ethiopia."

In the hallway, Joseph stops me. "Eden, I wanted to talk to you."

"What about?"

"You should be proud," he says, beaming. "Orion has been completing mission after mission. Finding artifacts and disproving them. As of right now, we've been weakened as a whole with Sarah's death and Jamal's retirement. We need another Judge."

"Olivia would be a good choice. She's been here for six years. She knows all of Sarah's work and she's an asset to the organization," I say.

There's a blank look on Joseph's face. "I'll consider your choice, but I was thinking that Orion would replace Sarah. He's completed twenty missions since joining the organization, Eden. He's completely dedicated to the House and to be honest with you,

I want him to succeed." Joseph pauses, studying me. "You're not happy. Why?"

I step back. "He hasn't been here long enough to be even considered a Judge. Just six months ago his entire family was taken from him. He's unstable. Joseph, you can't be considering him. His fighting skills are still nowhere near up to par."

"Don't let your feelings get in the way, Eden. If you look at the facts, you can see that he has been a great Captain."

I punch the wall. "It's not about the facts Joseph! Have you ever seen what he's doing in the missions? How he's killing people?"

"You used to be reckless on your missions too, Eden. You killed people, too."

"Joseph, this isn't the same kind of killing. If I need to kill, I do it clean and quick by attacking the vitals. Orion isn't doing that. He's brutally killing people. He even tortures them before he kills them. Why would you want to promote someone like that so quickly? I know you don't believe in torturing."

A hint of hurt flickers in Joseph's eyes. "I won't be here long, Eden. I would like you to replace me someday. Whether you like it or not, Orion will become a Judge one day. The sooner he becomes one, the more valuable he becomes to the House."

Joseph disappears down the hallway. I continue with my plan to go to Ethiopia. I need my Deathscythe so I head to the weapons room, where I see Joshua.

"Where are you heading off to, Eden?" he asks as I grab the scythe and head for the door. "Are you going to Ethiopia?"

"Why does it matter where the hell I'm going?"

He advances towards me. "If you're going then I'm going. I don't know what's going on with Orion but what he did to that guy on our last mission—that was probably the cruelest thing I have ever seen in my life. I want to go because he's my friend and I see how painful losing his family has been for him. I want to be there for him."

"Well, he's on this mission with Luka. I'm pretty sure Luka will not let this get out of hand but regardless, they don't know we're coming. We'll monitor covertly and if we need to, we'll step in."

A few hours later, Josh and I are on the helicopter on the way to Ethiopia.

"Eden," Joshua says. He's sitting across from me. "Captains aren't taught many things about the House of David. I mean, I've been a Captain for many years now and I don't know much about our history at all. Will you tell me about how it all started? I'd like to hear it from your point of view."

"Well, the history of the House isn't actually that well-defined. You already know about the story of David saving the house and finding the Finger of God. But there's another story. I don't know how true it is, but it was one of the stories that was written down in one of our oldest books." Joshua looks eager for me to continue.

"The story goes like this. In 45 A.D., our founder, David, discovered a piece of blood-stained wood that was said to be a part of the cross that Jesus died on. One day, while he was traveling to Rome, he was attacked by a man named Saul. Saul beat him to death for being a follower of Jesus. It is believed by some that David died that day, however, something happened. He didn't die, in fact, his wounds mysteriously closed and healed. Could it be true or not? Everything is up for interpretation, just like the Bible. People interpret it according to how they see it."

Joshua just nods in agreement. "I see. There are so many secrets in this organization."

"No, my friend, there are not. You just need to see what's in front of you. Then you'll see the truth of it all."

He smiles at first then, as if remembering something, turns thoughtful. "I need to tell you something else. I heard this from the other Captains, I don't know if it's true or not."

"What is it?"

He takes a deep breath. "Whenever Orion kills someone, apparently he mumbles the words 'the weak must die.' The idea of it scares me, to be honest."

"Thank you for telling me. I think this is something we'll need to look at thoroughly."

I watch the sunset from the window before we get to our destination. The helicopter lands in a field about three miles from the capitol. As we exit the plane, I notice a black 2018 Tahoe waiting for us. I get into the passenger seat. Joshua takes the driver's seat and we make our way to a forest just a little bit outside the capitol.

Orion and Luka recently reported activity in this area so we're checking it out. We've been on the road for three hours before we see an old two-story brick house. Even though the red bricks in front looked clean, it's obvious the house is abandoned. After seeing the wood pillars of the overhanging porch, I knew that the materials used to build this house are not even found in this region. They must have been imported meaning whoever owned this home must be wealthy. There are two motorcycles parked in front of it.

We drive around the house a few times to survey it. After the third pass, shots fire off from the top floor window. *So much for monitoring the scene first.*

"Stop the car!" I yell. Joshua slams on the brakes.

We shrug into our STP armor and we hurry to the front door, carrying two semiautomatics between us.

"I'll go in first because I have the Finger of God. You should cover me," I tell Joshua. With my back against the wall, I slowly twist the doorknob, which, to my surprise, is loose. I push the door open. It's extremely dark in the house and a pungent smell of rotten flesh floods my nostrils. I shine my flashlight around the room to find the source of the smell. There are bodies all over the place, blood on every surface, limbs ripped off of bodies, arrows sticking out of walls and corpses.

I pull an arrow out of the closest body. "This looks like one of Luka's arrows." Then, silently, I signal to Joshua that he should take the downstairs and I'll take the upstairs. He nods and I head up the second floor feeling the wood planks creak underneath my feet.

At the top of the stairs, I find a dead body that was shot in the head with an arrow. I step over it and continue advancing down the rest of the hallway until I see a light at the end of it coming from an open room. I approach the door carefully and push it open.

"Drop the weapon," I say sternly with my gun locked and ready.

"What are you doing here, Eden?"

I flash my light at the person inside and it's Luka with his bow dripping blood.

I drop my weapon. "I thought you might have needed backup. I heard Seditio was around the area."

"Planning on showing them the God of Death? Got it," he says with a grin, getting down on his knees to examine one of the bodies.

"What happened here? Where's Orion? Isn't he on this mission with you?"

"We met a very rich family in the capital." Luka picks himself up. "We made friends with them and eventually they let us stay at their house which worked well since the house was located so close to where the Arc of the Covenant had been spotted. So, we've been here a few days laying low until we came out to investigate these ruins nearby. When we got back, all of these men were here." He spits.

"Were they Seditio?"

He shakes his head. "No. They were Djiboutian. I talked to

the leader. What I got from him was these men who attacked us were rogue soldiers from the 2008 Djiboutian-Eritrean border conflict. They hid money in this area during the crisis and decided to come back to get it, saw this nice house, and assumed we took it. The leader kept asking for the money, but before we couldn't talk much, the soldiers started firing shots and went into the house. Orion chased after the rest of them into the forest."

"Why would they come back to this place now?" I ask him. "That conflict happened over fifteen years ago."

"I don't know, Eden. I thought about that too and it makes no sense to me. I feel there's something else to this story. I plan to report all of this back to the House."

We're interrupted by footsteps rushing up the stairs. Luka and I aim towards the door, but it's only Joshua.

"The bottom floor is clear," he announces.

We drop our weapons and sigh in relief.

"Jesus, Eden, didn't you guys bring headsets?" Luka asks. I hit my head with my hand realizing we indeed forgot them in the rush of leaving.

Luka sighs. "That is the most rookie thing you can do, Eden."

"Let's go check up on Orion."

Luka asks Joshua for a brief of the mission as we shuffle down the stairs.

"Here's what we know. Three years ago, we heard that there were sightings of a gold box located in Ethiopia. The first thing we checked was the Ethiopian Orthodox Tewahedo Church who claimed that they possessed the Ark of the Covenant. Further research showed us that they did not have the Ark—at least, how it was described in the Bible. So, while we were here, Orion was able to sneak into the heavily guarded church called Our Lady Mary of Zion."

We step out of the house.

"In the treasury of that church, there was a similar object that we thought might be the Ark, but it turned out to be something called the Axum Tabot. Orion also found a little scroll that must have been hundreds of years old and written in old French. I translated it and found out that the Ark was hidden in some old stone ruins just about three miles from the capitol. This house sits right near the only ruins we could find in this area, so we're assuming that the artifact is located somewhere around here."

It makes more sense to me now. "The mission is more like an investigation of the Ark of the Covenant," I clarify. "The Ark has been lost for centuries. I doubt it's in those ruins. We've known for some time that it might be in Ethiopia but we don't know if it still is."

"That's right," Luka says. "But this wasn't supposed to be a hard mission. It was just supposed to be an investigation of the sighting. I didn't think we'd be fighting people or that I'd be killing someone today."

We walk to the car and I grab my Deathscythe from the trunk. "I was lying about backing you up," I confess to Luka. "I came to monitor Orion. He's been extremely busy with missions and I want to see for myself how my Captain is performing."

Luka frowns. "I've noticed he's been kind of off lately. He's more one-track-minded and doesn't talk as much anymore."

I pass Joshua two more guns. "It seems like Seditio might be here, though. They're probably coming for Orion again."

Luka nods. "That would make sense. Why are they so obsessed with Orion?"

We walk towards the forest with our weapons. "In the Whiteface mission report, Orion stated the leader wanted to recruit him to their organization and that they had been following him for a while. At first, I thought it was because his family had some ties to Seditio. But when I looked into it, it didn't seem to be the case."

Joshua and Luka look confused. "What conclusion did you

come to then, Eden?" Joshua asks.

"I think Whiteface wanted him because they thought Orion was weak. I think they thought they could break him. After all, if he's a member of the House, he at least has some of the skills needed to push Seditio motives.

All of a sudden, Luka interrupts as he motions us into the forest. "Follow me, it's this way."

Joshua continues. "The report also stated that they killed his whole family. I didn't know Seditio would kill innocent people like that."

I move through the brushes. "Seditio is still a mystery to us," I tell them. "We truly don't know their motives at all. Orion stated that they have a new leader and even the Seditio members don't know what she wants."

Joshua stops in his tracks. "Wait the leader of Seditio is a girl?"

No wonder he's still a Captain; he never reads the paperwork. "Yes. It was in the report!"

As we move through the trees, I catch a whiff of something fresh.

"Eden, do you smell that?" Luka asks.

"Yes. I know the smell all too well."

It's the smell of death and we were getting close to it. Either Orion slaughtered the men he was following or they killed him. We're about to find out.

We run into two bodies that are both cut up to pieces. One is missing his head and the other is missing an arm.

"This was done with a sword," Joshua concludes as he inspects the bodies. "I'm pretty sure Orion did this."

"The ruins are right in front," Luka says.

We walk to the edge of the forest. Luka points at something. A soldier is pinned to the wall with a sword in his shoulder. His tormentor is circling him like a hawk. Orion.

"Where is the Ark?" Orion asks.

The soldier is panting and cringing in pain. "I don't know," he manages to say.

Orion pulls out his knife and slices the man's cheek slowly. "I'm not a fucking fool. You're not a rogue Djiboutian soldier. Why did Seditio send you? And where is the fucking Ark?"

Joshua starts to charge towards them, but I grab the back of his jacket.

"I need to see what he does. Right now, he's getting intel. Nothing more," I mutter.

Orion pulls the knife. "You have two choices," he tells the soldier. "Tell me what I what to fucking hear or die a horrible death. Your choice."

The soldier is crying even harder. "She hired us and told us to find you because you have gold with you. We weren't supposed to fight you. She heard about the rumors of the Ark in this area."

Orion looks up at the sky in frustration, then in one swipe, swings down to cut the man's arm, gashing him deeply.

"Then why did you attack us?"
The soldier is barely conscious at this point. "Because we wanted to steal the gold."

Orion punches him in the face to keep him awake. "Who is she? The Seditio leader?" But it's too late. The soldier has bled so much, he's unable to answer. This angers Orion even more. He pulls the blade out of the soldier's shoulder and swings so hard at his head that he cuts it off. After that, he starts stabbing the man over and over until Luka grabs his arm.

It was just like Aiden described.

"That's enough, Orion! He's dead," Luka yells.

I walk up to him solemnly. "What are you doing, Orion? You beat him. You won. You got the information. There's no need to cause more damage."

A look of surprise comes over Orion. "What are you doing

here, Eden?"

"I came here for backup."

"We didn't need backup," he says quietly.

He walks past me, blood running off the blade of his sword. I grab his arm.

"Head back to the Gate," I enunciate.

He jerks his arm away from my grip. "The mission isn't over."

I stare at him coldly, but his eyes are even colder than mine. "I'm your Judge. And you are my Captain. You will do as I say."

Luka interjects. "The mission is over, Orion! We got what we needed. The Ark isn't here. It was a ploy by Seditio."

Finally, Orion nods at Luka and walks back towards the abandoned house.

"Orion needs a purpose," I tell Luka. "Right now, he's lost."

"I don't think that's what it is, Eden," Luka replies. "He already knows what he's looking for."

Chapter 12: Your Own

AFTER A LONG flight back to the Gate, I make my way to my room for some downtime. As soon as I open the door, I hear a voice inside.

"We need to chat, Orion." I turn the light on and find Eden leaning up against the wall with his arms crossed, waiting for me, but we don't talk in my room. He leads me instead to the Gift Room.

"Why did you bring me in here?" I ask.

"We're in here because the Gift Room blocks out sound. This way, no one will be able to hear us." I already know what he's going to say.

"I don't care what you have to say, Eden," I say, shrugging.

He takes a step towards me. "You may not care what I have to say, but you will listen to me, you hear me? I don't care that you're killing people, but I have a problem with how you're destroying the bodies. Once they're dead, there's no need to do anything more."

"It shouldn't be a big deal since I always get the job done."

"I understand what you're going through, Orion." Eden's tone softens, which grates at me more.

"Do you, really?"

"Yes, I do."

"You don't fucking understand anything I'm going through. My fucking family was killed right in front of me. Whiteface didn't kill my family. My curiosity did."

"No, Orion! Whiteface was a murderer. You shouldn't blame yourself. I've experienced loss, too."

"Maybe you're right. Maybe I shouldn't blame myself. I

should blame you. You're the God of Death, right? I should blame you."

"You can't blame me for what another person did. You knew the risk of being a member of the House. You knew your family was coming to Paris. I was the one who told you it wasn't a good idea. It doesn't matter, though, Orion. What happened to your family was no one's fault except Whiteface's. They were victims."

"I don't care anymore. What has happened is already in the past. I'm alone now. The only thing I can focus on is the House, nothing else," I say calmly. "I have work to do."

I walk away from Eden before he can say anything else. I make it to the laboratory which is surrounded by glass mirrors. Glancing inside, I can't help but notice what looks like a piece of skin with what looks like a sliver of wood on it sitting on one of the lab tables. *Is that the Finger of God?*

I look through the glass windows closer to see if anyone is in the room. It's empty, so I walk in and get a closer look. To my surprise, the piece of wood is actually stitched to the skin. *How fascinating.* I've never seen a Finger of God close up before. This is something completely new to me. I reach down to touch it but I'm stopped by someone's voice.

"Hey, you can't touch that!"

I jump, startled by the voice. I had never seen this woman before. "Who are you?" I ask.

She walks up closer to me. "I'm Judge Abigail Ramirez. And you're the new Captain. Captain Orion Bachman. You're Eden's Captain. You shouldn't be in here."

"I didn't know. I've never seen this room before. Sorry."

"Only Judges can know about this room." For someone who's reprimanding me, she has a very gentle tone.

"I haven't seen you on the Gate before. Are you a new Judge?"

She laughs at the question. "I travel around a lot and find

the leads. That's why you never see me. Judges usually don't stay on the Gate, unless you're Eden who's always in the library or drunk."

"Is that Sarah's Finger of God?" I ask her innocently so she doesn't build any more suspicion about me being in there.

"No. This is an experimental Finger of God. It came from Joseph. I'm running tests on it now. We're trying to see if the bacteria in the wood can be mutated so we can create more pieces. We've tried it before, but never been successful."

"Why are you doing that?"

"That is something only Joseph and I know." There's an edge to her voice.

I head to the door to leave. I take one more look on my way out and see her remove the wood and put it in a vial.

Even as I get to my room I can't stop thinking about what Abigail did. I have to go back and look into it later. *Are we missing a Finger of God? Why would we test it if it's been tested before?*

I wait until later to go back when the Gate is quiet. I head to the server room to look at Abigail's file. The coding is extremely easy, and I'm able to get into her file in only a couple of minutes. One of the first things that come up is an email chain between her and Joseph. *Bingo.*

August 23, 2027, 11:00 am

Hey Joseph,
During the Whiteface Mission, Eden reported that Sarah sustained horrible injuries. When I examined the body, it seemed as if the Finger of God was ripped out with a blade. I know that Eden said she was slashed. Do you know if this was recovered?
Thanks,
Abigail

August 23, 2027, 1:00 pm

Abigail,

The hideout was examined, but the Finger of God wasn't recovered. We need to keep this between us. This could have major implications on the integrity of the House of David. I pray that the Finger of God wasn't destroyed once it was removed from the body. I would like for you to test my Finger of God and see if it could be destroyed once removed. If not, then we need to be on the lookout for anyone rising from the dead.

Thanks,
Joseph

August 25, 2027, 3:00 pm

Joseph,

We can keep this secret. I will go back to the site with my Captain to investigate further. If we hear anything about people healing from injuries, we will assume it's been stolen and we'll need to restrain those suspects immediately.

Thanks,
Abigail

August 28, 2027, 1:30 pm

Abigail,
    We will only inform the Judges if we begin
hearing stories about people recovering from near-
death experiences. Until then, investigate and
perform the research on mine. I don't want to make
our Captains concerned either.
    Blessings.
    Joseph

So, Sarah's Finger of God is missing? Interesting. Maybe they're planning a mission to search for it. It sounds like Joseph didn't even tell Eden about this. He probably doesn't want to cause panic, which is a good idea. *Who has the Finger of God? Does Seditio have it? How did it get stolen?* This could be a fun mission if it turns out to be a case that we investigate further.

***

Two days pass and the tension between Eden and me continues to build. He has been keeping an eye on me more lately and I'm not sure how I feel about it. He doesn't trust me at all, but I understand why because I don't entirely trust myself either.

It's midafternoon when I go to the shooting range on the Gate to get a few rounds of practice in when I hear Joseph's voice.

"Orion, I have a mission for you. Meet me at the War Prep Room at 0800 tomorrow," he says and continues walking past me.

"Yes, sir." Part of me is extremely excited, but the other part wants to cry. Maybe Eden is right. Maybe I need some time to heal. Regardless, I need to redirect this pain to my work. After getting my shots in at the shooting range, I see Joshua leaving the weapons room.

"Hey, O. Want to grab some dinner? It's been a while."

I always appreciate his enthusiasm, but I don't have time

for dinner at all. I don't stop and just shake my head because I don't want to get into a long conversation about it. I need to focus on getting ready for tomorrow. Missions are what I live for now.

I wake up at 6:00 am to get a morning jog in and put in some time in the weight room. I arrive at the control room an hour and a half later with Joshua, Judge Abigail Ramirez, and Joseph. We are just about to start our mission brief when we hear footsteps running down the hallway.

"Sorry, I'm late," Eden says, breathing heavily as he sits down next to me at the conference table. "Luka kept me up drinking last night and, well, never mind . . . Let's get started."

Joseph sighs and Abigail giggles. I can smell the alcohol on Eden. He also smells like he hasn't showered in a few days.

"Since everyone is here, let's begin." Joseph stands up and points at one of the computer screens on the wall. "Judge Eden Dowler, Judge Abigail Ramirez, Captain Joshua Honore, and Captain Orion Bachman are assigned to this mission. The name of this mission is 'Mission: Blood' and this mission encompasses a recurring issue. I want to note, at this point, that in the House of David, recurring problems are not something we deal with often. In the past twenty years, we have only dealt with two other recurring issues. Captains, Judges, this is an important one. You four will be sent to Dublin, California." A topographic map of the city appears on the server screens.

"That is where I went on my first mission," Eden says, putting his hands on the table. "So, you guys finally saw the connection between the recent deaths in Dublin and France?"

Joseph nods. "At first I thought it was a coincidence. But later I found a police report that stated that the Virgin Mary had been seen by five people. The cop investigating these people wanted them tested for drugs. When they did, the hospital found an unknown bacteria in all five of these people's blood."

"What happened on your first mission, Eden?" I ask.

"We were investigating someone who claimed they had the blood of Mary in a tube. This man claimed that Mary gave him the vial herself and that he needed to cleanse the world with it. He killed his whole family and the group that had started following him. On the mission, we killed him and took the vial for more testing. It's a bacteria that kills people from the inside out. We have kept a close eye on this strand of bacteria ever since. Traces of the same bacteria were found on the Chains of Peter in your house, Orion."

"The bacteria was in my house?" I didn't even know that the Chains of Peter were even there. I just knew my Dad had an old box out in that shed that hadn't been touched since he died.

Joseph turns another screen on behind him to show a picture of the Chains of Peter. "I think that the box in Orion's house was placed there to make us believe that his family was involved in Seditio. Regardless, we have seen this bacteria in three places now: a crime scene in France years prior, the vial in Dublin and, most recently, the Chains of Peter in Orion's house. The goal of this mission is to contain the bacteria for good. It's way too dangerous to have it floating around."

The screen behind Joseph changes back to the map of Dublin, California. He grabs a pointer off the table and points at a spot slightly to the left of the center. "I chose you four for multiple reasons. First and foremost, Eden has experience with the area and the mission. The rest of you are some of our most ruthless, so it will be less alarming for you if Seditio is there looking for the same bacteria. If this is a trap and you run into Seditio, I'm confident this group of four will be our best warriors. Show no mercy!" We all nod and Joseph continues with instructions.

"You will leave by helicopter at 8:00 am tomorrow and we will land twenty miles south of Dublin. From there you'll work your way to the house. Your agenda is to go in, sweep the area, find the source of the bacteria, and bring back whoever is behind this. Eden and Abigail will survey the property from a distance at noon and Joshua and Orion will hit the house later at night. We will follow this plan unless we need to engage sooner. Now go prepare for the task at hand. Your briefcases will be placed at your door before the mission. Be up at 7:00 am. You're dismissed."

I head towards the door, but as I'm about to leave I notice Eden staying behind to talk to Joseph. He's making an unusual face, almost like he's nervous. *Is he scared of me being on this mission? He shouldn't be.*

As I walk to my room, I run through the details of this mission in my head, I can't help but think about the missing Finger of God. I wonder where it could have gone until it was almost morning and I grab my briefcase to get ready. Inside, there is the usual mission attire: My sword, Michael the Archangel, is clean and propped up against the wall next to the briefcase. I quickly put the armor on, grab my sword, and head toward the deck.

Outside, the mission members congregate with their weapons before boarding the helicopter. This is my first mission with Abigail. Normally she doesn't bring a weapon since she only does intel on missions. But this mission is different. Her tool is a six-foot-tall staff made of Damascus steel. I heard from Joshua that she's amazing in long-range combat using the staff. Inside the helicopter, Eden sits next to Abigail, and Joshua is next to me. The flight only takes three hours and four motorcycles are waiting for us at the local airport. We ride the motorcycles from the airport to the hotel, which is surprisingly rundown.

"Eden, this place is a shithole," Joshua says.

"Indeed. This, Joshua, is the first hotel I ever stayed at. This shithole is where Joseph and I stayed at on our mission," Eden says with a nostalgic smile. "It will always hold a part of me. Think of it this way, I'm sharing a piece of me with you by letting you see this place." Then, he gets everybody's attention. "Alright! We don't need to survey the area, I did the research beforehand.

I've narrowed down places to investigate. If you all check your phones you'll see two different locations. Orion, Joshua, and I will go to the first location which I'm assuming will be the trickiest. Abigail, you'll go to the second one listed. It requires more investigation."

"Do you think you guys will need help?" Abigail asks.

"No, we should be fine," Eden responds. "I realize that both Orion and Joshua don't have a Finger of God, but I'm more comfortable with them in combat. We've done this together before. Since you have a Finger of God, it would be optimal if you go to the other location alone. If anyone surprises you there, you have that to protect you." Abigail gives Eden a thumbs up and we head to our motorcycles. We put our headsets on and hop on our bikes until we get to the neighborhood as planned. The location Eden had pinpointed is a ranch-style home with a very open and empty yard. We stop a few houses before the targeted one to avoid being seen.

"This is the place where it all began for me. Interesting that it's the place where the bacteria is located. Almost funny to be back here," Eden says with a hint of sadness in his voice. Then he gives out instructions. "All right, Orion, when we get in, you take the upstairs. Check it and make sure there isn't anyone in there. I'm pretty positive that Seditio is behind this, so your instructions are to wound and not kill. We need to use them for information. Joshua, you clear out the downstairs of the house. I will handle the back and front yard and stay outside in case any reinforcements come. I'm pretty sure they will."

"Let the games begin," Joshua mutters as we divide into our assigned tasks.

We head down the street towards the right of the house and make our way around the back. Sure enough, ten men appear in front of it. They instantly begin to fire at us. Eden jumps in front and uses his body as a shield; the shots are not penetrating his STP

236

armor. He takes out three of the guards right away. With incredible speed, he disarms them by slicing through their arms. Then he shoots the other two; one in the leg and the other in his lower abdomen.

Running alongside Eden, I move forward to handle the other five guards. Within a few minutes, I shoot two in the head and cut another's head off. For the last one, I slice at his ankle before slitting his neck. Then I turn to Eden, who is pointing to the back of the yard indicating that he's going back there. I wave Joshua to come with me and we hear guns fire and men screaming.

As I approach the side door, I try to take a quick look inside but the window has blinds covering it so I make my way to the other window and do the same. Inside, there are four men. I grab a smoke grenade from my belt holster and throw it crashing through the window. I signal over to Joshua and, within seconds, he kicks down the door and fires to the left. I enter after him and see a guard running towards me with a knife. I grab his arm and slice at his throat with my sword.

Once he's down, I press down on my earpiece and say, "I'm heading upstairs." As I make my way up, I move as carefully as I can, making sure I don't make a sound. There's a noise from a room two doors down from the right. I raise my gun before proceeding forward.

I approach the door and I open it to find Mary standing in the middle of the room.

"Did they kidnap you?" I ask, surprised to see her here. But she twirls around in a circle and the black and yellow dress she's wearing flutters.

"Do I look like I've been kidnapped?" she replies, giggling and still twirling.

"Then what are you doing here?"

She takes a step towards me and traces her fingers across my cheek. "I'm here to save you," she whispers.

I lower my head into her hand. "Save me from what?"

"From yourself," she says as she backs away.

"Myself? What do you mean, Mary? Why are you here? What's going on?" I can hear the fight raging on downstairs.

"You don't have to worry. We have enough men to keep the Judges entertained for a while so we can talk," she says calmly.

I look around the room and see pictures all over the walls of people with an "X" brushed over their faces. Some of them are mother, grandpa, Joseph, Jacob, and Matthew. Others are of an old woman, a young man, and an entire family.

"Mary, tell me. What's going on?"

She rolls her eyes and sighs. "Well, here's the thing, Orion." She pauses for a moment. "I'm the leader of Seditio."

I drop to my knees. The leader of Seditio murdered my family.

"Mary," I spoke slowly. "Did you kill my family and friends?"

She looks at me with unremorseful eyes. "No, Orion. I killed liars, fakes, and evil people."

I can't help it. Tears start to come and once they do, they don't stop. "Then why my family?"

She tilts her head to the side. "Here's the thing, Orion. Your so-called 'family' didn't love you. Matthew sold you out for money, and the other two just hung out with you because they knew you would help them."

"But my mom and grandpa! What about Rebecca? Did she have to die?"

Mary raises her eyebrows. "Who's Rebecca? Oh, yeah, the cashier girl. Caldwell was only supposed to kill Matthew, Jacob, and Joseph. The others were not supposed to get involved. But Whiteface paid his price in the end, you know this. Who do you think freed you back in Whiteface's chamber? I did."

Shaking my head, I start to question everything I thought

was right.

"Oh, Lord!" Mary has no emotion in her voice. *Who is this person?* "You're doing the Orion thing again, overthinking things like you always do. I've known you for years. All I ever tried to do was push you in the right direction. I didn't know that that Judge was going to come looking for the Chains of Peter in Mobile. I didn't poison anyone in Mobile. I liked the quiet time I was having there. You did make things fun, though." She smiles.

"I don't even know who you are."

She walks closer to me with her lips pushed together. "You knew who I was the whole time, baby. You accepted me. I know that you're smarter than this, Orion. Me, being in Paris the same time you were? Running in the middle of the night when the Judge was there? I know Whiteface told you the leader was a girl. I was even there when your parents died, remember?"

"No, you weren't!" I start to think back to that day. Then I remember the girl's strawberry blonde hair back in the chamber. *Why would he bring a random innocent girl if he was trying to teach me a lesson? If he had my whole family then he would've had Mary too.*

"I can tell by the look on your face that you finally fucking realized it. That dumbass Whiteface always hated me as a leader, but he didn't know you. He thought you were like your selfish friends and would kill me instantly, but you did what you always do." She pauses and looks out the window. "I didn't really like that he tried to kill me, though so, you know, he had to die."

Everything is clear to me now. "Why did you put the Chains of Peter in my shed?"

She smiles. "I was curious to see if he would want to recruit you. I wanted to see how this would play out. Whatever you went through has made you into this killing machine. It's pretty hot, actually."

I throw up my arms in frustration. "You don't know who

239

the hell I am! This isn't me!"

Mary laughs. "Stop hiding behind that fucking mask, Orion. This is who you are. This is what you wanted to be, anyway. That's why you went with Eden. You didn't have to. It was your choice. Remember?"

"No. No! NO!" I shake my head.

She comes up to me, then in a quiet voice, says, "Yes. Yes. Yes. You hated that fucking life. You were hiding behind a mask, just like me. And you know what? I only helped you break free from it. I know who I am, Orion. You always saw me for who I was. I never needed to wear a mask for you. I wore one for Eden, but he could see it was a mask. But never for you."

"Then what do you want, Mary?" I wipe tears from my eyes. She walks to the wall beside her and talks as she studies the pictures.

"I want you to see things as I see them. I've been bored lately. Will you have fun with me? We're the only family we have, right? I don't have anyone. They're all dead, the same as you." She reaches her hand out to me. "You believe in family. I'm your family. Come with me, Orion. Join me."

She was right about a few things. Back in Mobile, I was just going with the flow. I went with Eden because I wanted to get away from that life. I wanted to unmask myself.

Suddenly, the door creaks open. Joshua peeks in. "Orion, is the room clear?" He pushes the door even further and sees Mary. "Is she a hostage?"

I hesitate. "Yes."

He looks skeptical. He walks up to Mary and just like I did, looks around to see the various pictures on the wall. Mary and I stand in silence.

"Wait," Joshua says. "Didn't they say the leader of Seditio was a girl? Orion, why are there so many men here if there's only one hostage?"

Then he turns to Mary with the coldest stare. "She is the leader, Orion."

I put my hand up in between them. "Stop, please, Joshua, stop."

I slice his throat before he can reach for the button on his earpiece. His body falls to the ground as he clutches his throat, choking on blood and gasping for air as he tries to stay alive.

"See! You protected me! You do care!" Mary squeals.

I step away from Joshua's body but can't look away from what I had done. "No, it's not like that. I don't know. Joshua, I'm sorry! No! No!" I fall to my knees and collapse over his body.

"Orion, it's okay. Come with me." Mary grabs my arm, but I pull away.

"No. I must pay for what I've done. I must meet Death," I say.

"You keep surprising me every day, Orion. You can meet Death, but I'll be waiting at Hell's door for you."

"I don't know about that, Mary. Go! You're right, I can't forgive you for what you've done to my family. But you are my family. So instead of killing you, this is my gift to you. Leave now."

She folds her arms. "I'll leave, but let's make this a game. If you beat Death, then you get me. If you lose to Death, though, you'll get to see your family again." Before I can respond, she pulls the yellow wallpaper down to reveal another door. "I'll see you soon, O." She steps through the door. "We aren't done playing."

She closes the door and all I can think about is how much my life has changed. How has my life come to this? Maybe she's right, this is who I am. I'm not a hero. In reality, I spent too much of my life being the hero, but this journey would allow me to be the villain of my story.

"Where is everyone? Over," Eden says in the earpiece.

"Come upstairs. Over," I respond. I drop my guns. I only have my sword in my hand. *To be honest, this is what I wanted since I met Eden. I told him before that life was about being the better man, and he said that giving that man death was being the better man. If I kill Death, would I be the better man?*

Eden walks through the door. "Orion, Rebecca found the vial with the bacteria at her location. I don't know why there were so many men here. It's over, though." Then he glances down to see Joshua's lifeless body on the ground.

"Did you do this, Orion?"

Motionless, I reply, "Yes."

"Why?"

I don't have any more energy in me. "I don't know."

He tightens his grip on his scythe. "You don't know? You killed a comrade and you don't know? He was family."

"But he isn't my family."

"I'm taking you in."

I back away. "No. I must pay for what I've done. I want my punishment now. Me versus you."

"No," he says angrily. "There's no you versus me. Let's go, Orion. This isn't a game."

"Eden, either you fight me or you're going to die. Choose."

"If you kill me you won't escape."

"Yeah, I know, but I would have beat Death." I lunge with my sword and dodge to the left. Then I swing at him and he blocks me with his scythe.

"Stop, Orion! There's no need for us to fight," he yells.

I kick him in the chest. I have no more words for him. I've made up my mind that I'll fight. He falls back and lands on his ass.

"You've gotten better," says Eden, breathing heavily.

I swing downward; he tries to block the blade but it swipes his right leg and he grunts in pain. Then I slice across his arm, piercing his armor. He manages to push me and I fall back. I know

242

I can beat him. I've been on so many missions that my fighting style has improved. I've watched hours of combat film and trained with everyone at the Gate.

He stands up and looks at the blood flowing from his arm. "If it's the God of Death you want, Orion, then the God of Death I shall be."

We both charge with our blades clashing. He headbutts me and I fly back. I catch myself on the wall and swing forward at him. He ducks under my blade and slashes me across the chest, piercing my STP armor. I fall to my knees, gazing down at the wound. It's bigger than I expect.

"I'm sorry I failed you," he says as he walks up to me. "I ruined your life, my friend."

I crack a smile at him. "You must kill to live, remember?" My vision starts to darken. A calming feeling takes over and all I can think about is that I'll finally get to see my family again. I see it now. I see what all of those men who have died fighting Eden see. It is a presence. And it is a soothing feeling. I fall deeper into sleep. Slowly, as I slide onto my side, I hear Eden's voice one last time. "Your . . ."

Chapter 13: Truth

EVERYONE WANTS to be the hero of their own story, but the reality is that in every story there are villains too. My whole life I've felt like I've had an ordinary upbringing, well, ordinary to me, at least. I was the oldest child. My father had two jobs and my mother was extremely religious. We lived in France for most of my life because of my family's ancestry. I was born on the thirteenth of December and have always been told about the unluckiness of that day and the unluckiness of the number thirteen. As I grew older, I realized my birthday couldn't suit my true self more. People fear it, just like they fear me.

My father always told me that our family was very important, and we grew up hearing lots of stories about our ancestors. I'm the descendant of the famous conquistador Panfilo de Narvaez. During his travels through the Gulf of Mexico, there was an Israeli stowaway. Instead of killing the man Panfilo listened to the man's stories. The man told tales about artifacts and religious people. He believed that people could use them to help society, but the problem was that the people he worked for only wanted to keep them hidden away from the world. He couldn't allow that.

One day, he took an artifact from the vault in Israel and traveled up to Spain with it. He wanted to escape to the new world. The entire time, Panfilo thought that this man was making up nonsense stories until one day, the stowaway showed Panfilo the artifact. The stowaway called the artifact the Chains of Peter and stated that they have the power to kill sinners.

According to the story our father told us, the man kept saying things like he was a sinner and that the House would find him. He told Panfilo, "No, no, no. I don't have much time. I don't have my Finger of God anymore. They took it out of me," and lifted his shirt to reveal a huge chunk of flesh missing from the side of his body. The gash looked like it had been burned to keep the bleeding in.

"I will show you the Chains, but you have to believe that they work first," he told Panfilo. "Promise me you'll hide the Chains and keep them hidden from the world," the man said panting in pain.

"You show me the power and I will decide what I will do," Panfilo told him. According to history, Panfilo was a stubborn man, but a religious one too. He needed proof to believe in the artifact's power. It's amazing the power that belief has on the minds of the weak. The story goes that, the stowaway cut his wrists and put the Chains of Peter on himself. Two hours later, he was bleeding out of his mouth, ears, and eyes.

Panfilo fell to his knees at this sight and started praying to God. He was so in shock at what he witnessed that he couldn't do anything but cry. That day, he decided that he wanted the world to see the power of these artifacts. Panfilo would later end up dying by drowning in the Gulf of Mexico, but his children would keep his dream alive and continue to preserve the Chains of Peter and collect the rest of the artifacts.

A century later, his descendants founded a group called Seditio, which in Latin means rebellion. Seditio's goals are to follow Panfilo's footsteps and collect artifacts and rebel against the Judges. But because the organization was so disorganized, they've always been unsuccessful.

Eventually, the Chains of Peter were put in our possession, and my father became the new leader of Seditio. While he made it very structured, he was weak. To society, he was a good father, but he wasn't good for me. I used to kill the little birds that would fly into our yard. Seeing them covered in blood was so pretty to me.

Once I was done playing I would put them in a box and hide it under my bed. One day when I came home from school, my dad was waiting in the living room for me with the box of dead birds. He screamed at me and called me a heathen. He said I was going to hell for what I had done, and that I needed to pray to the Lord for forgiveness. He said that I needed to act like a good girl.

From that day on, I did what I was told. I acted like a "good girl." I wore pretty dresses, I played with dolls, and I had tea parties until one day, he brought me to a Seditio meeting.

Listening to them talk disgusted me. They didn't fear my father. He was too stuck in the old ages and I could barely handle it. After the meeting, we went to see a movie and, in the movie, someone died a brutal death. It was beautiful: the pain, the suffering, the cries for help, the praying for God, the blood, and more of the blood. It just warmed my heart.

Even in my early years, my dad saw my passion for blood and kept me away from the movie theater and told me to be a good girl. "Go pray and repeat," he would tell me. I realized then that my dad was not going to accept me for who I was. I would be wearing a fucking mask all my life.

I knew that he had to die. They all had to die. So, I killed them. I made it seem like someone broke into our house and killed them so that I wouldn't be blamed. When they were dead I called my father's friend, Don, from Seditio. He came and picked me up that night along with the Chains of Peter. He assumed if the cops where there with me, then I would be taken and the Chains of Peter would be taken. That could not happen.

He took me with him and inducted me into the organization at the age of thirteen. I learned all there was to know about Seditio and quite a bit about the House of David. To be honest, I thought all of it was stupid. Organizations, religions, and governments—they're all stupid. They make these rules that keep us from becoming what we truly are—animals.

Even with Don, I couldn't be myself. He saw me as this sweet, determined girl that wanted to get revenge on her family, but he was so wrong. I couldn't care less about my family. I just wanted to live my life the way I wanted to live it. Don always cared about me, but the fact that he couldn't see me for who I truly was bothered me. Eventually, I became sick of my life in France so I made plans to move in with my grandmother in Mobile, Alabama.

Before I left France, though, I decided that I needed to experience the true power of the artifacts and test out the Chains of Peter. Don kept them in a safe in his study so it wasn't hard for me to get the codes. I was very well-developed for my age, so all I had to do was flirt with him a little, rub his leg, and he was mine for the taking. He told me the codes and I got my first taste of an older man, all in one day.

As soon as I had the codes, I took the Chains, put them on his wrist and cut his wrists to see what would happen. Nothing happened for a few hours besides him screaming and calling me a psycho cunt and to let him go. After about two hours of that, something magnificent transpired. Blood started oozing out of his eyes, ears, and nose. It was beautiful.

He was screaming in pain and kept saying that he wanted to live. He even asked God to save him. I told him there was no God there for him before I grabbed a butcher's knife from the kitchen and skipped back to his room singing "Hush Little Baby."

I could hardly contain my bloodlust. Then I stabbed him over and over again until I was covered in his blood. It smelled so nice, like freshly picked roses. I even rubbed it into my skin like lotion before I showered and put a change of clothes on.

Next, I met with a few members of Seditio to discuss how I should take over as leader. I was sixteen and still living in Europe, so we decided to meet in Rome. I arrived two days later to meet with four of the most powerful Seditio directors: Roberto Cruz, 36, from Cuba, Erwin Rivera, 32, from Guatemala, Heath Coker, 56, an older white American man, and Whiteface, age unknown, from Germany.

We discussed the death of Don and why I should be a leader. Whiteface wasn't too fond of the idea of me taking over. He believed he was stronger willed than me. He thought I was too young, immature, and inexperienced to lead. He argued and fought with the other members but due to my lineage, everyone agreed that I should take over, even though, I believe that Whiteface was too incompetent and would probably betray me. Everyone believed that he was dedicated to the organization. He also emphasized that he just wanted what's best for Seditio.

I saw through him, though. He was a coward at heart. He was violent and did brutal things to people to make himself feel strong, but this all stemmed from his insecurity because deep down, he was weak and pathetic. To prove myself a worthy leader I told them about my plan to bring awareness to the divinity of God. The plan was to poison people at a festival and we would do this with the Chains of Peter. I'd give them the blood from Don by spiking people's drinks, telling them that it's the blood of Mary and that those who drink it will be saved, and those who don't will die horrible unholy deaths.

The plan was approved, of course, and what made it easy was the first man I convinced to take the blood, Marco, was heavily taking drugs at the time. He was seeing all kinds of visions, which made it easier to approach him with this plan. All I did was tell him I was Mary and that I chose him to give my blood to the holy ones, and that those who took my blood will be saved.

Little did he know that if anyone tasted just a little of the poisoned blood, they would die most horrifically. He took the vial without any protest, and my plans went in motion easily.

A month later I traveled to Dublin, California to see where he lived. I monitored him and saw that he had gained many followers too, just like Seditio wanted. One of his followers even told me that he was having visions of poisoning people with the vials of blood at Coachella.

I alerted the caudillo and they were very pleased with what was happening. Because of my plan, more people were going to be aware of the power of God. Caudillo is Spanish for a team leader. To become a caudillo, a member has to have been with Seditio for at least five years, has killed a Captain in the House of David, and has contributed to the success of the organization. There had been only six who had gotten to the status of caudillo.

All was going well until two days later when the Judges took our main house down and killed Marco. I didn't care about Marco dying, but the caudillos were very upset. I assured them that everything was going to be fine. Eventually, they realized that this was the closest Seditio has been to bringing awareness of God's miracles to the public. All because of my brilliant idea. That was when they made me the leader. They claimed much of it had to do with my father, my lineage, and family connection to Panfilo. But I knew I was better than them.

As the newly appointed Seditio leader, I wanted to lie low at first so I decided it was a good time to finally make the move to my grandmother's house in Mobile, Alabama. It had been two weeks since the Judges took down Marco and I was walking down the street of my grandmother's neighborhood. I was in my world, reminiscing about my life when a boy riding a bike approached me who would change my life forever. He had blond hair with a bowl cut and caught right up to me.

He came up to me all willy-nilly and introduced himself as Orion. He gave off this happy-go-lucky vibe and I kind of hated it. It was disgusting. He kept walking with me though then kept talking to me. I wanted him to go away but I indulged him. He asked me where I was from and I told him California. He asked me about my name but I didn't want people to know my last name so I told him my name was Mary Scotland. I had to lie about my last name because if he was a smart kid he might look up my real last name, Denau, and find out that I should be dead.

We walked down the street together after that. I just remembered him looking at me with this creepy ass smile. His voice was charming but there was something there. I could hear a bit of fakeness in him. From my experience, people with the kind of smile he had kept a lot of secrets. He seemed like he was hiding his true self. Something we had in common. I thought I was alone this whole time.

He told me about his religious upbringing and his family. However, when talking about them he kept looking down and his eyes relaxed, as though he was ashamed of them. But when I asked about it he would put up that hideous fake smile. I could see right through him because I was him once. I hid who I truly was just to make people think that everything was all right when it wasn't.

He continued to walk with me for a while but then I wanted to be alone. We said goodbye. I finally felt like I met someone like me. I wanted to get to know him more.

Years went by and I continued to monitor Orion. I studied him and I learned all that I could about him. I hated his friends. They were liars, users, and thieves. They used him because he was smart, popular, and rich. Orion saw it too, but he never acted on it. I truly wanted them to just die and rot in the ground.

I hated his family the most, though. His family was full of uppity, self-righteous assholes that would also never accept who their son was. He didn't need them in his life. They were just holding him back from who he truly could become. He was brilliant, athletic, and ambitious but his family always kept him from reaching his full potential.

Besides keeping an eye on Orion, I worked at a wine bar to keep up with the image of a normal hardworking girl. I still did Seditio missions on the side, but I made our overall objective to find these artifacts. If the Chains of Peter had bacteria in them that could kill people, then maybe the other artifacts had the same power. I didn't give two shits about Seditio's mission, but as the leader, I needed to make them believe I did. The lies I told them would keep Seditio going. It's also so much fun using people.

I knew the only way to get Orion to join me was to break him, so I plotted his whole tragic story. In truth, I had been bored for so long that this allowed me to finally have a little fun too. I brought more Seditio members to Mobile by telling them that I lost the Chains of Peter and that we needed to find them before the Judges do. That got the attention of the House and I knew they would want to get the Chains.

The Judge came into the bar, met Orion, and saw what I figured he would see in Orion—that he's something more than a simple kid from Mobile. I arranged for some Seditio members to attack the Judge outside the bar and we uploaded false files about Orion's family being related to Panfilo.

Anyway, after the Judge killed the Seditio member, I knew that he would be in contact with Orion. I continued to keep tabs on Orion from a distance and eventually, I saw him and the Judge talk at the Bachman family bakery. Weeks went by with the slow monitoring, and eventually, I had to explain what I was doing to the Caudillos.

After killing all of the men during his time in Mobile, that Judge was on standstill to avoid suspicion, which wasn't unusual. I knew I had to move, though, so I placed the Chains of Peter in an old box in Orion's garage. I sent Seditio men to kill the Helton family, knowing that this would draw attention to the Judge and he would end up at Orion's house to get the Chains.

Finally, it was Orion's graduation and, for a second, I thought my months of monitoring this mission had failed, but sure enough, the Judge came and told Orion's family that he was going to take Orion to join the House of David.

The day after Orion left for the House of David, though, my grandmother died. I didn't know how she died, but when I went back to the house her lifeless body was on the floor. It looked kind of beautiful, actually. She was truly dead, yet she finally glowed.

I was going to have to make Orion suffer true pain which would allow me to get rid of his fucking waste of space family too. Their presence in this world just annoyed me to no fucking end. So, I sent Seditio men to Paris to look for a sword at the Notre Dame Cathedral. I knew they'd never find this sword, but since I wanted to make sure their top Judges came, I sent Whiteface.

As usual, Whiteface was reluctant to go because he was involved in other missions. I convinced him when I told him that the mission would allow him to meet the new candidate and give him a nice Seditio greeting. He accepted on the terms that he gets to test him on his agenda.

Whiteface went to Paris ready to make his presence known. I knew everything was going according to plan when one day I got a call from Orion saying he was about to leave for a mission in Paris. So, I planned a family trip with all his friends and family.

We arrived in Paris and got to the hotel. I wanted to let the House know that Seditio was there, so I told Whiteface where we were and to first kidnap Joseph, Orion's jackass friend, and make an example of him. I wanted Whiteface to shoot him in the head and hang his body up high so the Judges could see, and he did exactly as he was told.

Orion came over later. I didn't know what it was, but I got so turned on by the thought of that asshole Joseph dying that I wanted to have sex with Orion. I didn't think he would want to but to my surprise, he needed a distraction, I guess.

After Orion drifted off to sleep that night, I left the room to call Whiteface and have him pick up the rest of Orion's family. I also told him to do what he wanted with them, but at the end of the day, they must die. He chuckled on the phone and told me he would need my assistance, so I made my way there.

Whiteface had two hideouts: one was the decoy and the other was his real house of horror. Whiteface had captured a few innocent people and put them in the decoy house so that it looked like they had weapons. I waited at the house of horror until Whiteface picked up Orion. He arrived at the house injured so our doctor, Jo Bernad, stitched up his wounds so he was in good shape when Whiteface started testing him.

Days later, I got word that the Judges were heading to the decoy house with French troops. I rallied up a few Seditio members and we ambushed and defeated the French troops. We stole their uniforms afterwards and pretended we were them.

Why do people need a reason to do things? Why can we just do things just because we like to do them? Society gives this predetermined ideology of what good and evil are. But how do we know that society is right about good and evil? What is good for you might not be good for me. What's evil for me, might not be evil for you. How do we know? The answer is we don't. You might see me as a villain, an evil girl. But maybe it's you that's evil.

When that Sarah Judge didn't make the choice I wanted, I told my guy to kill her. And he did.

Whiteface asked for my help, so I headed to the house of horrors. He put a bag over my head and placed me next to Orion's family. Then he gave Orion the choice to kill me or his family. What pissed me off most was that he told Orion I was a horrible person. Orion wasn't going to decide to kill and Whiteface knew he couldn't kill me, so he killed Orion's family.

This broke Orion, and he faded. Then that sick Whiteface tried to have sex with me.

"You like this gory shit don't you, Mother Mary," I remember him saying as he pushed me down and got on top of me. He took the bag off my head and I stared deep into his eyes.

"If you continue to touch me, I will assume you're ready for the worst death imaginable."

He let me go and told me he was just playing. I left the room, but I knew that Judge would be back for Orion soon. I came back to the room a while later after Whiteface had gone to let Orion loose. Afterwards, I drove a mile or two away from the site and found a spot to hide. Using my night vision binoculars, I watched that Judge massacre Whiteface and his members. All I could do was laugh because it was such a pretty sight. I fucking hated him, so getting rid of him and his flunkies was wonderful. I called the Caudillos right away and told them that Whiteface went rogue and strayed away from the original plan, so we decided to get rid of him.

From there, I drove to the decoy location. Seeing all the carnage where that stupid girl Judge died made me feel fantastic. It was like seeing beautiful roses everywhere. It was so delightful that I took my time enjoying the scene. Eventually, I noticed a piece of skin on the ground. When I looked at it closer, I realized that there was a piece of wood attached to a chunk of skin. It was stitched into it. I took it with me.

After Whiteface died, we waited two days before me and the Caudillos discussed what to do next. Only the Caudillos had a central place where they meet members and talk. I headed to Erwin's central location called the Lion's Den in Calhoun, Georgia, where he kept data about the House of David. There I researched this piece of wood. I discovered that their founder gave it to his Judges because this particular wood allowed them to recover from serious injuries. This was a game-changer. I could use this piece of wood to keep my game going.

Over the next few months, my Caudillos updated me more on Orion's progress. I got word that Orion was doing a lot more than just killing his victims; he was torturing them. The mask had finally been broken.

I had one final plan to that would get O to join me. The plan was fairly straightforward. I sent hundreds of lower-tier Seditio members to Dublin where I first distributed the vial of poisoned blood. The Caudillos were skeptical of how many Seditio members I was using for this mission, but I assured them that this mission would bring a new Caudillo.

The day came and the plan was set. I arrived at Marco's house where it all started. I thought it would be a fitting location since this was one of the first places where I murdered forty people. To help cover my identity, though, I put another vial of Don's blood in a different location with fewer men.

I had a large group of our men guarding us. I needed a large amount so that I'd have enough time to talk to Orion. I told Orion I was the leader of Seditio and that everything that happened to him was because of me. I confessed that I wanted him to break the mask he's been wearing for him to become a better man and not be what society wants. He was hesitant but I knew he still had feelings for me when he killed his comrade to protect me. He couldn't fully forgive himself for doing that, though, and his pride took over him. He wanted to see who was better, him or Death, and I encouraged him. I made a game out of it. When I walked into the other room, Death struck him down. I walked up to Orion's body quickly after; he was still breathing, but barely.

In life, we must find our truth. Orion still needed to figure his out and I wanted to help him. Also, I wasn't ready to stop having fun. "I'm not done with you yet," I had told Orion.

I snuck downstairs and saw Death sitting on the porch, crying. There were so many dead bodies on the ground. So much blood. It looked so beautiful. It was amazing. It made me feel alive.

I hid in the kitchen under a dead body for a while. At this point, there were cleaning men taking out the bodies. One of them came into the kitchen, and I tripped him. When he fell, I stabbed

255

him in the eye while covering his mouth. I dragged his body into the closet so that I could put his outfit on and his mask to cover my face. Disguised, I had one of the other masked men help me and we put Orion in a black body bag and carried him out.

On my way out, I noticed that Death was still on the porch, but he wasn't crying anymore. Instead, he was looking into the distance, his face devoid of any emotion. Once Orion was inside the van, we all got in and drove off a couple of miles away.

"Wow, that was a massacre! Can't believe two Captains died," the other man said as he wiped his brow after taking off his mask.

I took my mask off, too. "Make that three."

He gave me a puzzled look. I grabbed the gun and shot him in the head. Then I fixed my eyes on the body bag that carried Orion.

"Don't worry, Orion."

I stopped the car, took out the Finger of God from my pocket, shoved it into his wound, and resumed driving.

***

A week passed since that day and I was back in Mobile. According to what I've read, the Finger of God only healed the living, but nobody knew if it would work on a half-dead body. I've been checking up on Orion regularly; he's still barely alive. I had put him in the storage room of the wine bar. I scheduled myself to work the whole week, which worked well because the rest of the owners were in South Africa for three months.

One day in the middle of my shift, a familiar face came into the bar. It was that Judge Aiden kid from the House. I welcomed him with a smile.

He ambled up to the bar with that same dull look he always had. "Are you Mary? Do you know Orion?"

"Yes, I'm Mary and yes, I do know him. Why do you ask?" I hoped I looked curious enough that he wouldn't suspect anything.

"Well, I'm sorry to tell you this, but Orion died last week and his body is missing. I wanted to tell you because you're the only person left who knows him deeply."

Deep down I was laughing because Orion wasn't lost. I have him.

"What do you mean? Did someone steal his body?" It was taking every bit of my strength not to laugh out loud.

"We think so, yes."

I slammed my hands on the counter. "Well, you need to find him now!"

"We will find him," he reassured me in the same monotonous voice. He was halfway to the door when suddenly, he paused and turned back to me with a slight look of disgust across his face. "Why do I smell death from you?"

"What did you say?"

This boy is very perceptive. I need to watch out for him. Luckily, I'm a good actor.

"Nothing. We'll be in touch."

After he left, I locked the door and flipped the 'Open' sign to 'Closed.' I let out a deep breath and let my forehead rest on the door. *What a day.* Then I heard a voice behind me.

"Mary?"